PRAISE FOR *LOVE SOLD SEPARATELY*

"A breezy, fast-paced contemporary with elements of suspense... Readers looking for a light beach read will enjoy the engaging writing and compelling plot."

—*Library Journal*

"Anyone entranced by QVC will adore this glimpse behind the scenes of televised home shopping, while the novel's twists and turns will keep fans of Kimberly Belle and Tana French guessing until the last page."

—*Booklist*

"With plenty of red herrings and plot twists—along with a dash of shopping...—this quick, breezy read is the perfect late summer escapism."

—*New York Journal of Books*

"A smart, dishy romp that serves up murder, romance and pages of fun."

—*Augusta Chronicle*

"Witty, clever and full of original characters, it kept me up reading way past my bedtime! A great romp of a read."
—Candace Bushnell, *New York Times* bestselling author of *Sex and the City* and *Is There Still Sex in the City?*

"An absolute delight... Meister has created a complex and comic main character who pitches cool fashion (as well as some hideous designs) on a cable TV shopping network...all the while maintaining her smarts and satirical eye. What fun!"
—Susan Isaacs, *New York Times* bestselling author of *Compromising Positions* and *Takes One to Know One*

"Completely charming!... Wise, hilarious, and with a determined heroine you will instantly adore, the oh-so-talented Ellen Meister brings her special _____ to this shopping-and-the-city delight."
_____ estselling and
_____ e *Murder List*

"A clever cockta_____ _____or with the perfect twist of _____
—Tami Hoag, *New York Times* bestselling author of *The Boy*

Also by Ellen Meister

Love Sold Separately
Dorothy Parker Drank Here
Farewell, Dorothy Parker
The Other Life
The Smart One
Secret Confessions of the Applewood PTA

Ellen Meister

the Rooftop Party

mira

mira™

ISBN-13: 978-0-7783-0951-2

The Rooftop Party

Recycling programs for this product may not exist in your area.

This edition published by arrangement with Harlequin Books S.A.

For questions and comments about the quality of this book, please contact us at CustomerService@Harlequin.com.

Mira
22 Adelaide St. West, 40th Floor
Toronto, Ontario M5H 4E3, Canada
BookClubbish.com

Printed in U.S.A.

For my mom

the Rooftop Party

1

Dana Barry raised her fist to knock on the door and paused. She wasn't easily intimidated, but walking into Eleanor Gratz's office was like trying to open an umbrella in a hurricane, and she needed a moment to anchor herself.

Not that Dana wasn't used to stormy weather. Until she got this job at the Shopping Channel, her life had been one shitstorm after another. The last monsoon hit six months ago, when she was fired from her job at a mall store in Queens. With no acting auditions on the horizon, Dana didn't know how she would pay her rent, let alone her student debt. So she did the only thing she could think of. She got drunk. And high. Thank god for her friend Megan, who burst in and dragged her to an open call. Now here she was, with a steady gig as a Shopping Channel host. And she was crushing it.

Dana took a breath and rapped twice on the door.

"If that's not Anthony Bourdain with an exotic drink and two tickets to Fiji, get lost," Eleanor called.

Dana opened the door and stuck her head in. "You know he's dead, right?"

"Like this whole place might be if I don't get my work done."

Despite the warning, Dana stepped inside. The sun-drenched office of the Shopping Channel's head buyer was a study in whites, grays and aqua blues. Eleanor sat behind a long desk the color of sea pearls. She was sixtyish, with shoulder-length salt-and-pepper hair, offset by hammered-silver hoop earrings. She wore a jewel-toned top with bell sleeves, bohemian-inspired but sophisticated. A pair of tortoiseshell reading glasses rested low on her nose. Through the window behind her, the Manhattan skyline flexed its might against the sky.

"You want me to come back?" Dana asked.

"Like a yeast infection," Eleanor said, but she sighed, relenting. "Sit down."

Dana took one of the chairs opposite her desk and the two women studied one another.

Despite her bluster, Eleanor's demeanor was open, and Dana took a moment to reflect. She could hardly believe how long she'd been at this job without screwing it up. Usually, she'd be cleaning lead out of her foot by now and filing for unemployment. But somehow, every self-sabotaging shot had missed. So she was living the life of an actual adult, with a paycheck that covered her expenses and then some. And sure, she missed the rush of going on auditions and the thrill of getting callbacks. She even missed nursing the hurt of rejections. But she didn't miss getting threatening notices when she was late on her student loan payments. Or being so broke she couldn't afford tampons without a discount coupon.

So for now, her acting ambitions were on hold. (Or at least the ones she could be public about.) In the meantime, the Shopping Channel gig was so much more than she had imagined.

But lately, Dana worried it could all blow away. Despite her personal success, the company's sales were down overall. They had even brought in a new CEO, sending a ripple of anxiety through every department.

That's why she wanted to present her idea to someone important. And sure, it might be impolitic to leapfrog her boss to talk to the head buyer about it. But going straight to Sherry Zidel with the idea wasn't an option, especially now that the business was so wobbly. Sherry was always tightly wound, but these days her jaw was tense enough to crack teeth.

"They tell me you're our resident action hero," Eleanor said, "saving us all from imminent demise." She laced her fingers, and her emerald-cut diamond ring took center stage. It was flanked by sapphires, showcased in an art deco platinum setting. The piece was tasteful despite the size, and Dana could imagine cooing over it on the air.

"Some heroes wear capes and fight crime," Dana said, offering a self-deprecating smile. "Me? I can talk for hours without taking a breath."

Eleanor shook her head, her expression serious. "Silly girl, you don't even know your own superpower."

"Enlighten me."

"It's your eye for detail."

Dana shrugged. She'd heard that kind of thing before. She noticed minutiae on an almost atomic level. It enabled her to talk about the quality of the polished rivets on a pair of jeggings with the same gushing enthusiasm she could rally for a diamond ring.

"I've been told it's pathological," she said.

"As long as you move products," Eleanor said, "I don't care *what* you call it."

"That's what I came to talk to you about—products."

Eleanor shrugged as if to say, *What else is new?* People talked to her about products all day long.

Dana hoped she could break through, and leaned forward to study Eleanor Gratz's age-defying complexion. Though her face was softening around the jawline, there was barely a wrinkle. And nothing about her appearance suggested Botox or a face-lift.

"What kind of moisturizer do you use?" Dana asked. It was a question she had formulated on the elevator. She would flatter her way in, but earnestly.

Eleanor pulled off her glasses. "I know an opening line when I hear one."

"There's a reason I'm asking."

"I would hope so."

Dana regrouped. Eleanor wouldn't respond to fawning or manipulation. She had to get right to the point.

"Look," she said, "I know we're not doing as well in apparel as we used to. And Sherry is leaning on me hard. But the fact is, there's no way we can compete with the internet. All those fashion websites—they're creaming us."

Eleanor snorted. "With cheap rags. Made with cheap Chinese labor."

"Awful," Dana commiserated.

"Disposable clothes held together with spit and a prayer."

Dana nodded, agreeing. "They can't touch us on quality, but that's hard to demonstrate on TV. Skin care, on the other hand…"

"Please don't tell me you're suggesting a skin care line."

"Why not? I can sell it, Eleanor. I know I can. All I need is a couple of models and a tight shot of disappearing crow's-feet."

Eleanor laughed. "Honey, you really think this is an original idea?"

"I don't know if it's original. I just know I can make it work." She had been studying the industry giants—HSN and QVC—and knew that any product with a strong demo moved like beer at a frat party.

"Twenty years ago, when this was still a young company, I brought in a skin care line and it was a disaster."

Dana straightened her back. "Maybe it wasn't the right time or the right host or... I don't know. Point is, twenty years is a long time. It's worth another shot, don't you think?"

"Which is why I've been pitching the idea every few years. But the board always knocks it down. It's like they have PTSD from one loss on the books two decades ago."

"What about that hand lotion Kitty used to sell?" People at the Shopping Channel rarely brought up Kitty Todd—the former star hostess who was found with a bullet in her head—but this was important.

Eleanor waved away the comment. "That California Dreams crap? It was a loss leader. The board holds it up as further proof we would always fail at skin care. I'm telling you, they're *dug in*."

Dana considered this as she pictured the man now occupying the largest office in the company. He had the look of an aging preppie, with a full mop of white hair and webs of burst blood vessels on his nose and cheeks. Evidence, she assumed, of a hard-drinking past, though today he seemed as sober as a judge.

"But we have a new CEO now," she pressed. "Maybe he'll be open to it."

Eleanor released a bitter laugh. "Ivan Dennison."

"He was brought in to shake things up, wasn't he? Maybe this is just the—"

"He'll never go for it."

"Are you sure?"

"Trust me, Dana. I'd never get anywhere with Ivan..." She trailed off, as if she were burrowing deep inside an idea.

"What is it?" Dana asked.

Eleanor pursed her lips in thought. After a few beats, she lowered her head as if confiding something. "Dana, there's a particular kind of man to whom women become invisible at a certain age. We've served our usefulness, and now we're dispensable. Ivan Dennison wouldn't hear me if I came in with a bullhorn."

"You?" Dana asked. Eleanor was such an imposing presence this was hard to imagine.

"Trust me, I could burst into flames and he'd lean forward to light his cigar."

Dana squinted, struggling to understand. "If he's such a sexist, why did the board—"

"Because they're desperate, and he's a ruthless fuck."

Dana sat back and tried to reconcile this description of Ivan with the friendly man who had been introduced to her on set. He'd been flattering and collegial, conspicuously straitlaced. The sort of man who found a way to work his marital status into every conversation with a woman.

"He seemed nice enough to me," Dana said.

Eleanor indicated the entirety of Dana's lanky twenty-nine-year-old appearance with a sweep of her hand. "Of course he did."

"What if *I* pitched him the idea?" Dana asked, energized. "He seems to like me."

"He probably wants to bang you."

"So what?" Dana said. "He's got this whole choirboy vibe going on. Like a born-again something-or-other. I don't think he'll come on to me."

"And if he does?"

"He won't."

Eleanor raised an eyebrow, and Dana got it. Guys who constantly mentioned their wives were covering up their darkest urges. Caged beasts posing as carpool dads.

"I can handle it," Dana said. "I promise."

Eleanor stared at her, fingers tented, and Dana held her breath. She could tell the formidable buyer was actually considering it. Without warning, Eleanor rose and walked to a tall wooden armoire on the left side of the room. It was a pretty piece—more suited to a bedroom than an office—painted white and stenciled with delicate aqua waves. She pulled open the doors and stood on her toes to drag a navy-blue box from the top shelf. She brought it back to her desk and placed it in the center. It was a shiny, oversized cube, with the word *Reluven* stamped in gold foil on the side. Dana had never heard of the brand, but assumed it was a skin care company.

Sure enough, Eleanor opened the lid and began pulling out products and placing them on her desk, narrating as she did so. "One-step facial cleanser, exfoliating body scrub, firming mask, shower gel, nighttime eye serum, daily moisturizer with SPF 30, hydrating body lotion, retinol antiaging miracle creme."

Dana studied the Reluven products, lined up before her like obedient soldiers in color-coordinated uniforms. Eleanor closed the box and picked up the scrub—a round gold jar about the size of a tub of whipped butter—and unscrewed the top. She held it toward Dana. "Smell this."

Dana leaned forward, closed her eyes and breathed in. It was a delicate scent, fresh and young and nostalgic all at once, with a hint of gardenias. "That's...sublime." She took another sniff.

Eleanor's voice went wistful. "It's the best skin care line I've ever come across. If only I could get it on the air."

Dana pointed to the body lotion. "May I?"

Eleanor nodded her assent, so Dana picked up the bottle, pumped a dab into her palm and rubbed her hands together. The feel was rich and velvety. She took a whiff, enjoying the same sensual smell as the scrub, and smoothed it onto her neck. Dana imagined her boyfriend, Ari, reacting to it as he kissed her there. The thought was enough to distract her, but she brought herself back to her mission.

"I can do this," Dana said, studying Eleanor's face. "I can get Ivan to agree to let us give this a shot."

The buyer leaned back in her chair, considering it, but Dana sensed she had already decided. She held her breath.

"Maybe," Eleanor said, "but we have to approach this strategically."

Dana inhaled a tingle of success. *Eleanor was on board.* "What's the plan? Should I pop into his office? Better to make an appointment? I'm afraid he might ask what it's about and then—"

"Easy, tiger," Eleanor interrupted. "I admire your determination, but you need to keep your impulsivity in check. This has to be done methodically."

"I'm listening…"

"You need to schmooze. Flatter. Build a relationship first."

"The anniversary party!" Dana said, bringing her hands together. It was a big rooftop bash the company was throwing the following week to celebrate twenty-five years on the air, and as soon as she said it, Dana knew it was the perfect opportunity to pitch Ivan Dennison.

"It's a good place to start."

"It's a good place to *finish*," Dana insisted. "If I talk up the idea when he's happy and relaxed, the center of attention…"

Eleanor shook her head. "Honey, you might know how to sell on TV, but there are nuances to the one-on-one pitch with a narcissistic executive."

"What if he seems open to it?"

"Trust me, you have to play the long game. Get cozy with Ivan at the party, but do not bring up business. Eventually, he'll come to you."

"I don't know," Dana said. "I might need to strike while the iron is hot. It's not like he's going to fall in love with me. I think you have too much faith in my appeal."

Eleanor tsked. "And I think you have too little."

2

"What fresh hell is this?" Dana said when she answered the phone.

It was just after 9:00 a.m. on Saturday. She had been up since her boyfriend, Ari, slipped out of bed in the obscene predawn darkness to work his morning shift as a New York City homicide detective, so the call from her friend Megan was actually a welcome distraction. But so was busting her chops.

"Were you and Ari in the middle of it?" Megan asked.

"I pushed him off me so I could answer the phone."

"As if," Megan said. "You wouldn't push Ari off you if the roof caved in."

Dana took a sniff of her blanket, where his scent lingered. "With Ari, the roof always caves in."

"Lucky you."

Dana fluffed the pillow behind her back and sat up. She couldn't argue. "What's going on?"

"I found you an apartment."

Dana was not in the market for a new place. Not yet, any-way. But Megan—who doubled as best friend and manager—was always looking out for her.

And sure, Dana and Ari had talked about moving in together. And they would need a new place to make that happen, as his was in south Brooklyn—a difficult commute—and hers was so small she once told a date, *I can invite you in or I can invite your ego. One of you has to stay outside.* And it wasn't just cramped, but dark, with just two tiny windows, one with a partial view of First Avenue, and the other a full panorama of a sooty airshaft.

Unfortunately, Ari didn't want them to look for a new apartment until he got a promotion and could afford steeper rent. Dana insisted she was making enough money to handle it on her own, but he refused. It had to be fifty-fifty or he wouldn't do it.

"Bad timing," Dana said to Megan. "We're not ready."

"At least look at it," Megan said. "Two bedrooms, West Side. I got an inside scoop because my friend Carrie's aunt died last week and it's going to be snatched up in a matter of hours."

"They all get snatched up in a matter of hours," Dana said, but at the same time, the words *second bedroom* made her pulse quicken. That was the kind of luxury New Yorkers dreamed about. All that space! It could be a library or a gym or they could plant a small meadow and tend sheep.

"I just sent you some pictures."

Dana pulled her phone from her ear to look at the text Megan had sent. It showed a living room flooded with light from a wall of massive windows. She put the phone on speaker.

"Is this for real?" she asked.

"Would I lie?"

Dana kept staring at the picture, aching with envy. "I wish I could," she said. "Ari would kill me."

Then Megan told her the rental price.

It was a steal. More than double her current rent, of course, but well below market value. And she had enough in her bank account to cover the deposit. She thought about all those years she struggled to make rent on this tiny place. And now here was a glorious apartment on the other side of town, and she could actually afford it. Her skin tingled.

"When is it going on the market?"

"Today."

"What *time* today?" She had plans to meet her father and sister for brunch, and a part of her hoped the place would be listed and snatched up before she had a chance to look at it.

"First showing is at two p.m."

Damn. That left her just enough time and a decision to make. Dana let out a long breath. If she looked at the apartment, she probably wouldn't be able to resist it. And then she would have to find a way to convince Ari it was the right thing to do. It was a risky proposition.

"I don't know," Dana said. "I shouldn't. Ari's not on board."

"Bring him with you. Maybe if he sees it…"

"He's working. And he wouldn't come anyway."

After a pause, Megan asked what she wanted to do.

Dana looked back down at the photo. High ceilings. Tall windows. Sunlight pouring in like it was spilled from a bucket of joy. She knew this was the trap of real estate—this feeling that an opportunity like this would never present itself again. And yet.

"Give me the phone number," she said quickly. "I'll make an appointment." Suddenly, it felt right. Like destiny.

"Too late," Megan said.

"Too late?"

"I already scheduled you for the first showing."

Dana wanted to arrive at the restaurant to meet her family on time so she wouldn't look like such a shit for ducking out early to get to the real estate appointment. Of course, her father would judge her no matter what, but she couldn't help herself. Despite learning the same lesson again and again, a part of her always thought that this time might be different.

So she scrambled through her morning routine. Unfortunately, one wardrobe malfunction after another cut into her prep time, followed by a frantic search for her cell phone, which she finally found buried under a pile of discarded outfits.

"Sorry, sorry," she said to her father and sister when she arrived. She gave them each a quick kiss on the cheek. "Crazy morning."

Kenneth Barry wore a wool blazer and crisp Oxford shirt along with his usual scowl. Since remarrying that summer, the retired neurosurgeon had put on a little weight, softening his sharp cheekbones. Dana thought she even noticed a little more hair on the top of his head, and wondered if he'd started using Rogaine to please his new wife, a cardiologist more than twenty years his junior. When he was married to her mother, who was now remarried and living in Boca Raton, he never would have considered improving himself for her.

Chelsea, Dana's sister, was suburban chic, as always, in a Stella McCartney off-the-shoulder silk blouse and statement necklace. Despite being the mother of a four-year-old, she always looked entirely put together, with impeccably highlighted blond hair. The only time Dana saw her slip was some months ago, after she suffered a miscarriage. She had sunk so low Dana worried she wouldn't recover. And then, just like that, she was back—cheerful and functioning. It was some kind of miracle. People often joked about "retail therapy," but in Chelsea's case there really did seem to be something to it. For her, the only thing better than shopping was more shopping. Which was why Kenneth had asked Chelsea, and not Dana, to help him pick out a birthday gift for his wife today. That was the reason for the brunch. Afterward, Kenneth and Chelsea would be heading to Tiffany's, leaving Dana free to shop for an apartment she had no business considering.

"It's *Saturday*," Kenneth said to Dana as he tapped his watch. The implication was that she couldn't possibly have anything important on her schedule on a weekend morning.

"And tomorrow is Sunday," she said, "so it looks like we both passed the neurological assessment."

One day, her snarky remarks might get a rise out of her father. But not today. As she took a seat, Chelsea scrutinized her outfit, which included a red sweater and indigo skinny jeans.

"So cute," her sister said, indicating the entirety of it.

"Even the boots?" Dana asked, surprised her fashionista sister approved of her appearance.

Chelsea shook her head. "No, not the boots. The boots are revolting. But you know that."

She did, in fact, know the boots were revolting. That was pretty much the point. They were a last-minute addition to the outfit, which had been carefully selected to make a good impression on the Realtor. But Dana couldn't bring herself to arrive at a brunch with her father looking the part of the perfect daughter—that was the push-pull of her relationship with him. She wanted his approval and wanted to piss him off, all at the same time. So she dug through her closet for the beat-to-hell combat boots that had seen her through the leanest times. She bypassed the smart-looking saddle-brown pair she had just bought, as well as the black ankle booties with a stacked heel that needed repair. Dana was well aware of how bad the combat boots looked, as she had spent years covering up the scuff marks with a Sharpie so she could wear them to auditions. Dana resurrected them today so her father would know she was still the same person he had judged so harshly for her money problems.

Dana smiled at her sister and shrugged—a gesture that said, *Guilty as charged.*

"You're an idiot," Chelsea said affectionately, as she leaned forward to rearrange a lock of her sister's hair. Dana still wore it short and bark brown, but now, thanks to the Shopping Channel's stylist, the edges were tipped in ashy blond. It was, he had assured her, the perfect complement to her gray-green eyes.

"Fuck you very much," Dana said.

Their father, who never understood the camaraderie of their banter, told them not to be childish. Dana fought the urge to burp a response.

Kenneth looked at her over his menu. "How are you doing at the Shopping Station?" he asked.

"Shopping *Channel*," she corrected, "and I'm doing fine." She considered adding that she had been the top-selling host for four weeks in a row, but managed to keep her mouth shut. There was no way it would get the reaction she desired.

"I hope you're behaving yourself," he said. "That's not a job you want to lose."

"Thanks for the vote of confidence, Dad."

"You don't have to get sarcastic."

The waitress came to take their drink orders, and Dana noted that Chelsea requested a Virgin Mary. She didn't want to read too much into it, but it was hard not to wonder if her sister was pregnant again. She wouldn't say anything, of course. If Chelsea wanted to tell her, she would. Dana imagined that following a miscarriage, one might want to keep a pregnancy quiet until it was further along.

Later in the meal, Dana's suspicions were tweaked when Chelsea put her hand to her abdomen and furrowed her brow.

"You alright?" Dana asked.

"Yeah, fine. Why?"

Dana shrugged and went back to her meal, but several minutes later Chelsea seemed to sink, and then excused herself to the bathroom.

Dana looked at her father, the medical doctor, to see if he picked up on any of this, but he was fully concentrated on his egg-white omelet.

When Chelsea returned, her face was pale and worried.

"What's the matter?" Dana asked.

"Nothing, I... I just have an upset stomach. I think I'm going to head home."

"Home?" Dana said.

"Might be food poisoning," Kenneth said, signaling for the waitress. "I'll tell the management."

"No, Daddy, please," Chelsea said. "Don't make a fuss. It doesn't feel like food poisoning. I'm probably just tired."

"Let me take you to Penn Station," Dana said, concerned about her sister's trip back to the suburbs of Long Island.

Chelsea shook her off. "It's fine—I'll take a cab. But will you do me a favor and go shopping with Dad?"

Dana swallowed. "Me?"

"Please."

"I... I have an appointment," she stammered. She pictured the wood floors. The tall windows. The second bedroom.

"Can't you reschedule?" Chelsea said.

Dana opened her mouth to argue, because she couldn't reschedule. She had to be at the apartment in an hour or it would be gone. But her sister looked so forlorn, her voice so plaintive, that all she could say was, "Of course. Feel better."

3

Dana wanted the errand to be quick, so as they walked toward Tiffany's, she tried to get her father to focus on the kind of gift he wanted to buy. If they hurried, there was still a chance she could make the appointment.

"I hadn't thought about it," he said. "I counted on your sister for some ideas."

"How about a bracelet?"

He nodded thoughtfully. "Yes, perhaps a tennis bracelet."

Tennis bracelet? Was he kidding? It had been the last gift he bought her mom before the divorce, and she wanted to smash him in the shins with a racket just for suggesting it.

"No, Dad," she said through her teeth. "Anything but a *tennis* bracelet."

"I thought women liked tennis bracelets."

He sounded genuinely confused, and Dana realized he probably hadn't meant to be insensitive. He was simply that unimaginative. It was easy to forget how robotic his thinking could be, because on the outside he looked almost like a real human. She regrouped.

"I noticed Jennifer wears a lot of silver," she said. "Maybe a big chunky cuff."

"A *cuff*?" he said, as if it were an inconceivable suggestion, and she knew he was picturing the double-stitched fabric at the end of his shirtsleeve.

She tried to describe what she was talking about, and he couldn't picture it. At last she said, "Did you notice that thick gold bracelet Chelsea was wearing at lunch? That's a cuff."

"Ah, yes," he said, as if seeing the light at the mention of Chelsea's name. "I think that will work."

Dana bristled. "From now on I'll qualify all my ideas by saying they came from Chelsea."

"Your sister knows quite a bit about fashion."

I should have seen that coming, Dana thought. But no matter how low her expectations, he always managed to limbo under the bar.

"I *sell* fashion," she said through her teeth.

"You haven't even been there a full year," Kenneth said.

"So?"

"Dana," he said with the practiced patience of a doctor who has to explain complicated medical procedures to simple lay folk, "there's a learning curve with any new job. But you've never stayed at one place long enough to know that."

Her nostrils flared. "I'm a loser. Check. Thanks for the reminder."

"I didn't say that. You just have to keep your nose to the grindstone."

Dana rubbed at a migraine nipping the edge of her forehead. She was quite sure that if the Shopping Channel went down, her father would think she was the one who sank it.

She needed to end this errand asap. If not for the apartment, then for her sanity. Dana directed the conversation back to the bracelet, and by the time they arrived at Tiffany's he had a budget and a vision of what he wanted. The store was crowded, but Dana was aggressive in getting the attention of a sales associate, and in a short while Kenneth had settled on an extra-wide Elsa Peretti silver cuff.

"Jennifer will love it," Dana said as she glanced at the time. If her father didn't ask for it to be wrapped, she still had a chance to make her appointment.

Then the sales associate said something that made Dana wince. "Would you like that engraved?"

Dana said, "Oh, I don't think that's—"

"Of course," Kenneth said. "Of course I want it engraved."

And just like that, she knew it was over. She wouldn't be getting out of this store anytime soon. Some other lucky New Yorker would be whipping out their checkbook to snatch the apartment—*Dana's* apartment—before she got a chance to look at it.

"Fine, Dad," she said, sighing. "Let's talk about what you want inscribed."

"Don't worry about it," he said.

She looked at him. "What do you mean?"

"I mean I can take it from here. You can hurry off to whatever *pressing appointment* you have on a Saturday afternoon."

He pronounced "pressing appointment" as if it were in quotes. As if she couldn't possibly have something important to do. But if he meant to make her feel guilty, it didn't work. Or at least, it didn't work well enough to keep her there. Dana wished him luck, moved in for a perfunctory hug and flew out the door and onto Fifth Avenue, where she saw a waiting taxicab. Perfect timing. She practically knocked over a heavyset guy in a plaid jacket to get to it.

Then it registered. Plaid jacket. Hybrid sneaker-loafer walking shoes. A subway map sticking out of his pocket. The guy was a tourist. The guilt she had been able to ignore just moments ago now stabbed at her. *Don't do it*, said the guilt. *Give up the cab and tell him to have a nice day. Then he'll go back to wherever he came from and explain that New Yorkers aren't really all that bad.*

But the apartment. This taxi might be her last best hope.

They locked eyes, and he seemed so earnestly shocked that Dana had no choice. "It's yours," she said, backing away as her eyes swept the street for an empty cab.

"Hey," he said, "I know you. You're that HSN lady."

"Shopping Channel," she corrected, offering a weak smile. It was a common enough mistake. HSN was an industry powerhouse. Her struggling company was third tier at best.

He grinned wildly. "I just knew I'd meet a celebrity!" He opened the cab door. "Please," he said, gesturing for her to get in.

"Are you sure?"

"You kidding? This is the best thing that happened to me since I got off the plane."

Dana wasn't going to argue. She slid into the car and thanked him. "If I didn't have a pressing appointment…"

"My pleasure," he said. "Just do me one favor?"

"What's that?"

"Say hi to Lori Greiner for me. I love her!"

"Will do!" she said, and shut the door, wondering if he would later remember that the famous *Shark Tank* entrepreneur was actually from QVC.

Of course, traffic was abysmal, and by the time the taxi turned the corner on West Sixty-Ninth Street, she was fifteen minutes late. Her heart thudded as she looked down the block, which struck her as one of the prettiest streets in Manhattan. Immediately, she could envision herself living happily here. Making a life with Ari. It was a dream.

She dashed into the building, where the Realtor stood in the lobby on the checkerboard marble floor, chatting with another couple. Dana didn't know what to make of the tableau. Had they already seen the apartment? Were they ready to put down a deposit? She took quick stock of the young couple, and pegged them as trust fund kids, blandly good-looking and expensively dressed in muted colors.

"Sorry I'm late!" Dana cried. "My sister got sick and—"

"Are you Dana?" the Realtor asked, her professional smile steady. She wore a plaid shawl smartly draped over her expensive black blouse and gray slacks.

"Yes, I apologize."

The Realtor shook Dana's hand and introduced herself. "It's no problem," she said. "I was just about to show the Peabody-Lathams upstairs. We can all go together."

Peabody-Lathams? She knew immediately this wasn't a feminist joining of bride and groom names. This was his family name, which his wife took on. Dana would eat her Easter bonnet if these two weren't Old Money. She immediately imagined Grandmama Peabody-Latham furnishing the rooms and supplying the first year's rent.

When they reached the apartment, Dana noticed two things simultaneously. The herringbone wood floors were a rich, warm reddish brown—even lovelier than they looked in the photograph—but the living room wasn't nearly as sunny. It didn't dampen Dana's enthusiasm, but she hoped the Peabody-Lathams were at least a little turned off.

"I thought it would be sunnier," Dana said, pointedly.

"So did I," the man said. "How about you, Ainsley Beth?"

Ainsley Beth? These people loved burdening their kids with extra names.

"It gets sun in the morning," the Realtor assured them. "And it's an overcast day. Let me show you the kitchen."

Even though she knew the answer, Dana inquired about a doorman.

"I was just about to ask that," said Ainsley Beth.

The Realtor explained that there were only twelve units in the building, so it didn't warrant that kind of staff. But it was a good neighborhood, she assured them, and there were never any security problems.

Dana had to fight the urge to gush over every detail. She needed to play it cool, pretend the place wasn't all that. In fact, it was all that and more. When the couple shut themselves into the second bedroom to have a private chat, Dana feared they were phoning Grandmama to get the money wired.

When they emerged from the bedroom, the husband put his hand on his wife's shoulder and told the Realtor they needed some time to think it over.

Time? Ha! Old Money could buy a lot of things, but not New York savvy.

Dana waited until they left, counted two beats and then turned to the Realtor with her decision.

4

On Friday, as Dana sat in the hair-and-makeup room getting ready for her set, she wasn't thinking about the rooftop party, the apartment she hadn't yet told Ari about or even the line of clothing she would be selling on that day's show. She was thinking about a conversation she'd had with Megan several months ago—a conversation she liked to replay at quiet moments.

"Was it great?" Megan had asked. "You look like the poster child for post-coital bliss."

It was the day after Dana had first slept with Ari Marks, and she was still floating in a dreamy haze.

"Great?" she had repeated, mulling over the syllable. "I think that word is too...*terrestrial*."

Megan's eyes went wide. "Tell me."

Dana studied her own hand, a shiver tickling the tips of each vertebra as she remembered the transcendence of Ari's touch, the spark of his desire igniting her. And sure, she understood that there was always hunger in sex, especially after the tease of a relationship that took so long to finally click. But this… this was an alchemy she never could have imagined.

"You know that specific sex feeling," she said, "that desperate *please, please, please*, you—"

"I get it," Megan interrupted. "You were in the elevator and wanted to reach the penthouse."

Dana shook her head. "Not just that," she said. "I'm talking about…the feeling that there's always more."

"Darwin 101," Megan explained. "It's what keeps us having sex—we're compelled to feel like we haven't quite reached the final destination."

"But that's exactly what I'm talking about," Dana said. "With Ari, it feels like I'm there. *Right there.*"

Megan reached out and gave her friend's hand a squeeze. "I'm glad, Dana. Just remember that this stupid wonderful feeling doesn't last. It can't. I'm not saying it won't work out with Ari—just that it'll change."

Megan's heart was in the right place, but on this, she was wrong. Because here Dana was, all these months later, and it hadn't changed. If anything, the feeling had intensified.

Now, she tried to focus on her show as the two most gossipy women in the company were busy making her camera-ready. But their chatter centered around what they planned to wear to the company party that night.

"Not a tank top," Jo, the manicurist, was saying. "More like a blouse, in a shiny copper."

Felicia, the makeup woman, nodded. "That color will be gorgeous with your eyes."

They had the kind of thick New York accents you heard in old sections of Queens or Brooklyn. Neighborhood accents, utterly unselfconscious. It was like overhearing a conversation on a stoop, and Dana loved the music of it. As an actor, she listened for the nuances she could imitate if a role ever called for it. *Dat cullah will be gawjis wityawreyes.*

"What are *you* wearing tonight?" Jo asked Dana, as she worked on her nails.

As a Shopping Channel host, her hands were everything, and Dana got a fresh manicure before every show.

"I brought a dress to change into. Black V-neck." The party was just after her segment, and she would have enough time to make a quick change in her dressing room and go right up to the roof.

"Clingy?" Felicia asked.

Dana nodded. It was her favorite cocktail dress, and she worried that it might be just a little too sexy for a work event, especially since she planned on cozying up to the ostentatiously pious Ivan Dennison. But she hardly ever had an excuse to wear it. And besides, the rest of her wardrobe was still evolving from her days as a Hot Topic cashier, and she knew that a concert T-shirt and ripped jeans weren't going to cut it tonight.

There was a knock on the open door, and Dana looked up to see Ari, his tall form filling the doorway. Her heart bobbed in a bath of pure pleasure. She hadn't been expecting him, but wasn't surprised he had been able to get past security without her permission. Being a New York City homicide detective had its advantages.

Still, he rarely popped in, and she took a quick scan of his expression to make sure nothing was wrong. As a detective, he had perfected his poker face, never giving too much away. But over the months, she had come to read him, and could discern a hint of joy dancing in his winter-blue eyes. She wondered what good news he had received, and hoped it had to do with the exam he had taken to qualify for a promotion to detective sergeant. She had been waiting breathlessly for those results so she could tell him about the apartment.

"Look who's here," Jo said, switching to a kittenish voice. "I hope you brung your handcuffs, Detective."

Dana shook her head, amused. It was harmless flirting, and Jo couldn't help herself. Few men were as tall, dark and smoldering as Ari.

"Did someone break the law?" he asked, playfully.

Jo fanned herself with her hand, as if the room were getting too hot. "Oh, I'm a bad girl." She tilted her head coquettishly.

"Okay, cool it," Dana added, good-naturedly enough for everyone to laugh. She looked up at Ari. "You have news?"

"I passed," he said, trying to keep his expression in check. He wasn't entirely successful, and his smile warmed her like cognac.

"Passed what?" Jo asked.

"An NYPD promotion exam," Dana explained.

"You got a promotion?" Felicia chirped. "Congratulations!"

"Not so fast," Ari said. "It's just step one. I have to be recommended by my superiors."

"An important step," Dana said. "I'm proud of you."

He walked inside the room and gave her a careful hug, avoiding her nails and makeup. And even that small touch felt significant, as if he were conveying a message about their future. *If this promotion comes through*, he seemed to be saying, *everything will fall into place for us.*

He released her and she looked into his eyes, certain she had read his message correctly.

"You got to suck up to your bosses?" Jo asked.

"Something like that," he said. "In fact, they'll all be at the captain's birthday party with their wives tonight, and I think it's important for me to show up."

"You want me to come with?" Dana asked.

"Always," he said, "but you have your office thing."

"I could meet up with you afterward. This party shouldn't go too late."

He offered a grateful smile and then gave her the details.

"We'll make sure she don't drink too much," Jo said.

"Or flirt," Felicia added. "She's wearing a sexy number. I'd be worried if I was you."

Dana and Ari locked eyes again. His expression remained stoic, but his right eyebrow betrayed him, rising a pica-width. Dana understood. The beginning of their relationship had been fraught with tension, as he came into her life just as she was ending something with a coworker. She moved mountains, drained oceans and rearranged the planets to convince him she and the sound guy were history, but some of the hurt lingered. Besides, Lorenzo still worked at the channel, which meant daily intimate contact as he threaded a microphone wire under her clothing.

Felicia looked from Dana to Ari. "You know I was just kidding, right? You got nothing to worry about. She's *insane* for you."

"How could she not be?" Jo said.

Ari's tension released into a laugh as he gave Dana's shoulder a final squeeze, and left. She imagined showing up at his event and charming his superiors. Then she could tell him about the apartment, and he'd be mad, but maybe not too much. And once he saw the place he would understand she had done it for them, and that it was an opportunity she couldn't pass up. In the end, he'd be grateful, and eventually they would laugh about it.

A short while later, as Felicia stroked mascara onto Dana's lashes, another unexpected visitor appeared in the doorway. Ivan Dennison.

"Hello!" he called jovially. Dana intuited that he intended

to be booming, but his voice was thin and tinny, concentrated in the space behind his nose.

Still, he managed to suck the relaxed energy right out of the room. The three women returned his greeting, but he made his next comment looking straight at Dana.

"I hope you're coming to the party tonight. Big news!" Then he winked, and left.

"What do you think *that* means?" Felicia asked.

"I bet Dana's getting the prime-time slot," Jo said.

Dana shook her head, as that would be good news for her, but bad news for Vanessa Valdes, who currently hosted that show. "I don't think he'd be announcing that at the party," she said.

Felicia put the mascara wand back in the tube and twisted it shut. "What, then?"

Dana shrugged. She couldn't figure it out, but one thing was certain. Ivan wanted her there, and she would use that to her advantage.

Less than an hour later, Dana was on set, standing next to a rack of hooded tops made by SoftChic, a line of cotton knits that bridged the gap between sweats and casual wear. Her live running commentary was accented by constant rubbing and touching and cooing to drive home the sensual softness of the fabric. She spoke directly into the camera as if sharing a special secret with her closest friend, and listened as her segment producer, Jessalyn, whispered into her earpiece: *Heather blue is moving—push desert sand.* Dana pulled the tan shirt off the rack and did a riff on the sumptuousness of the color, explaining how great it would look with jeans. She ran her hands up and down her own sleeves, giving herself a hug to show how much she loved wrapping herself in the cozy cotton. She twirled to illustrate the loose and forgiving fit, which she insisted would flatter every body type.

At last, the show wound down and Jessalyn said, "Good work. You were 1.2 percent over projections."

Dana let out a breath. It was a squeaker.

She hurried to her dressing room, where her manager—who also happened to be her best friend—was waiting for her. As Dana's official rep, Megan had been invited to the company party, and was decked out for it in a short red dress and high black boots.

"Wow," Dana said. "You look *hot*."

She meant it. Megan Silvestri often complained about her looks, but Dana thought she nailed it with a dress that flattered her ample curves and complemented her olive skin and lush, dark hair.

"Only because you're still in that *schmatta*," Megan said. "Once you slither into your dress, I'll go back to looking like a troll by comparison."

"Trust me, if we were going to a bar, guys would push me out of the way to get to you."

"Good thing you're an actor. You almost sold that."

Dana gave her friend a hug and told her she was a pain in the ass.

Less than a year ago, they were just ordinary besties. But then Megan announced that she was giving up on her acting career, and in the same breath offered to be Dana's manager. She made a strong case, insisting that she believed in her friend's talents, and would get her more auditions than her overtaxed agent. Megan's enthusiasm was contagious, and Dana agreed. She never could have imagined that in a matter of months—just as she was at the end of her financial and emotional rope—Megan would sober her up and march her into an audition at the Shopping Channel.

Dana pulled off the hooded top that would be going back to wardrobe, and took her black dress off the rolling chrome rack in the alcove of her dressing room. She slipped it over her head and smoothed it out. It was long-sleeved, with a plunging neckline and a flouncy skirt that emphasized her long legs. She opened the shoebox she had brought, and pulled out a pair of glittery silver platform pumps with dangerously high heels.

"You sure you want to wear fuck-me heels to an office event?" Megan asked.

"Bad idea?"

"Not if you want to get laid."

Dana bit her lip, thinking about her later rendezvous with Ari, and the amorous mood that would surely follow. "I'll take my chances."

5

When Dana first learned that the company was throwing a rooftop party in November, she thought she had gone to work for a group of sadists.

"We'll freeze out there," she had said.

But they insisted the Shopping Channel always held rooftop parties in the fall, with the help of massive outdoor heaters and a semi-enclosed tent. Coats and scarves, she was assured, were unnecessary, and it would all be quite lovely.

Still, she was unprepared for the transformation of the rooftop. When she and Megan pushed open the metal door, they found themselves in a twinkling urban wonderland, right there on the West Side of Manhattan. Strings of delicate white lights outlined every surface. Even the George Washington Bridge, arching majestically over the Hudson River in the distance, seemed part of the enchanted décor. The only thing that broke the spell was the deafening volume of the party. An industrial generator had been brought to the roof, and a band on the far end had their amps cranked up to overpower the pulsing noise. It was a little bit like holding a party inside the engine of a Boeing.

"It's beautiful," Dana shouted.

Megan cupped her hand to her ear. "What?"

"I said it's beautiful!"

"I can't hear you."

Dana took a deep breath and boomed, "It's beautiful!"

Megan laughed. "I'm fucking with you, Dana."

"What?" Dana said.

Megan opened her mouth to repeat herself, but stopped when she caught Dana's expression. "Funny."

Dana pointed to a setup on the other end of the roof, beyond the white tent. "I think that's the bar."

The tent was more like a canopy they had to pass under to reach the two bartenders—one male, one female—who were moving with the quick grace of experience as their nimble hands shook and squeezed and poured and plunked to meet the needs of a line of impatient New Yorkers.

It was warmer under the vinyl, with all the bodies concentrated and the giant heaters at full blast. There was a clear plastic square in the center of the tent's ceiling, so people could look up at the stars. Dana preferred the open air, but passing through the crowd gave her a chance to ogle all her coworkers and their plus-ones. Eleanor Gratz was there with a man Dana presumed to be her husband. He was about her height, with blond hair and a scruffy beard. When Dana got close enough to say hello, she could tell he was quite a bit younger than his wife. Maybe by about ten years. Eleanor introduced him as, "My husband, Philip Wagoner," and Dana understood that since Eleanor hadn't changed her name, she made a point of giving her husband's full name so no one would make the mistake of referring to him as Mr. Gratz.

Dana introduced the two of them to Megan, and soon learned that Mr. Wagoner taught at a private middle school in upper Manhattan.

Before the conversation wound down, Eleanor put a hand on Dana's shoulder and gave a nod toward the area of the tent where Ivan was holding court amidst a circle of eager sycophants. Dana made note of it. She would approach him when the party settled down a bit. At very least, she needed a drink first.

Dana's new temporary assistant, Ashlee St. Pierre, was also surrounded by admirers trying to get her attention. She was an imposing beauty—over six feet tall and defiantly big-boned, as if her very existence (and certainly her confidence) told the fashion industry it could just go to hell. As a child, Ashlee had done the pageant circuit in her home state of Tennessee. It was, Dana assumed, where she learned her poise and self-assurance. And like so many Shopping Channel staffers, she had acting ambitions.

Megan grabbed Dana's arm, breaking her reverie. "Who's that guy?" she asked, pointing to an unfamiliar man at the bar. He was mid-to-late twenties, with a big square head and a pleasant face. To Dana, he wasn't particularly handsome, but Megan had a type, and this guy was custom-made, from his tousled hair and nerd glasses to his rumpled sports jacket and jeans. Dana hoped, for Megan's sake, he wasn't someone's date.

"I've never seen him before," she said.

As if sensing he was being watched, the guy turned to look at them. But his eyes swept past Dana and landed on Megan in her smoldering red dress.

Dana elbowed her friend. "I *told* you."

"He's probably some breast-obsessed creep with arrested development." But even as she said it, Megan didn't take her eyes off him.

Dana shrugged. Her friend had the kind of figure her mother would call top-heavy, making it hard to find clothes that fit properly. But she thought her own lean body, practically pubescent in straightness, was the kind that appealed to the arrested development set.

"There's only one way to find out," Dana said.

They began to move through the crowd, but Dana was waylaid by Sherry Zidel, the Shopping Channel's supervising producer. Sherry was fierce-eyed and angular, with a sharp chin and a pair of thick glasses she seemed to wear like armor.

And she was even less fun than she looked. Months earlier, she had discovered that Dana was in breach of contract for moonlighting with her downtown acting troupe—a gig that meant so much to Dana she simply couldn't give it up. At the same time, Dana learned that Sherry had broken one of HR's most rigid rules. And so the two had reached an uneasy truce, vowing to keep one another's secret.

Sherry gripped Dana's arm to stop her. Even in a party setting, her hold was viselike, and Dana assumed she was about to be chewed out.

"I know," Dana said. "My numbers weren't that strong today."

"It's not that."

Sherry always seemed to be angry with her, and Dana studied her face for clues on her current grievance. Did she find out about the conversation with Eleanor Gratz? That could mean serious trouble.

"I wanted you to meet Anna," Sherry said.

Dana peered up to see a willowy Asian woman at Sherry's side. She had the look of a former model and wore a pleasant expression along with her silver satin jumpsuit. Sherry had always been intensely private and rarely mentioned her significant other, so Dana was surprised to see Anna at a company event.

They exchanged introductions, and Dana searched Sherry's expression for any tenderness now that it was after business hours and the imperious executive had her partner at her side. But Sherry's jaw was rigid, her eyes tight and blinking as if expecting an assault.

Dana was stopped by several more people on her way to the bar, including her assistant, Ashlee, who hadn't been in New York that long and was still stunned and delighted by the sights.

"That span!" she said pointing. Her Tennessee accent was unmistakable. "It just takes my breath. What do y'all call it?"

"That's the George Washington Bridge," Dana said. "And trust me, it's a lot less impressive when you're trying to inch across it in daylight."

Dana moved on and was greeted by Charles Honeycutt, the company president. Everyone had assumed he would be promoted to CEO when the last one was ousted, but the board recruited Ivan Dennison from a retail electronics giant, assuring shaky investors he would help the company blaze new trails. Dana didn't know much about corporate intrigue beyond what she saw in the movies, and wondered why Charles had been passed over. She liked him. He was smart and congenial, and understood the Shopping Channel's business more than some guy who traded in motherboards and baby monitors. She hoped it wasn't racism that kept this capable Black man from advancing.

As they chatted, Dana noticed Felicia and Jo inching toward them, and she knew these girls from the makeup department rarely got a chance to rub elbows with the president. So she signaled them over and they happily complied, clicking forward on their teetering heels. Dana left them cooing over Charles Honeycutt while she made her way to the bar.

By the time she got there, Megan was deep in conversation with the large-headed man.

"Dana," Megan called over the music, "this is Jamie Dennison."

"Dennison?" Dana repeated, while she shook his hand. "As in—"

"Ivan Dennison is my father," he said. "I hope you don't hold that against me."

Dana smiled. She appreciated the joke, though it was hard to tell if he really disliked his father or was just being glib. "Nice to meet you."

"Jamie is a reporter for the *Daily Beast*," Megan said, clearly impressed.

Dana could see her friend's cynicism dissolving, and gave her a grin. "What are you drinking?"

"Vodka martini. I ordered you one but I don't know what happened to it."

"I think it got pushed down the bar," Jamie said, pointing.

The woman bartender, dressed just like her male counterpart in a black vest, white shirt and yellow bow tie, overheard the conversation and seized the drink. Dana held out her hand for it, but the bartender spilled it out and grabbed a clean glass.

"I'll make you another," she said.

"Why?" Dana asked, taking a glance at the bartender's name tag. It said Margaux, and Dana wondered if it was a stage name. It was an easy assumption, because in New York, attractive young people who worked for caterers were usually struggling actors.

"A woman should never let a drink out of her sight," Margaux said.

Dana was about to make a joke until she saw the expression on the woman's face, which looked as serious as an open wound, and Dana surmised that bartenders were on high alert since the Bill Cosby disgustathon.

Margaux made the cocktail in a matter of seconds and was on to the next order without missing a beat. Her movements were so precise that Dana changed her mind about the actor thing. Margaux was a dancer. She even wore her hair tied back like a ballerina, held in place by a golden yellow ribbon that matched her bow tie. Her forehead had a pronounced widow's peak pointing right down the center of her symmetrical face.

Before returning to the hectic, pulsing noise of the party, Dana took her drink to the north side of the roof, where it was a little quieter. She leaned on the waist-high railing, enjoying the view. The Hudson River looked almost supernatural, like a living black mirror reflecting the lights of the city. A chill wind blew over her, and she took a warming sip of her drink. After a few moments, Dana became aware of a presence next to her, and looked up to see Ivan Dennison.

"Nice view," he said. His eyes lingered on her for a moment before he gazed out at the George Washington Bridge. It seemed flirtatious—a far cry from the choirboy innocence he affected during business hours—and Dana thought about Eleanor's warning.

"Are you enjoying the party?" she asked.

"It's nice seeing everyone let their hair down."

"I hope you still feel that way after everyone's had a few," she said. "I heard these parties can get a little wild."

He nodded, barely listening. "What are you drinking?"

"Vodka martini. You?"

"Club soda." He held it up. "Cheers."

Dana tipped her glass toward his, feeling sure her original suspicions were correct—he was a teetotaler with a hard-drinking past.

"I like those shoes," he said. "They make a statement."

And that statement has nothing to do with you, she thought, and changed the subject to something safer. "Is Mrs. Dennison here?"

"Couldn't make it. What about your boyfriend?"

She folded her arms. "How did you know I have a boyfriend?"

He looked her up and down so thoroughly she wished she'd worn a parka. Or a yurt. This was no glance—this was a leer. "How could you not?" he said, his eyes lingering on her chest.

Now there was no denying it. Eleanor Gratz was right. Ivan Dennison—who looked older than her father—was coming on to her. She would have to play this with finesse—friendly and open but with a clear message about her unavailability. It was a fine line to walk.

"We're going to be moving in together." She made sure the remark sounded pointed.

"If he likes you, he should have put a ring on it," Ivan said, grinning with pride, and she supposed he thought he was being cool, quoting a thirteen-year-old Beyoncé song. She noticed that his teeth were as tiny as baby corn kernels.

"I can take care of myself, Ivan." She offered a friendly but tight smile.

"I bet you can." He took a step closer.

"Did I mention my boyfriend's a cop?" She said this as if it were only half a joke.

"Should I be scared?"

"Not if you behave yourself."

"What fun is that?"

He advanced, and Dana backed up until she was leaning against the roof railing. He was too close, and a chill of danger swept through her.

"You know, I think we'll get along better if we keep it strictly business," she said, hoping he would step away.

For a moment, they locked eyes. And they were so close she could even see the outline of his contact lenses in the gleam of the overhead light. He looked menacing, and Dana's pulse quickened, her fight-or-flight response triggered. She glanced around to see if there was anyone nearby whose attention she could get. The only person close enough to see them was Lorenzo DeSantis, the sound guy she had been involved with when she was first hired. But he was engaged in conversation with Brenda, the executive suite receptionist, and she couldn't catch his eye. She tried to will him to look her way.

Ivan touched her neck with the back of his fingers. "You're irresistible."

"I'm unavailable," she said firmly.

He leaned in. "Don't you like powerful men?" he whispered.

"Back off, Ivan."

He waited a beat, as if she might change her mind, and then took a step away. "You take things too seriously," he said with a laugh, as if the whole thing were a joke, as if he hadn't meant any of it. As if he hadn't come within an inch of threatening her. In truth, he probably sensed she was about to call for help.

"I'm getting a refill," he added. "Can I get you something?"

Dana wondered if that meant he would search for another victim—someone more amenable to his advances—or if he'd be coming back for her.

"I'm fine," she said, indicating her nearly full glass, but as soon as he left she downed the rest of her drink, and then waited until he cleared the bar before getting herself another. She needed to steady her nerves.

"I thought you were going to take it easy tonight," Megan said when she saw Dana sipping her second vodka martini.

Dana was eager to tell her friend what had happened, but she couldn't do it with Ivan's son standing right there. It would have to wait until later.

"This will be my last one," she said, because she really did want to stay sober for Ari. It was important to make a good impression on the cops who held his future in their hands. In fact, she wouldn't stay at this party one minute more than she had to. After the speeches, she'd make a quick and quiet exit.

Dana nursed the rest of her martini as she chatted with other coworkers, making sure to keep her distance from Ivan. But a short while later, the band stopped playing and everyone gathered in the tent for the speeches. Dana's glass was empty by then, and she got another martini just so she would have something to hold on to. She told herself she would not take more than a sip, especially since she was already a little light-headed.

Charles Honeycutt spoke first, thanking everyone for coming. He had been there since the company's inception, and spoke a bit about the history with great pride. Clearly, he felt he had helped build something worthwhile, and expressed his confidence that such a talented group of people could weather the current difficulties and that they would emerge stronger than ever.

"We've done it before, friends, and we can do it again." Everyone raised their glass and drank to that.

He introduced Ivan Dennison with carefully chosen words of praise, restrained yet collegial.

When Ivan took the mike, he thanked Charles and the entire staff, but in a way that pointed to how magnanimous he was for acknowledging them. Then he proceeded to talk about himself and the success he had leading an electronics chain through some terrible trials to emerge as one of the country's biggest retailers.

"I vow to do the same thing for the Shopping Channel," he said. "But of course, that's going to necessitate some difficult changes. It will take toughness and grit, and I hope you're all up for the challenge."

A murmur of concern rippled through the party. Did this mean layoffs? Who would be fired? Dana glanced around and could see the worry in everyone's eyes. Sherry Zidel looked like she was made from poured cement. Her girlfriend gently rubbed her back, but Sherry was unyielding as she stared at Ivan, a glass of champagne in her fist.

Dana took a sip of her martini and then another. She was getting drunker, but it was okay. She could handle it. She just needed to get through whatever bomb Ivan Dennison was about to drop.

"Relax," Ivan said with a forced smile. "At this point, nothing has been decided about changes in personnel. But we will be taking the company in a bold new direction."

Dana's dainty sips gave way to an indelicate gulp. She wiped her mouth with the back of her hand.

"As you know," he continued, "the fashion industry is going through a sea change. Online retailers are gobbling up our business. We've tried everything, including bringing aboard great new talent." He paused to make a subtle gesture in Dana's direction, and nearly everyone at the party turned to look at her. She couldn't think of any response beyond taking another sip of her drink. Dana put her other hand on the back of a chair for balance.

Everyone turned their attention back toward Ivan, and Dana's eyes swept the room. It seemed that no one knew what was coming—not Eleanor Gratz, who had her hand to her heart as if attempting to keep it inside, not Charles Honeycutt, whose head was down in the intense concentration of someone trying to hold in an explosion, and certainly not Sherry Zidel, still as static as a rooftop gargoyle.

"So it's time to look to the future," Ivan said. "To embrace reality—we live in a technical world. And that's why the Shopping Channel is going to become a leader in computers and electronics. No more *fashion*." He pronounced the word as if it left a bad taste in his mouth. "No more...*handbags* or *accessories*." He articulated those words with even more disdain, as if they could only exist within quotation marks because they had so little meaning. "We'll be selling laptops and desktops, cell phones and tablets, speakers and headphones, smart appliances, drones, things that haven't even been invented yet!" He reached a crescendo of excitement, so wrapped up in his own drama he had no idea that he had completely lost the room. He thought he was impressive and inspiring, when in fact there wasn't a person listening who didn't wish to see him collapse in sudden cardiac arrest.

"We'll be on the cutting edge, people. And I am so excited to lead the Shopping Channel into this brilliant future."

The room fell silent for several uncomfortable beats before a smattering of polite applause rippled through the crowd.

Dana downed the rest of her drink, and wanted to bolt. But for the moment, she was too dizzy to move. Suddenly, Felicia and Jo were upon her, asking what she thought it meant. Who would be fired and how soon? Were their jobs safe? Would Dana and Vanessa and the rest of the hosts be able to sell electronics, or would they be bringing in some geeky types?

Dana had no answers, so she kept repeating, "I don't know, I don't know."

"Are you okay?" Jo asked.

"I'm fine. I just need some air."

Dana crossed out of the tent and back to the quiet section of the roof, where she steadied herself on the railing as she looked past the Hudson River and toward the bridge. She lost track of time, but soon became aware that Ivan was back at her side.

"We have to stop meeting like this," he said, resting a heavy hand between her shoulder blades.

She turned to him. Was he really going to come on to her again, after that bombshell? She saw no reason to hold back.

"You got to be kidding me," she said, angry.

"Aw, c'mon," he said. "It's not that bad." He leaned in close to her ear and breathed, "Besides, I like you."

She backed away, trying to unpack his implication. His use of the word *like* seemed loaded with innuendo, as if her job would be safe if only she "liked" him back.

He held up a martini glass. "Here, I brought you a peace offering."

She folded her arms. "No, thanks."

"Don't be like that," he said, and forced the glass into her hand.

She looked down at the drink and then pointedly put it aside, resting it on the building's ledge.

"Ivan," she said slowly, trying to regain control of the conversation. After all, she had an agenda of her own. "If you want to talk business, we can be friends. In fact, I have some great ideas that can help turn things around without abandoning our brand."

She thought she sounded pretty articulate for someone who was drunk, but he laughed at her.

"Dana, you're adorable, but leave the marketing to the executives."

You condescending fucker, she thought, but before she could utter a response, Megan was at her side.

"I was looking all over for you," she said, casting a glare at Ivan. "Come on. Jamie is waiting for us on the dance floor." She grabbed Dana's arm and pulled her away.

When they were out of Ivan's earshot, Megan was in business manager mode, though Dana could tell she'd knocked back a few. "Don't worry about that bastard's speech," she said. "You have a contract. They can't fire you. Understand?"

"I don't even know if I want to work for such a pig."

Megan studied her friend's face. "Did he do something?"

Dana shuddered. "It was gross. He's older than my dad. It was all so...so Harvey Weinstein."

Megan bit her lip in concentration, and Dana waited. Her friend could hold her liquor well enough to fool most people, but Dana understood that when Megan slowed down, it meant she was buzzed. "Don't worry," she finally said. "We'll...document everything—take him to court if we need to."

"I should really get out of here," Dana said. "Ari's waiting for me."

Just then, the band launched into a rendition of "Firework," and Megan's face lit up. The two of them had partied to the song in college.

"Not yet," Megan said. "We have to dance to this. Please!"

Dana figured one dance couldn't hurt. In fact, blowing off a little tension was just what she needed. And so she let her friend drag her onto the dance floor, where they joined Jamie Dennison as the musicians did a very passable job with the Katy Perry number.

She had promised herself that would be it, but the band segued into "Forget You," which was just too much fun to pass up. But Dana was perspiring now, and wanted just another sip or two of a drink. She rushed back to the ledge where she had left the cocktail and downed a big gulp before realizing Ivan, that idiot, had ordered a gin martini, which was piney and bitter. Still, it was better than nothing, and the song was playing on, so she had a couple more sips and joined her friend on the dance floor.

Within moments, a different kind of dizziness began to overtake her. How strong had that drink been? Dana continued dancing, but her limbs began to float, and when the band started playing Beyoncé's "All the Single Ladies," she glanced up to see Ivan across the floor, holding up a drink as if toasting to her.

After that, Dana lost a sense of where she was, as everything blurred into random images played against a muted, driving beat. It seemed to go on and on and on. She waited for it to end, for the vertigo to clear, as there was something she needed to do, someplace else she needed to be, though for the life of her she couldn't remember what it was. The world stopped making any kind of sense. Her body. Her brain. Everything was strange and disconnected, impossible to track. She seemed to strobe back and forth between here and elsewhere. At one point, a man was standing very close, saying something important, but it was as if she were suspended on a string, swimming through space and unable to reach the earth. Someone grabbed her arm and she reacted in anger, wrenching it away and saying...something. Time collapsed on itself and she didn't know if she was back on the dance floor or elsewhere. Then, just like that, it all went black and silent, as if the world had ended. Until one sound broke through the haze of her thick trance: a piercing scream.

6

"Dana, are you okay? Wake up."

For a moment, Dana thought she was still on the dance floor, and wondered why she was on her back. But no, the room was warm and a soft expanse cradled the length of her.

She opened her eyes to discover she was on the couch in her dressing room, looking up at Megan.

"What happened?" Dana asked.

"You don't remember?"

She sat up and rubbed her throbbing head. "I don't think so."

"How many martinis did you have?" Megan handed her a glass of water and Dana took a gulp.

"I remember a gin martini, dancing with you and Jamie, and then...not much. What happened to me?"

Her friend's brow tightened. "You were dancing with one person after another and then I lost track of you. You don't remember what happened after the lights when off?"

She focused hard and bits of it came back to her. She recalled that everything went dead very suddenly—the music, the lights.

"Was it the generator?" Dana asked.

"Yes, the generator died. And then…" Megan looked away, as if hoping Dana would complete the sentence.

"Then what?" Dana said.

"You really don't recall?"

Dana studied her friend's face and realized she had the pale, faraway look of someone who had been traumatized.

"Tell me," she pleaded.

Megan's hand went to her throat, as if she had to find her own pulse before continuing. Finally she said, "Dana… Ivan Dennison is dead."

Dead? Dana blinked, trying to understand. Her brain seemed to need an extra beat to process the simple sentence.

"One minute the lights went out," Megan continued, "and the next minute someone screamed. Everybody rushed to the side of the roof and looked down. There he was—on the sidewalk right next to a lamppost. His whole body…" She trailed off and shuddered. "Poor Jamie. He went white as stone."

"Someone pushed Ivan?" Dana asked, picturing the impossible drop from the railing to the street below. No one could survive that fall.

"The railing is too high for someone to trip over accidentally, so…"

Dana held her head in her hands. She didn't need Megan to complete the sentence—Ivan was murdered…and she remembered none of it. "Where was I?"

"I found you in the crowd. You didn't look right. Your eyes were glassy and blank, and you couldn't speak. Next thing I knew, you passed out. I caught you just before your head hit the ground. I didn't know what to do. Jamie was freaking out and you were unconscious. Thank goodness for Charles Honeycutt, who carried you here like you weighed nothing."

"Where is he?" Dana asked, glancing around the empty room.

"Went back up to the roof to try to calm everybody down while they waited for the police to arrive. He asked me if you'd done any drugs."

Dana closed her eyes and tried to remember if anyone had offered her a pill, a joint, a bump. Nothing came back to her.

"What did you tell him?"

"Just that you'd had a few too many. But you sure seemed fucked up. I've been waiting so long for you to wake."

Dana took several slow breaths, absorbing this new reality. Ivan Dennison was lying dead on a sidewalk. She tried to imagine how his family might react to this heartbreaking news, and with a shudder, she realized what his son had witnessed. She looked at Megan.

"And Jamie?" she asked.

"All I know is that Sherry and Eleanor were with him."

Dana reached out and gave her friend's arm a squeeze—a thank-you for staying with her.

"I don't know why I passed out," she said. "I didn't take anything. At least I don't think I did." She stopped to recall about how far away she'd felt, how altered her consciousness had been, and a terrible thought occurred to her.

"You okay?" Megan said, when she saw her friend's expression.

Dana shook her head and swallowed. "I think somebody doped my drink."

Megan's eyes went wide. "You mean like Rohypnol?"

A date-rape drug. Dana shivered. "I don't know, but that was not an ordinary drink."

"Maybe that bartender just made you paranoid."

Dana sat up and swung her legs over the side of the couch. "I've been drunk plenty of times. This was different."

"Who would have done something like that? Ivan?"

Dana shrugged. "He's the one who got me the drink, so maybe. Probably. But it could have been anyone. I left it on the ledge."

Megan sat on one of the chairs facing the sofa. "Did he try to get you to leave the party with him?"

"I don't know."

"Did anyone else come on to you?"

Dana concentrated, but the memories were so elusive, like wisps of smoke. She closed her eyes and tried to recall. There were flashes—a man trying to get her to understand something, the feeling of someone grabbing her arm, followed by some kind of argument.

"I think someone got...physical," she said, "but someone else intervened."

"Do you know when it happened?"

Dana sighed. "It's all so vague."

"Think hard. Was it right before the lights went out?"

"Maybe."

"And who was it? Who intervened?"

Dana studied her friend's face to understand her line of questioning. She was still a little fuzzy and felt a few beats behind. "Why is that so important?" she asked.

"A man is *dead*."

"And you think my savior was the one who pushed him?"

Megan shrugged as her eyes narrowed in concentration. "Who knows? After that announcement, everyone on that roof wanted to see Ivan Dennison choke on his own tongue... or worse."

Dana thought about how complicated the investigation might get, and then she remembered something. Ari. She realized how late it was and knew where she was supposed to be. "Oh god," she said. "Ari was expecting me at that party."

"Somehow I think he'll understand."

Dana nodded. She knew from the sound of sirens that the police had already arrived on the scene, and wondered if he had heard about what was going on. She was about to get her phone so she could text him when there was a sharp knock on the door.

Megan answered it, and there stood a woman in a gray blazer over a black shirt and pants, a plastic-covered identification badge hanging on a chain around her neck. She had pale red hair and a delicate complexion, but the steely resolve of a police officer. She identified herself as Detective Byrne of the NYPD.

After taking their names, Byrne got a full account from Megan on what she saw. Then it was Dana's turn, and she had to explain why her memory was so hazy. The detective nodded sympathetically, but Dana could tell her wheels were spinning.

"But you're okay now?" she asked.

Dana nodded. "I feel like I just woke from a deep sleep. You think someone gave me a date-rape drug?"

"It's possible," Byrne said. "Will you consent to a drug test? It could be valuable information."

"Of course," Dana answered. She was eager to know what had been dropped into her drink…and by whom.

Byrne got the details on the type of glass Dana had been drinking from and closed her notepad.

"If you can stick around for a bit," she said, "I'll take you straight to the lab."

After Detective Byrne left, Dana retrieved her purse from her dressing room locker and fished out her cell phone. There were two texts from Ari. The first one was sent during the party, asking about her ETA. The second one came in only a short time ago, when he was in police mode.

Heard about the incident at your office. Hope you're okay. May get called in.

She understood that he needed to be vague, as it would be unprofessional for him to tell her anything specific about what he had learned. From her conversations with him, she also knew that *may get called in* meant the homicide squad was waiting to hear from the precinct detectives about the probable cause of death. If it wasn't an accident or a suicide, the murder police would be summoned.

She started to type back a message about what had happened with her drink, but thought better of it. No need to worry him with a few vague sentences. So she backspaced over it and simply wrote:

I'm fine. Come over when you're done.

His reply was quick:

We got the call. It'll be late.

It meant he was on the case, and some cop on the scene would probably tell him about the Shopping Channel host whose drink had been doped. He'd be worried as hell. But she would fill him in later. For now, she simply sent back two emojis: a key and a snoring face. It was her shorthand for *Let yourself in—I'll be sleeping*.

7

After the drug test, Detective Byrne drove Dana home with a promise that someone would call her soon with the results.

When she finally got into bed, Dana expected to toss and turn. But apparently the mysterious drug was still in her system, and the shade of sleep came down fast. Later, she roused herself to see if Ari had come in, but she was alone in bed. She glanced at the clock—it was two thirty in the morning. That meant he either went all the way home to Brooklyn, or was still working.

She fell back asleep, but got her answer in a few hours when she heard his key in the door.

"Ari?" she called out, bleary.

"Sorry to wake you," he said, and came into the tiny bedroom, which was actually nothing more than a walled-off alcove.

She squinted at the light coming in from the living area. "What time is it?"

"Just after six. It was an all-nighter. You okay?"

Dana struggled to prop herself onto her elbows. "Can't say I'm not freaked out."

He sat down on the bed, loosening his tie. She put her arms out for a hug and he embraced her, nosing into the warmth of her neck. They held still for a quiet moment before he pulled away and looked into her eyes.

"I spoke to Byrne," he said softly.

"She told you about the drink?"

He nodded, moving a lock of hair from her face. "We'll have the lab results next week. You feel okay?"

"I'm fine. I guess I was lucky—only had a few sips."

"You think someone was trying to get you alone?"

Here, in the intimacy of this dark room, his stoicism relaxed into worry. And she wished she could tell him it was all a big mistake—she had simply had too much to drink. But no. The more time passed, the more certain she became. She had been drugged.

"I don't know," she said. "It's a confusing blur."

"We'll figure it out, Dana. All of it."

She sat up straighter. "Does this mean it's your case?"

She hadn't meant to sound so excited. A man was dead, and here she was, focused on what it would mean for Ari's career… and for them. After all, if he took the lead on a high-profile investigation like this, his promotion was a shoo-in. But when she saw Ari's reaction, Dana wished she could take it back. His posture went rigid as he stood and turned away from her. He went through his ritual of taking off his suit jacket and putting it on the hanger she had left for him on a wall hook. He removed his gun from his waistband and put it in the night table drawer. She waited for him to speak.

"I think I'll have to recuse myself," he finally said, his back to her.

She sat up straighter. "What do you mean?"

"I'm…personally involved. It could be a problem."

"But you're not personally involved with the *victim*…or his family, or…"

"If the issue with your drink becomes relevant to the case, our relationship could be a liability."

"This doesn't make any sense," she said.

"This is going to be an important investigation, high profile. It has to be squeaky clean."

"But there's nothing dirty about—"

"Tomorrow I'm going to tell the lieutenant to make Lee the lead investigator."

"Lee?" she said, feeling suddenly very awake. Detective Kevin Lee—often Ari's partner on cases—was his competitor for advancement to homicide squad sergeant.

"It's the right thing to do." He sounded resolute.

"But your promotion."

Ari let out a heavy sigh and turned back to her. "It will have to wait."

She stared at him, wondering how all that ambition had drained so quickly. Surely there was a way to take the lead on this case despite their relationship.

"I think you're giving up too easily," she said.

"Dana, you think this is what I *want*?"

She considered it, recalling her hesitance to get involved with a guy who had been married. In her experience, divorced men were always terrified to make another commitment for fear of repeating their past mistakes. So maybe, on some level, it was exactly what he wanted, because the promotion would also mean fast-tracking their relationship. He had said it was what he wanted, but who knows? He wouldn't be the first guy to get cold feet.

"Maybe it is," she said.

He backed up. "How could you say that?" His voice was even, but she could tell he was holding back, and that only made her pricklier.

"You've been so resistant to looking for a new apartment with me. Maybe a part of you doesn't want it."

"Of course I want it. You *know* that."

"Then why recuse yourself? Why not just talk to the lieutenant about it and let him make the decision?"

"Because I know what he'll say, and I'm trying to be a professional here."

"What about us?"

"This has nothing to do with us."

"It has everything to do with us," she said. "Unless you've changed your mind about waiting for the promotion before moving in together."

He paused, inhaled. "You know how I feel about that."

Dana kicked off the covers and sat up, fear gnawing at her. He was pulling away. "You're sabotaging this relationship!" she said.

He grunted. "That's called *projecting*."

"You think *I'm* sabotaging our relationship?" She got up out of bed. "Then tell me this—how come I'm the one who went out and got us a perfect apartment?"

It took Ari a moment to find his voice. "You did what?"

Dana froze. Had she really just blurted that out? Well, there was nothing to do now but own it.

"I found an apartment," she said defiantly. "A steal. Two bedrooms. West Side. Crazy amounts of sunlight. For *us*."

His face went still. "You signed a lease?"

"It was either that or let it go." She took his hands. "Ari, once you see this place—"

He backed away. "You didn't even ask me?"

"I wanted to surprise you."

"But you knew I wanted to wait until after my promotion."

She turned on the light to get a better look at his face, and then turned it off again. His fury was mounting.

"I thought it would come through any day," she explained, "and I knew that once you saw it you'd fall in love. Ari, it's on this beautiful block, and it has gorgeous hardwood floors and massive windows. And they allow dogs!" She was sure that last part would be the clincher. Ari wanted so badly to have a dog, but they were strictly forbidden in his Brooklyn apartment.

"I don't care if they allow American Kennel Club meetings," he said. "You did this behind my back."

"Maybe it seems a little impetuous, but—"

"A little! When did this happen?"

"Last week. I was waiting for the right moment to tell you."

"And you thought I would just go along with it? After we talked about it? After I specifically said we had to wait until I could afford my share?"

"I knew you'd be a little mad, but—"

"But what? You thought you'd manipulate me even after we had a very clear conversation about this? *Several* very clear conversations."

"Will you at least look at it?"

He blinked at her, stunned by the question. "Not a chance."

She sat on the bed. "I… I don't think I can get out of the lease."

"Well then, I hope you're very happy there."

"Oh, c'mon, Ari."

"How did this even start? Were you scanning real estate sites?"

"No! Megan called me about this great rent-stabilized place that came on the market. It was an *opportunity*."

"But you didn't call me. Text me. Nothing. You just went

and signed a lease. Because you knew I'd say no if you asked me first."

"You would have! And then you'd have regretted it."

"Oh, please." He opened the drawer with his gun and snapped it back into his holster.

"You're leaving?"

"You don't get to make unilateral decisions for us, Dana. It doesn't work that way." He grabbed his jacket and slid it on.

"I think you'd feel differently if you were willing to take the lead on the case. It would change everything."

He turned to her, his eyes burning with fury. "I can't take the lead!"

"Why not!"

"Because my girlfriend was drugged and doesn't even remember if she pushed the fucking victim off the roof."

Dana's jaw unhinged as she tried to think of a response, but before she could find one, Ari was gone.

8

Dana knew it was useless to try to fall back asleep, but she could think of nothing else to do at that hour but lie in bed in the dark, listening to the white noise of traffic whooshing up First Avenue, punctuated by the occasional honk of an impatient driver. Well okay, she could think of two things. But right now, Dana wanted to stay sober and reason this thing out. She knew Ari didn't believe she murdered Ivan. He couldn't possibly. But she also understood that she couldn't be officially ruled out as a suspect. At least not yet.

But once that happened, he would forgive her for signing the lease on the apartment. She knew he would.

Or maybe not. Maybe she had really fucked up this time. Maybe it was a mistake to sign the lease. But there was nothing she could do about it now, except apologize. She picked up her phone several times, wondering if she should text Ari to say she was sorry. If she admitted it was a stupid mistake— a terrible error in judgment—he would forgive her.

She held her phone and tapped out:

I was wrong. I'm sorry. Let's talk.

She stared at the text, debating whether to send it. Maybe it was better to give him some time to cool off.

She tried to picture where he might be. Home, grabbing a couple of hours of sleep? Or maybe he went right back to the office and told the lieutenant he was recusing himself.

But no. Now that he had walked out, he didn't need to recuse himself. He was free of her, and free to take the lead on the case. If she apologized now, it would put their relationship back on track, but derail his career. And that would be a roadblock to moving forward. Dana felt caught in a loop of impossibilities.

Unless…

Unless she let him walk away. Then he could take the case and see it through. They could get back together when it was all over. It probably wouldn't even take that long. And by then, his anger over the apartment would be ancient history. They could get right back on the relationship train. He'd get his promotion and they'd have a beautiful future in the semi-sunny two-bedroom.

As far as Dana could tell, it wasn't even a big risk. He loved her. He would want to get back together.

She backspaced over the apology and thought about what she should say instead. At last she typed out:

I think we both need a break.

Dana's finger hovered over the Send button. *Just do it*, she told herself, *before you change your mind*. She swallowed hard and tapped the screen. There. She had done it, and hoped he understood that it was a gift. She was proud of her courage.

Dana stared at her phone, her heart thudding as she waited for a response. After a few minutes, she saw the gray dots indicating he was typing. Her hand began to sweat in anticipation, and then the dots disappeared.

"Come on, Ari. Say *something*," she whispered to her phone.

She kept staring, willing a text to appear. The longer she waited, the more she worried about his reaction. She hated the thought of hurting him. But he was strong. And they were strong as a couple. They could weather this.

And then, at last, a message:

Is that it? No apology?

Of course I'm sorry, she thought. *All I want is for us to be together.* But she typed:

You're the one who walked out.

There were no gray dots after that, just the cold chill of her empty bed, and a barren weekend stretching out in front of her as she tortured herself with the idea of calling Ari to explain that she didn't mean any of it.

Later, when she was in the shower, Dana heard her phone ring. She wrapped herself in a towel and rushed out, diving for her phone. It was Megan.

"You okay?" her friend asked.

"Not really." She put the phone down and wrapped her wet hair in a towel before picking it up again. "You?"

"I'm with Jamie and his mom."

"Jamie?" Dana repeated, surprised. She knew Megan had hit it off with Ivan's son, but that didn't qualify her for the role of caretaker in the aftershock of a death. "How did that happen?"

"After they took his dad to the morgue, Jamie went straight out to Long Island to be with his mom. She's disabled—did you know that?"

"No idea."

"She was obsessing on what exactly happened at the party. Jamie was too shook up to answer her questions, so he called me and I came."

"That's…a lot of responsibility. How is she?"

"Sad. Confused." Megan lowered her voice. "I think she has an inkling of the kind of guy her husband is. *Was*."

"Shit."

There was a pause, and Dana heard Megan take a breath. "I was wondering if you could come out here."

"Me?" Dana asked. It was the last thing she expected to hear.

"Jamie has some…information. He wants to talk to you."

"That's cryptic."

"I know. I'm sorry. But it's hard to do this stuff over the phone. And things are so weird here. I could use the support, to tell you the truth. It's me and the Dennisons, and it's a little awkward."

It didn't take Dana long to decide. Megan needed her. And besides, the trip to Long Island would give her a good excuse to pop in on her sister, who had been avoiding her calls. Dana worried that Chelsea was privately nursing the sorrow of another miscarriage, and she wanted to let her know she didn't have to keep it a secret.

9

Two hours later, Dana arrived at the Port Washington Station and took an Uber up to the Dennisons' address in Sands Point. She knew it was one of the most exclusive areas in Long Island—the coveted Gold Coast—but Dana was still struck by the beautiful drive through winding, wooded streets, with estates carefully tucked back and mostly out of sight down long driveways.

As the car turned onto an entryway paved in smooth white stones, a massive iron gate opened to let them in. The house itself was an oversized mansion that looked more like a hotel than a home, and Dana tried to imagine the kind of people who had enough money to afford almost any house they wanted, yet chose this one. The architectural style managed to look cold and impervious despite the obvious Tuscan influence. Perhaps it looked better in summer or spring. But in the fall, surrounded by northeast foliage and tucked in among historic colonials, it looked as if it were dropped into the wrong spot, like tomato sauce on a bowl of oatmeal. If it weren't for Megan standing outside in front, she would have been tempted to tell the driver to circle right back to the train station so she could clear her palate.

"Yikes," Dana said, as she got out of the car and surveyed the property.

"I know," Megan agreed. "It belongs in *Architectural Indigestion*."

Dana gave her a hug. "How's Jamie?"

"More focused on his mom than anything else. How are you? No offense, but you look like shit."

Dana let out a long breath and gave Megan the news. "Ari and I decided to take a break."

Her friend's eyes went wide in alarm.

"It'll be okay," Dana said. "I didn't want him to have to recuse himself from the investigation."

"And you broke up over that?"

"It's just temporary," Dana insisted. "We'll be fine."

Her friend looked skeptical. "I hope you know what you're doing."

Me, too, Dana thought, as Megan gave her arm a squeeze. Normally, this revelation would be followed by an hours-long conversation. But it would have to wait.

She followed Megan into the house, which was nearly free of walls, with one room flowing into the next and no interruption of the vast expanse of modern gray driftwood flooring—the kind favored by Californians and the decorators of cancer centers. The furniture was angular and pristine, as if untouched. It was the opposite of welcoming. *Don't sit here*, every carefully spaced piece seemed to say, *this is just for show*.

Megan led Dana into the kitchen, which had ornate white wood cabinetry, a dripping crystal chandelier and a massive center island with a marble top. A stout woman with dark hair was wiping down the counters, while Jamie sat at the long oak table with a woman in a wheelchair—his mother, Dana presumed. Though underweight, with bony wrists and brown circles under sunken eyes, she was still attractive. Her cheekbones were sharp and her small eyes crystal blue. Dana could imagine the healthy version of her in walking shorts on a golf course in Connecticut. She wished she had asked Megan what put the woman in a wheelchair.

Jamie introduced her by her full name—Blair Dennison—and added that the person at the counter was their house-keeper, Marta.

"I'm sorry for your loss," Dana said to the new widow. "I can't imagine how hard all this is."

Mrs. Dennison pulled a tissue from her cardigan sleeve and dabbed at her nose. "I always thought he would bury *me*," she said, in a husky voice.

A former smoker, Dana thought, and pictured Blair and Ivan as a young couple sitting in a club at some time in the distant past, drinking highballs and flicking cigarettes into overflowing ashtrays.

Jamie rubbed his mother's back. "Are you tired, Mom?"

She nodded. "I think I'll lie down for a while."

Marta offered to take her to her room, and she accepted. "Don't forget to offer your friend some tea," she muttered, as she was wheeled off.

"I hope I didn't drive her away," Dana said, when she was out of earshot.

Jamie shook his head. "Don't take it personally. I've been fending off calls from friends and relatives all morning. The news is spreading and the phone doesn't stop ringing, but she refuses to see or talk to *anyone*. Well, except for me and my brother, who's on a flight right now from California. But she's glad I have Megan here to keep me company so she's free to withdraw. It's all too much for her."

Last night, the noise of the party was so overwhelming Dana couldn't have any kind of conversation with Jamie. But now that she heard him speak, she could see why Megan was drawn to him. He wasn't just intelligent, but fast-talking and hyper-articulate. Dana had known people like him—there were a lot of them in the theater world—loquacious and outgoing types who had been gifted children with a lot to say and the need to blurt it all out while people were still listening.

He pulled a china mug from a cabinet and held it up to Dana. "Tea? Please say yes so I can tell my mother I'm a good host."

She accepted, and he filled the cup with hot water from a special spigot next to the sink. He placed it in front of her, then pushed forward a rectangular wooden box filled with an impressive assortment of teas. Dana rifled through the selections and chose an organic green tea, which she plunked into the hot water. Jamie took a seat across from her, where his own cup seemed to remained untouched.

"You must have a lot to do," Dana said. "Funeral arrangements, calling relatives."

"They have *people* for that," Megan said.

Jamie offered a small smile, as if grateful she lightened the mood. "She makes it sound worse than it is," he said. "My uncle is handling most of it." He paused. "But yeah, we have *people*."

"And you're okay?" Dana asked him.

"Not really," he said. "I just haven't taken it all in yet."

Dana nodded, studying him. He seemed composed for someone who had just last night seen his father's gray matter oozing onto a sidewalk. But grief, she knew, was a fickle beast, and could be kept at bay for long stretches. A lot of people couldn't begin the process until after the burial, when it finally became real.

After a pause, Megan looked at him expectantly. "Go on," she said. "Tell her."

"Tell me what?" Dana asked.

Jamie wrapped his hands around his cup and stared off, unfocused. "We had a visitor here about two weeks ago." He directed his gaze back at Dana. "Eleanor Gratz."

Dana blinked back, surprised. Why would the Shopping Channel buyer be paying a visit?

"Eleanor came to your *house*?" she asked.

"Uninvited."

"Why?" Dana asked.

"She wanted to talk to my mother, but my father wouldn't let her inside. I only heard a few seconds of the conversation before he stepped out onto the porch with her and shut the door."

This was a surprising piece of information. "What did she want with your mom?"

"I don't know for sure, but I have a guess."

Dana took a sip of her earthy tea. "Go on."

Jamie glanced at Megan and back at Dana. "It probably won't surprise you to know my dad was a bit of a...player."

He said it so pointedly that Dana surmised he knew what had happened with her last night. She gave Megan a look that said, *What did you tell him?*

Megan shrugged in response. "He's an investigative reporter. He asks questions."

"Anyway," Jamie continued, "my theory is that Eleanor knew about my father's behavior, and threatened to tell my mother."

"You think she was *blackmailing* him?" Dana was incredulous. It didn't seem at all like the Eleanor she knew.

"Maybe not for cash," Jamie suggested. "Maybe she was trying to force his hand with the company. I mean, if anybody knew his secret plans to abandon fashion for electronics, it was Eleanor. So maybe she told him to back off or she would expose him to my mother."

"I'm still trying to figure out if the dots really connect," Megan said.

Dana paused to consider it as she replayed her conversation with Eleanor. If the formidable Shopping Channel exec had known about Ivan's plans for the company, she had certainly kept it under wraps.

Dana took another sip of her tea and dabbed her mouth with a napkin, stalling, as she decided whether she should share a certain piece of information. At last, she let out a breath. "We talked about him."

"*We?*" Jamie said.

"Me and Eleanor. She warned me to watch out for him."

Jamie looked at Megan. "See?"

"On the other hand," Dana said, "your father went through with his plans for the company. Doesn't that disprove your theory?"

"He was a pretty wily guy," Jamie explained. "And determined—especially since he was always so protective of my mother. He tried to shield her from any kind of stress, because it can trigger a flare-up like that." He snapped his fingers, and Dana was tempted to ask how such an ostensibly considerate guy could act like such a pig, but she kept her mouth shut.

"I know my father," Jamie continued. "He would have found a way to deal with a threat to my mom."

"Such as?" Dana asked.

He shrugged. "I don't know. Maybe he threatened her back. I couldn't hear their conversation, but I watched from the window and could see the two of them arguing on the front porch before she stormed off."

"Does your mom know any of this?"

Megan leaned forward. "He wants to tell her."

Dana turned to him. "Why would you do that?"

"Well, obviously I have to go to the police with this. I mean…"

"Obviously," Dana echoed. The police would want to know about Ivan's possible enemies. And here was one who was actually at the party. Still, the idea that Eleanor could have murdered Ivan was preposterous. She was just so open, so quick to tell you what was on her mind. Hardly the profile of a killer.

Then again, the company meant everything to her. Was it possible in the heat of the moment she grabbed—or rather, pushed—an opportunity?

Jamie went on. "I'm afraid my mother will find out about Dad's indiscretions one way or another. And it could devastate her. So, I was thinking it might be best if it came from me—I know how to deal with her, and I think I could find a way to soften the blow. But Megan disagrees."

"My point is that it's possible his mother will never find out," Megan said. "I mean, if Eleanor is cleared, then none of this will come up."

"But the police are going to be digging pretty deeply into my father's behavior. And I just hate the thought of her being blindsided."

"The cops aren't going to tell your mother unless it's absolutely necessary," Dana said.

"I wish I felt confident that wasn't going to happen," Jamie said. "And I hate lying to her. She seems to suspect he was cheating—asked me all kinds of questions about what happened at the party. I feel like I have a duty to tell her the truth."

"I'm trying to convince him to at least hold off," Megan said.

Jamie rubbed his forehead. "It worries me."

"Maybe I can help," Dana said.

Jamie looked at her. "How so?"

"I have a rapport with Eleanor. Maybe I can get her to open up about her visit here. If it turns out it had nothing to do with your father's indiscretions, you don't have to burden your mother."

Jamie took a sip of his tea as he considered it. "How long do you think that would take?"

"Not more than a few days."

He bit his lip in contemplation, and although his expression softened, he stayed silent. It looked like he wanted to speak but was holding back.

"Say yes, Jamie," Megan pressed him.

He sighed, as if he had no choice but to respond with the tired joke, "Yes, Jamie."

But it was clear he meant it—he wanted Dana to do some digging.

10

"What are you doing here?" Chelsea asked, when Dana showed up on her doorstep.

She had taken an Uber straight from the Dennisons' house to her older sister's home in Roslyn. It was a sprawling colonial Dana had affectionately dubbed the House of Seventeen Gables, due to the abundance of rooflines. But the trendy suburban architecture, supersized as it was, felt homey compared to the cold and incongruous mansion.

"How warm," Dana said. "I'm touched."

Chelsea folded her arms. "Seriously," she said. "You've never just shown up unannounced."

Dana surveyed her sister's appearance looking for the signs of depression she had exhibited after her miscarriage, when she couldn't bring herself to get out of her bathrobe and into the shower. Today, Chelsea looked like her normal suburban self, dressed for yoga in one of those Lycra outfits that came via monthly subscription. It was the kind of ensemble wealthy

Long Island women were more likely to wear to Starbucks or the hairdresser than to a workout.

"You've been avoiding me," she said.

"So you came all the way out to Long Island just to visit me? Without even checking to see if I'd be home?"

"Is it a crime to pop in to see my sister?" Dana said, hedging the question.

Chelsea squinted at her. She wasn't buying it.

"Have you turned on the news today?" Dana asked, testing whether her sister might have heard about Ivan's murder.

Chelsea shook her head. "Should I?"

Dana shrugged. "You going to let me in?"

Chelsea pushed open the door and Dana followed her into the kitchen.

"Where are the boys?" Dana asked, referring to Chelsea's husband and four-year-old son. The house, she had noticed, was especially quiet.

"Soccer."

"How come you didn't go?"

Chelsea took in a quick breath. "I had things to do."

Dana bent to look at the laptop on the kitchen table. The browser was open to a shoe store website featuring a cream-colored wedge in satin, with an ankle strap and a bejeweled toe. "I can see," she said. "Planning a mountain hike?"

Chelsea huffed and closed the computer. "So now you need a blow-by-blow on my day?"

"With video, if you don't mind."

Chelsea didn't laugh, but the joke seemed to soften her defenses. "Look, I know you're worried about me. But I promise, I'm fine."

Dana scanned her sister's face. If she'd had a miscarriage, she was handling it much better than last time. But maybe that wasn't it. Maybe she had simply gotten her hopes up about being pregnant this month, and got her period when she was at the restaurant. That would explain the sudden drop in her mood. They were usually so open with each other, but perhaps this time Chelsea just felt the need to keep her cards close to the athleisure-wear. Dana could understand that—her sister probably felt like dealing with her own disappointment was enough. She didn't need it compounded by having anyone else keep track of her ups and downs.

Dana placed a hand on her sister's shoulder. "I don't mean to be nosy. I just want to know you're okay."

Chelsea looked into Dana's face as if deciding what to say. At last she exhaled. "And I don't mean to be so secretive," she said. "I'm just…not ready to talk about it yet. Tell me about you, first. Didn't you have that company party last night?"

If Chelsea wanted Dana to distract her with light chitchat, this wasn't the topic. Still, she didn't want her sister to think she was punishing her by withholding her own news. "Let's talk about it over lunch," she said. "I'm starving."

Chelsea admitted that she was hungry, too, so the sisters went to work grabbing food from the fridge, chopping salad at the counter and hip-checking each other when they got in the way. At last they sat down at the center island to eat, and Chelsea brought the conversation back to the Shopping Channel party. "So how was it?" she asked, a smile indicating she was ready for some juicy gossip and inside dirt.

"Brace yourself," Dana said, and went to work having a few more bites of the salad to fortify herself for the appetite-suppressing conversation.

"Didn't you have fun?"

"Fun," Dana mused, as if the word were almost too difficult to contemplate. "There were a few things in the way."

"Such as?"

"Let's see…someone drugged my drink and the new CEO

was pushed off the roof and fell to his death. On the plus side, Megan met a nice guy."

Chelsea blinked, stunned. "Are you serious?"

"Yeah, they really hit it off."

"Dana!" her sister scolded.

She finished chewing a piece of cold chicken and swallowed. "It's just hard to explain everything."

"Did the CEO really get killed?"

"Dead as your old Tamagotchi key chain."

"What happened?"

Dana stirred her salad thoughtfully. "First, the generator died and everything went dark. And after that, I don't know. There was a scream and then…" She closed her eyes to search for any hidden memory.

"Then?" Chelsea prodded.

Dana shrugged. "I passed out."

Chelsea studied her face as if she needed to decide if Dana was telling the truth "Were you really drugged?"

"It seems somebody decided to make the roof party a roofie party, and slipped something in my drink. At least, that's my guess. I had a drug test, so I'll know in a few days."

Chelsea poured herself a glass of water from a pitcher that had pieces of fruit floating in it. She took a long sip. "This is all so chilling."

They were both quiet for a moment before Chelsea asked Dana if she had seen the body.

"Not that I can remember. But I got a pretty gruesome description."

"That poor man."

Dana shuddered, thinking about how she felt when he had her cornered against the railing. "To be honest, he was kind of a pig."

"I'm sure he didn't deserve to *die*."

"I suppose," Dana said, with little conviction.

"What about his family?" Chelsea asked.

"Disabled wife, couple of adult sons. That's where I was just now—visiting with his wife and younger son."

"Oh, Dana. They must be devastated. But what happened? Do you have any idea who pushed him?"

Dana shook her head. "But I can tell you this much—there were a lot of people at that party who wanted him dead. He had made this terrible speech, saying he was changing the whole direction of the company. He tried to sugarcoat it, but everyone knew it meant their jobs were at stake."

"The whole direction of the company?"

"No more fashion."

Now Chelsea looked truly stricken. "I...don't understand."

"He said the Shopping Channel would be an all-electronics network. No clothes, no handbags, no shoes, no jewelry. But Megan assures me my contract is rock solid—they can't fire me."

"No *jewelry*?" Chelsea repeated, as if her sister had just questioned the existence of God. Or Balenciaga.

"Don't panic," Dana joked, "we could always broadcast from your basement." It was meant in good fun—Chelsea's lower level was where her shopping addiction manifested. The whole space was lined with deep shelves stocked with every nonperishable item imaginable, including household items, gifts and clothes she couldn't wear in ten lifetimes. Dana didn't often tease her sister about this, as it was so clearly an illness. But she also didn't think she should normalize it.

Chelsea took it in stride. "The company spent years building its fashion reputation. I don't understand how he thinks this could work."

Dana nodded. Her sister had a good point. "He's an electronics guy. That's his background. To him, I guess this seemed like the only road to success."

"I get it," Chelsea said. "To a hammer, the whole world looks like a nail."

"And to Ivan Dennison, the whole world looks like something he *wants* to nail."

Chelsea made a face. "He came on that strong?"

"I literally felt like he was threatening me."

Chelsea put down her fork, her face turning even more serious. "Was he the one who drugged you?"

Dana thought about how aggressively he had insisted she take the drink he brought her. "Probably." In the past, she would have been more emphatic. But dating a detective had taught her to be circumspect about conclusions.

Chelsea's eyes flashed with fear. "But you weren't…" She trailed off, and Dana understood her point.

"No, no!" she quickly assured her. "That much I can say for certain—thank god. My memories are fuzzy, but I know I never left the party."

Chelsea rubbed her forehead like it was all too much for her. "You're sure?"

"I wasn't assaulted. I promise."

"Oh, Dana," Chelsea said, reaching out for an embrace. As they hugged, she whispered into her sister's shoulder, "If anything had happened to you, I would have killed him myself."

"I know."

Chelsea released her. "What does Ari say about the whole thing?"

Dana let out such a long, extended breath she was pretty sure it pushed all the oxygen from the room. And then she proceeded to tell her sister what had happened with Ari.

When she was done, Chelsea shook her head. "Sometimes

you are so stupid it's hard to believe you can put your own pants on."

"I don't know what else I could have done."

"First of all, you shouldn't have taken the apartment."

"You wouldn't say that if you saw it."

"Yes, I would."

Dana put down her fork. "Like you're the model of restraint."

"That's different. My shopping doesn't hurt anyone."

"I didn't think I was hurting him. I did it for us. It's such a great apartment, Chelse. I know we could be so happy there."

"So you're going to move in, no matter what?"

Dana pictured living in that spacious apartment, and the tingle of excitement almost equaled her anxiety. It only she could get Ari on board, it would all be so perfect.

"Have to," she said. "I signed a lease. But don't worry. Ari will come around. *He will.*"

Chelsea considered it. "I know he loves you like crazy. I just hope this isn't some subconscious effort to push him away."

"Stop it," Dana said. It was infuriating to have her family question her every decision. Sure, she had made some mistakes in the past, but this was different. There was no subconscious sabotage going on. She was trying her best to make this work.

"*You* stop it," Chelsea said.

"Stop what?"

"Stop being an idiot," Chelsea said. "Stop wrecking your life."

Dana stood. "Maybe I should go."

Chelsea held up her hands in surrender. "Fine. I'm sorry. I'm sure it's a great apartment."

Dana sat back down. "You don't have to be such a shit about it."

"I'll make it up to you with a housewarming gift."

"Can't I just go shopping in your basement?"

Chelsea sighed in mock exasperation. "I hate you," she said, her tone light.

"I hate you more."

Her sister winced, and Dana at first thought she had misinterpreted her banter. But when Chelsea put a hand on her stomach, it was clear she was having some kind of gastrointestinal distress.

"What's wrong?" Dana asked.

Chelsea held up a finger. "I'll be right back," she said, and excused herself to the bathroom. She was gone for quite a few minutes, and when she returned, it was clear she had touched up her makeup and applied fresh lipstick—a soft matte pink shade.

"I vomited," Chelsea said, as she sat down and resumed eating.

Dana pushed her plate aside. "Was it something I said?"

Chelsea took the last bite of her salad. "Hormones," she explained. She waited a beat and smiled. "I'm pregnant."

Dana gasped and smacked her sister's shoulder. "You fucking idiot! I thought you miscarried or something. Do you know how worried I've been?"

"If it makes you feel any better, I thought I miscarried, too. That's why I dashed out on you and Dad. Turned out it was just spotting."

Dana gave her a hug. "Well congratulations, you little shit."

"I'm sorry I didn't tell you sooner. I wanted to wait until I cleared the first trimester. It's hard not to get superstitious about these things."

"When are you due?"

"May fifteenth. Pretty close to Wesley's birthday."

"Is this why you didn't go to his soccer game?"

"My doctor wants me to take it easy for a bit. I'm not even supposed to get myself worked up about anything."

"*Now* you tell me," Dana said, understanding why her sister hadn't turned on the news. "After I dumped an avalanche of misery on you."

"It's okay. I would have been more upset if you kept all that from me."

Dana sighed, and started clearing away the dishes. When Chelsea stood to help, Dana pushed her back down with a stern warning.

"Tell me what else I can do to help," Dana said when she finished.

Chelsea bit her lip as she thought about it.

"Anything," Dana pressed. "I'm at your disposal."

"There is one thing," Chelsea said.

Dana scraped out a chair and took her sister's hands. "Name it."

"Try not to be an idiot for a couple of weeks."

11

On Sunday morning, Dana headed downtown to meet with her acting troupe, the Sweat City Company. For almost six years, the experimental theater group had felt like the beating heart of her life. In fact, she almost didn't sign on with the Shopping Channel, because there was a clause in her contract forbidding her from participating in any acting gigs without getting an official waiver from her boss, the granite-hard Sherry Zidel. Dana knew Sherry would never grant permission, so she solved the problem by signing the contract but continuing with the group in secret, playing the lead role in a powerful drama under the stage name Kayla Bean. She almost pulled it off, too. But on opening night, Sherry got wind of the performance, and actually showed up backstage to tell Dana she was through.

For Dana, it was the climax of her vexing relationship with Sherry. It seemed that nothing she could do would please her impossible boss. Fortunately, Dana found out that Sherry had a secret of her own—one that could have cost the stony supervising producer her job, too. And so, they reached an uneasy truce, keeping one another's secrets…and their jobs.

Today, the Sweat City players were doing a table read of a new script, written by their director, Nathan Thompson. It was their first comedy, and there were several roles Dana would have been happy to play, though of course she desperately wanted the lead. Entitled *Harte of Brooklyn*, the story revolved around Penny Harte, a hyper-earnest life coach from Park Slope with a touch of OCD that manifested in an obsession with fitness. There would be a treadmill onstage, and Penny was on it so frequently that most of her dialogue was delivered from that spot. But the core of her character was that she wanted desperately to prove her political correctness to everyone in her sphere. She had a habit of sticking her foot in her mouth on that front, which gave the play its humor, but also an edge of danger. The critics would either get it and love it, or want to eviscerate everyone involved for getting so close to the red zone.

"If it's not at least a little dangerous," Nathan had said, "it's not art."

It was a tense morning, because everyone knew Nathan would be announcing the casting before the table read. The unwritten rule in the theater was that as long as you were cast, you showed appreciation. No small roles, and all that. And with this group, they were so much like family that any pang of dejection was overshadowed by genuine happiness for your fellow actors.

Besides, they all had some level of daddy issues when it came to Nathan. The cast had talked about this both drunk and sober. He was only in his late thirties, but he had a quiet authority about him that made everyone in his orbit eager to please him. For his day job, he taught theatrical design at a college in Staten Island. Dana imagined that his students felt the same way about gaining his admiration.

So when they took their places around the table, Dana knew that reactions would be small but energy high as Nathan dropped a copy of the script in front of each actor and unceremoniously announced their character. Dana was pretty sure she would get either Starlight, the weird bohemian next-door neighbor, or Penny the life coach and lead.

Nathan tossed a script in front of her friend Tyrel and announced, "Curtis," who was the landlord and love interest—essentially the male lead. Tyrel gave a constrained raise-the-roof pump with his hands, and then quickly corrected himself, arcing his arms into a muscle flex to illustrate that he could play a masculine role, despite his natural inclinations. The group tittered.

Raj and Sylvia got the married next-door neighbors, Yvette got the androgynous office assistant.

Nathan dropped a script in front of Carolyn Beattie, who locked eyes with Dana. She was Dana's main competition for the lead, and they both knew it. One of them would get the part, so this was the moment of truth for both. The microsecond pause between the thud of the script and the director's pronouncement seemed to stretch and stretch and stretch as the two women held their breath.

Nathan coughed, and Carolyn rolled her eyes, as if to say, *Can you believe this?*

"Starlight," he pronounced, and Carolyn gave a nod of acceptance, followed by a silent acknowledgment of congratulations to Dana. It was a small movement—her hand went to her heart and then opened toward Dana—but it said everything she needed. Dana put her hand to her own heart in gratitude. Then they moved on and read the play through, with Dana as Penny. She couldn't tell if it was going to be a hit, but they would have a blast.

Afterward, Dana had to fight the urge to call Ari and tell him about the part. Her joy felt incomplete, as if it wasn't a real victory until she shared it with him. She stuffed down the feeling and told herself it would happen soon enough. After all, this investigation couldn't possibly linger very long.

Besides, Megan would be happy for her. As her best friend and manager, she was fully invested. And Dana would be able to tell her in person, as they had already arranged to meet up for a bite to talk about what the rest of the day with the Dennisons had been like.

"You look better than yesterday," Megan said, as she slid into the booth across from Dana. They were in Moran's, a pub they had long ago identified as being more or less equidistant between their apartments. Besides, the cozy wood-paneled bar had the most perfect French fries that ever came out of a kitchen. Dana would gladly do an extra hour in the gym for a couple of handfuls.

"I *am* better," Dana said. "I just came from a table reading."

"You never told me what play you were doing."

"Didn't want to jinx it before casting. But it's a comedy—something Nathan wrote. It's brilliant."

"Sweat City is doing a comedy?"

Dana understood her friend's confusion. Sweat City had established a reputation for its drama. "It's really offbeat," she explained. "But…accessible. I could almost picture it as a TV series. Such great characters."

"And?" Megan's expression was coy. She knew Dana well enough to understand the news would be good.

Dana smiled. "I got the lead. And it's not a straight man kind of lead. It's going to get laughs. At least I hope so."

"We should celebrate," Megan said, her eyes bright. She

signaled the waitress and ordered two martinis with top shelf vodka.

When the drinks arrived, they clinked glasses.

"You're going to clear this with Sherry, of course," Megan said.

Dana stared at her friend, surprised. "No way."

"You have to."

"But we have an understanding."

Megan shook her head. She was in manager mode now. "At this point, all bets are off." She took a sip of her drink and leaned toward Dana. "Listen, I don't know how things are going to go down at your company now. If the board nixes Ivan's plan to cross over into electronics, you're fine. But if they go through with it, they might be looking for any excuse to cancel your contract. We can't give them one."

Dana set down her glass. "Are you serious?"

"Not usually. But this is important."

"Come on, you know what a pain in the ass Sherry is. What if she decides to fuck with me?"

"Frankly, she's got bigger things to worry about right now. I don't think she'll hassle you much."

"This is Sherry Zidel we're talking about."

Megan seemed to give that some thought. "Tell you what— give me a heads-up when you're meeting with her and I'll join you. We'll make this happen."

12

At first glance, the mood at the Shopping Channel the Monday morning seemed somber. But under the surface there was a charged mix of schadenfreude and the excitement that goes along with being up close and personal with a shocking tragedy. Sure, everyone acted appropriately mournful, but the energy had a certain tingle. There were hushed conversations in every corner, and a buzz of gossip seemed to bounce around like skittish electrons.

Dana went straight to her dressing room, where her recently assigned temp, Ashlee, was waiting for her. The girl was Dana's third assistant, and she hoped it would work out. After her first one left, the HR department brought in an intern who was getting a graduate degree from NYU. Since it was Dana's alma mater, they thought it would be a good fit. But Talia was so disdainful she managed to alienate everyone from the security guard to Sherry Zidel, who didn't appreciate job tips from a twenty-four-year-old who thought a month in a creative writing MFA program made her the smartest one in the room. After she was fired, they brought in Ashlee St. Pierre, a leggy ex-pageant girl with wide cheekbones and a movie-star smile she highlighted with bright red lipstick. Dana could imagine her commanding the stage in all those competitions her mother pushed her into back home in Tennessee.

At first, Dana worried the girl wouldn't take the job seriously. After all, it wasn't too long ago that Dana had been in her shoes—an aspiring actress trying to stitch together a living between auditions. And she sure as hell wouldn't have been a star employee. But things with Ashlee seemed to be working out. For now, she was technically a "floater"—on staff, but not assigned a permanent job. In another month, it would be up to Dana to decide whether to make Ashlee her official assistant.

"I'm sure glad to see *you*," Ashlee gushed in her Tennessee accent. "There's more gossip flyin' around than backstage at a pageant."

"What are they saying?"

"Some think Mr. Dennison took a swan dive off the roof to hurt the company image. Others think Mr. Honeycutt must've pushed him. There's one rumor Eleanor Gratz was havin' an affair with him and her husband did it in a jealous fit. I don't know whether to scratch my ass or check my watch."

Distracted by the colorful expression, Dana took an extra beat to process the information. She remembered what Eleanor had said about Ivan's attitude toward older women.

"An affair?" she said to Ashlee. "Why would they think that?"

"I'm sure I don't know. But I do not think that man was faithful to his wife."

This caught Dana's attention. "Oh?" she said, prompting Ashlee to elaborate.

"I could swear he was flirting with me. He put his arm around me and said with a smile like mine I could be on the air. Said he'd buy whatever I was sellin'."

God, the man was shameless.

"So what did you do?" Dana asked.

Ashlee waved it away. "Oh, I've dealt with hornier dogs than that, believe it. I just pushed him away and laughed like I thought he was joking. That usually does the trick." She looked toward the door. "I think Miss Irini from wardrobe was looking for you. Should I let her know you're in?"

"Thanks—tell her I'll be ready in a bit. Could you also tell Sherry I'd like to see her after my show?"

"Yes, ma'am."

A short while later, Dana's segment producer, Jessalyn Grage, came in to go over the day's program. She looked a little like Rashida Jones with darker skin and a fuller face, framed by soft coils of black hair that floated around her head like a cloud. An ambitious young woman, hypercompetent and laser-focused, she was hard to get close to. But Dana admired her, and was glad to see her promoted from talent coordinator. She deserved it.

"It's Barlow and Ricci day," Jessalyn said, referring to the line of handbags that usually sold well, despite the internet's encroachment on fashion.

Dana nodded. She knew this had been on the schedule, and that any possible shifts in the Shopping Channel's branding would take weeks if not months, as the buying was done pretty far in advance.

Jessalyn used the images on her tablet to review the styles and colors Dana would be pitching on her show, including info on which colors needed to be pushed the hardest. That part was always a delicate balance, because the purchasers bought more of the colors they assumed would be popular. But if Dana pushed those too hard, the rest could flatline. On the other hand, if she ignored those in favor of the less popular colors, the whole show could wind up with a bust.

After finishing the review, Dana asked Jessalyn what she had been hearing about the company.

Jessalyn shrugged. "All the execs are meeting with the board this morning, so maybe we'll have an answer later today."

Dana asked who was in the meeting, and Jessalyn gave her the rundown, which included Charles Honeycutt and Eleanor Gratz. Dana could imagine how hard they would be pitching the board to reject Ivan's plan for a complete shake-up.

A few minutes later, Dana was alone in her dressing room with Irini, the wardrobe supervisor. She slipped into a quiet hunter-green midi-length dress and pulled on a pair of black boots. Irini had selected it as the kind of outfit that would showcase almost any handbag. Dana agreed—the woman had a great eye.

"Turn around," Irini instructed, in her no-nonsense Greek accent.

Dana did as she asked, and Irini tsked. "Take it off," she commanded. "It's loose. I'll baste some stitches into the back."

Dana pulled off the dress, and knew from experience it wouldn't take Irini more than two minutes to do her tailoring. Ashlee knocked on the door and poked her head in.

"Beg pardon," she said, "but they want to see you in the boardroom."

"Me?" Dana asked, feeling her heart speed up. She had never been summoned to the board of directors before, and couldn't imagine what they wanted from her. It didn't seem like it could be good news.

"Eleanor's assistant called me. She said they need you for a few minutes."

"I'm on the air in less than an hour and I still have to do hair and makeup."

"Good excuse to get out quicker than a scared haint, then."

Irini held the dress over Dana's head, and she slipped it on.

"I'm sure it is nothing to worry over," Irini said, as she signaled for Dana to do another twirl. She gave a nod, picked up her sewing kit and left.

Dana dashed to the elevator and up to the top floor, where she stepped out and looked at Brenda, the receptionist, behind her mile-long desk. She was a striking Black woman, with a model's complexion and the crisp appearance of a TV news anchor. But like so many Shopping Channel employees, she was an aspiring actor.

"I've been summoned to the board meeting," Dana said, trying to sound calm.

"I heard," Brenda said, and pointed toward the hallway that led to the big corner conference room.

Dana smoothed out her dress and headed down the carpeted hallway, her heart rate rocketing. What on earth did they want with her? She thought about the new lease she had signed. Dana had worked it out so that she could retain her current apartment through the end of December—a full month after taking possession of the new place. It meant a massive outlay of cash, not just for rent, but for decorating. Of course, when she signed the lease, she hadn't thought about the pressure, but the fun of strolling through furniture stores with Ari to design their perfect home. Now, it was nothing *but* pressure. And she knew that if the board of directors wanted to find a way to break her contract, they would.

She reached the conference room and gave a firm knock. A knock that meant business. Dana refused to show her fear.

The door opened, and the scene before her was like something from a movie. At least, that's the way it seemed to Dana, who had little experience with corporate America before joining the Shopping Channel. Her resume was a series of terrible little stints strung together to help pay the rent between gigs. Jobs like waitressing, ushering and insulting teenagers at Hot Topic. For her, the word *career* had always conjured images of movie sets or curtain calls, not boardrooms.

Now, she stood before the Shopping Channel's corporate power machine—twelve men and three women sitting behind neatly placed legal pads and water glasses at a long mahogany table polished to a high gloss. Every head turned to look at her.

"Thank you for coming, Dana," said Eleanor Gratz. "I know you have to be on the air soon, so we won't take too much of your time."

At that, Dana noticed that there was more than a legal pad in front of Eleanor. There was a large blue box of *Reluven* products. She took a glance around to read the mood of the room, and could tell the atmosphere was strictly balance sheet. If there had been any mourning for Ivan Dennison, it had passed.

"What can I do for you?" she asked.

"I was telling the board about our discussion the other day—how confident you are that you can sell skin care."

So that's what this was about. Dana had been brought in by the head buyer to sway the board. She let out a long breath. It was showtime, and Dana knew exactly what character she needed to play. She was now a woman who wasn't intimidated by a roomful of people who had ice-chilled formaldehyde running through their veins and could destroy dozens of careers with the stroke of a pen. In fact, she was the boss. The alpha. She was there to school them.

She could do this.

"One hundred percent," she said, adding a disarming smile.

"Can you share your thoughts on that? I'd like the board to hear it from you."

I'll do better than that, Dana thought. She approached Eleanor. "May I?" she said, gesturing toward the box.

"Please."

Dana peered inside and pulled out the nighttime eye serum and daily moisturizer with SPF 30. Then she glanced around and saw a cart behind her that held a sweating pitcher of ice water.

"I'm going to need you all to use your imagination for a bit, and pretend we're on the air." She turned to the white-haired man who was closest to her. "Hold these for a second, will you?" She offered a smile that showed they were in this together. Buddies. He sheepishly put out his hands and accepted the products, then Dana turned and removed the water pitcher from the cart and placed it on the table. She pushed the cart in front of herself, and arranged the products on it.

Dana's mind wandered back to her financial anxiety, and she breathed into it. She would use that energy. If she was ever going to sell her heart out, this was it.

She pointed to a spot in the middle of the wall of windows facing her. "That's camera one," she said, "and all of you are the viewers at home. Got it?"

They murmured their assent and Dana launched.

"I'm so excited to be introducing the Shopping Channel's newest skin care line from Reluven!" She beamed, staring straight into the pretend camera. As always, she psyched herself into believing there was one person on the other end—her dearest friend. Someone she loved with all her heart. A woman who needed this very product to make her life complete. "I promise you, there is nothing like this on the market. Nothing that works this well at firming, toning and reducing fine lines." As she spoke, Dana opened the jar of daily moisturizer and dipped her finger in several times to illustrate the richness of it. "We would have brought this to you years ago, but our standards are higher than anyone else's, and we wanted to be sure the formulation was absolutely perfect." She rubbed the product into the back of her left hand and held it up. "Can we get a close-up of this so you can see how quickly it absorbs and changes the texture of my skin." She held her two fists side by side. "Look at the difference in my hands! Just look! And that's after only a few seconds."

The board members actually leaned forward as if straining to see magical transformation in Dana's skin.

"And the best news?" she said. "This jar normally sells for seventy dollars on its own. But today we're offering a special introductory price for our viewers of only *fifty-five dollars!*" She punched the price as if it were the most life-changing news a person could possibly hear. "And, we're giving you the night-time eye serum absolutely free as our gift! Normally, these products would cost a hundred and ten dollars, so you're getting it for literally *half the price.*" She was pulling the numbers completely out of whatever part of her anatomy had the most imagination. "Plus, our Easy-Bucks option allows you to get it home for eleven dollars!" She laughed, as if the news were almost too wonderful to believe.

"But I have to show you this eye serum because it's going to change your skin care forever. Even if you're someone who doesn't have a bedtime skin care routine, this is the one product you'll want to invest in. Honestly, I can't believe we're giving it away, because it's like liquid gold." She walked toward the white-haired man. "This is our gorgeous model, Antoinette."

An appreciative titter made its way around the table as Dana beckoned to an imaginary camera. "In a minute, I'll want a tight shot of her eyes, but first, look at this." She opened the serum, pulled out the dropper, and plunked one, two drops onto her fingertips. "It feels like the smoothest silk," she said, as she rubbed her finger and thumb. She stopped to sniff it, closing her eyes as if transported. "Even the smell is seductive," she said. "But check this out." She crooked her finger toward the make-believe camera and rubbed the oil onto the old man's crow's-feet. Dana could picture him going home that night and telling his wife what a good sport he'd been. But in fact, he seemed to enjoy the feeling of being fussed over.

"Watch closely as her fine lines disappear. Do you see? Isn't that extraordinary?" She took his head in her two hands and moved it to face forward. "Now look at the difference between the right and the left side. The lines are *vanishing!* And that's after one treatment!" Dana tapped her ear as if listening to a message from her segment producer. She was going in for the kill. "Wow! This is incredible. We've been on the air less than two minutes and we've already sold three thousand units! This is unprecedented. But I'm just a little worried, because I really want you to get this home at this incredible one-time price, so you're going to have to be fast. Please, if you want this— and I think that any woman at any age should—get to your phone now." Dana held up the products again, talked about the essentials oils in the list of ingredients, restated the prices and then stopped abruptly, as if getting a last message from her producer. "That's it! We are sold out! I'm so glad so many of you were able to get your orders in on time. Thank you!"

A shocked silence descended over the room. Dana wasn't just a pitch woman, but an actor, and she knew when she owned an audience. And she owned this one. They were all in, suspending their disbelief enough to be convinced she had actually sold all that merch.

Dana closed the products, walked toward Eleanor and put them back into the box.

"Is there anything else I can do for you?" Dana asked the group, and saw a grin spread across Eleanor's face. Dana grinned back. They both knew what had just happened. Dana Barry had convinced the board to give skin care a shot. And Ivan's plans to convert to an electronics-only channel had just short-circuited. At least for now.

13

After the boardroom meeting, Dana and Ashlee dashed through the halls to get to the nails and makeup department.

"What happened in there?" Ashlee asked, as they did a kind of run-walk.

"Damned if I know," Dana said. "But I think I may have convinced the board not to abandon our brand for Ivan's Great Leap Forward."

"Bless your heart," Ashlee said.

"I never know whether you Southerners are being sarcastic when you say that."

"And you never will, darlin'," she said, pouring it on, and Dana got the point. That was the whole idea. Ashlee followed it up with a smile so endearing it was clear she wouldn't need to worry about losing her job. This was a girl who could charm her way into or out of whatever she damn well pleased. Bless her heart.

When they reached the makeup room, Ashlee left Dana

and headed off to tell the production folks Dana would be along in a few minutes.

Meanwhile, the rushed schedule meant that Dana got only a bucket-sized load of gossip from Jo and Felicia, instead of the whole fetid vat. They did admit that just about every person in the company had been brought up as a possible suspect in Ivan's murder.

"Whoever done it," Jo said, as she swiped sheer pink polish onto Dana's nails, "did us all a big favor. I heard he was set to fire everybody except the mailroom."

"I heard he was going to fire them, too," Felicia added.

Dana thought about the power of rumor mills to churn out gossip. If there was a way to harness that energy, the world could get along without fossil fuel forever.

"If he was going to fire Honeycutt, he would have fired anybody," Jo agreed.

"You heard he was going to fire Honeycutt?" Dana asked.

"Yeah, from *him*," she responded.

Now this could be actual news. "What do you mean?" Dana pressed.

"We heard him talking to someone at the party," Felicia said. "That white-haired guy who dresses like he's from England."

Dana knew exactly who she meant—something about his suit and tie combinations looked decidedly British. It was the man she had used for her eye serum demo.

"Member of the board of directors," Dana said.

"That's him. We heard Dennison tell him Honeycutt would be gone before Christmas."

"Are you sure that's what you heard?" Dana asked. "It was awfully loud at that party."

"That's why they was shouting," Felicia said. "They was outside the tent but we heard them sure as anything."

Jo stopped to admire her handiwork, giving an extra swipe to the corner of Dana's pinky. "Point is, we'd all be looking for jobs today if that prick was still alive."

Dana had to agree with the assessment. If Ivan planned to ax Charles, it would have been a company-wide bloodbath.

"We might be out of work all the same," Felicia responded. "If the board sticks with his plan."

Jo reached for Dana's other hand and continued. "I heard Honeycutt was meeting with them today to talk them out of it."

Felicia stroked blush onto Dana's cheeks. "God bless that man. I hope he succeeds."

Dana wanted to tell them their jobs were safe. But it wasn't her place to add yet more grist to the mill, especially since it wasn't more than a good hunch at this point. So she simply said, "Honeycutt's a good guy. We should have confidence in him."

Felicia stopped working on Dana's face and took a step back. "You know something?"

"Not for sure."

"But you do," Jo said. "You got the inside scoop. Spill."

"I haven't heard anything official," Dana said.

"But unofficial?" Felicia asked.

Afraid anything she said would be repeated and altered and blown entirely out of proportion, Dana merely shrugged.

Felicia and Jo traded a look, and then bumped fists. They knew exactly what Dana had meant.

"How are you hanging in?" Dana asked Lorenzo DeSantis as he clipped the tiny lavalier microphone to her collar. She was on set, getting ready for her show, and knew the sound engineer had to be especially nervous about the rumors. Unlike the charming Ashlee St. Pierre, a tattooed, ex-con, single dad was not easily employed.

"Kind of wish I'd taken that job at QVC," he said, referring to an offer he'd received from a competitor earlier in the year.

"Between you and me," Dana said, putting a comforting hand on his arm, "I think things are going to be alright here."

He stared into her face, his large, black-brown eyes earnest and grateful. "Really?"

"I was summoned to the board meeting and got a good feeling about it."

He leaned in. "I could kiss you," he whispered.

She knew he didn't mean anything by it…or maybe he did. She took her hand off his arm just in case. Since they had a history—a short but intense relationship when she first came on board—she didn't want him to misconstrue her signals.

"Better not," she said, dismissing his comment with a light laugh as she nodded toward the control booth, where her segment producer and the technicians had a high-definition view of the two of them.

He flicked on her microphone and gave her a wink. "Go get 'em," he said.

And she did. Dana's successful presentation before the board gave her an extra boost of adrenaline for her show, and as soon as the camera went on she oozed over the pricey leather satchels, crossbodies, saddle bags, hobos and totes like they were the culmination of every advancement of mankind since the dawn of time. The words flowed from her like poured cream as she cooed over the colors and the textures and capacious lined interiors. She marveled at the hardware and the styling and the workmanship. Dana barely even glanced at the monitor that showed the sales numbers, because she could feel it in the sinews of her body. Her viewers were reaching for their phones.

"Those were your best numbers in months," Jessalyn said when she finished. "Sherry will be thrilled."

Sherry, thrilled? Dana couldn't imagine what that might look like, but she was glad to be going into her meeting with the supervising producer on a high note.

Dana went back to her dressing room, and dismissed Ashlee for the day. She changed into her street clothes as she waited for Megan to arrive. Earlier, they had confirmed the meeting with Sherry, and Dana was feeling just a little more confident about it now. Of course, Sherry Zidel was hard to predict, but between Megan's presence and today's sales figures, she thought she had a pretty good shot at getting official permission to perform in her Sweat City show.

A few minutes later, Megan arrived in her black power suit, ready to do battle. As they rode the elevator together to the top floor, Dana filled Megan in on that morning's meeting with the board as well as her sales figures.

"Excellent!" Megan said. "Now we have enough ammunition to slay every supervising producer from here to Burbank."

By the time they arrived at Sherry's office, her assistant and official gatekeeper had already gone for the day, so the duo walked right up and knocked.

"Come in!" Sherry called, and Dana pushed open the door to see that Sherry was not alone. Standing across from her desk, his arms folded, was Ari.

Dana shouldn't have been surprised. He was investigating a murder, after all, and needed to grill everyone who had been at the party. But she'd managed to tune her mind to a different frequency. This was a jolt, like emerging from a darkened theater into sunlight, and Dana felt blinded. She couldn't move.

Time seemed to slow as Ari turned to face her. She could clock the exact second of recognition. He was startled to see her, but surprise was quickly replaced by pain. *You hurt me,* his eyes said, and it cut right through her. And she knew then that he hadn't intuited her intention to merely put their relationship on hold until his investigation was complete. And his heart was broken.

"Anything else, Detective?" Sherry asked as she rose from behind her desk.

Ari turned his back to Dana. "We're good for now," he said to Sherry, and gave Megan a brief nod while heading toward the door.

"Ari, wait," Dana said.

"Sorry—I'm busy," he said.

"Will you be in the building for a while?" she asked.

He paused, avoiding her gaze, and she knew that he was deciding whether to brush her off or let her in. At last, his shoulders relaxed in resignation.

"Probably," he said.

Dana nodded. "I'll find you."

After he left, Sherry took a seat without bothering to invite Dana and Megan to do the same. Still, they lowered themselves into the pale pink side chairs—a carefully added touch to an office hardened by a wall of live monitors displaying every camera angle on set, as well as the actual live broadcast as seen by the viewers at home, and a real-time feed of the sales numbers. The wall behind Sherry's desk had windows spanning at least six feet across. But if the sunlight had any notion of casting a glare on the supervising producer's screens, the decorator had thwarted it with heavy curtains patterned in bold stripes of black and white.

"If there's trouble with you and Clark Kent," Sherry said to Dana, "I don't even want to know."

As if Sherry Zidel would make the list of people Dana might pour her heart out to. "Relax," Dana said. "I wouldn't dream of exposing you to human emotions."

"This meeting is looking up already."

"Have you seen Dana's numbers today?" Megan asked.

Sherry adjusted the glasses on her narrow face. "No," she said sarcastically. "I don't look at numbers. I sit here all day watching sitcoms. What's that new one that's all the rage? With Ross and Rachel?"

Great, Dana thought, *Sherry Zidel has decided she's a comedian.*

"I suppose you also know Dana got called into a meeting with the board today," Megan said, ignoring the joke.

"They keep me apprised." Sherry leaned back in her chair. "Tell me why you're here."

"We need to revisit that agreement you had with Dana— about Sweat City."

Sherry made a face. "What about it?" she said. "That show was over months ago."

"There's a new one," Megan said.

"Well, someone alert *Entertainment Tonight.*"

"This is serious," Megan said. "With everything that's going on at the Shopping Channel, I don't want to take any chances with Dana's contract. We'll need your official approval for her to appear onstage."

Sherry went quiet, as if retreating in thought, and Megan shared a look with Dana.

"Little problem," Sherry finally said. "I no longer have that authority."

"What do you mean?" Dana asked.

"Ivan stripped me of it about two weeks ago. Said he would be making those decisions from now on."

"You might recall—" Megan said "—Ivan is dead."

"Hard to forget, what with all of Munchkinland celebrating."

Megan leaned in. "So wouldn't the power revert back to you?"

"Damned if *I* know," Sherry said.

"Can you just *take* the power?" Dana asked. "I mean, you could certainly make a good case that you assumed the responsibility was yours."

"Do I need to remind you that it's a delicate time here for *all* of us?"

"Not as delicate as it was before Dana knocked the board's socks off this morning."

"Fair enough," Sherry said. "That bought us some time. But if those skin potions don't sell, we are all fucked."

"So what do you propose we do?" Megan asked.

Sherry shrugged. "If Dana wants to take a chance on being in breach of contract, be my guest. I won't make an issue of it. But don't expect me to sign off on it, either. If anybody finds out, we never had this conversation. I'm not sticking my neck out for *anybody*."

"And what if I threaten to tell the board about—"

"Then we're all screwed, aren't we? My best advice—don't do the damned show. But if you have to, don't tell anyone— least of all, me."

Dana couldn't imagine how Ivan even knew about that clause in her contract unless he went actively looking for it. "Why did Ivan take the power away from you, anyway?" she asked Sherry.

"He didn't say."

"Any guesses?" Megan pressed.

Sherry folded her arms. "Oh, I think we all have a pretty good guess."

The idea that Ivan had been strategically hunting her made Dana queasy. She looked down, and they all went quiet for a moment. At last, Megan spoke, addressing Sherry.

"You think he wanted the leverage for, uh…" She trailed off, the struggle apparent on her face.

"For a blow job?" Sherry said. "Yeah, that's exactly what I

think. He managed to convince the board he was some sort of holy roller, pious and above reproach. Meanwhile, the fucker thought he landed the gig of a lifetime here. Money, women, power. He had it all. Too bad for him pigs can't fly."

"Did he come on to you, too?" Dana asked.

Sherry's face went so tight she couldn't breathe without snorting. "Anna," she said through her teeth. "Can you imagine? What kind of entitled prick comes on to someone's girlfriend right in front of them? I could have…" She stopped herself, looking from Megan to Dana. "Well, I *could* have, but I didn't. I just refuse to pretend I'm falling to pieces over it. That bastard."

"I don't think any of us are too broken up over it," Dana added.

"Maybe this one," Sherry said, pointing a thumb at Megan. "She seemed pretty cozy with the son."

"Fortunately, he's nothing like his dad," Megan said.

Sherry snorted. "You'd better hope not."

When they left Sherry's office, Megan tried to get Dana to consider giving up the play.

"As your manager," she said, "I have to advise you to pass up the Sweat City show this time."

"No chance."

"It's just too big a risk. If things go south with the company, they're going to be scrutinizing every contract—especially the ones with high salaries."

The very thought made Dana's chest tighten. "Sweat City is more important to me than the Shopping Channel. You know that."

"I also know that you just signed an expensive lease you're going to have to carry on your own. If you find yourself out of a job, what'll you do?"

"I'll think of something."

"Be realistic," Megan said. "Your last steady job paid twelve dollars an hour, and you couldn't even hold on to it."

"Now you sound like my father."

"I'm just trying to be pragmatic here."

"Well, I'm not worried," Dana said. It was a lie. She was terrified. But that didn't mean she was willing to give up Sweat City. It just meant she would have to sell the hell out of that skin care line.

14

After saying goodbye to Megan, Dana went back to her dressing room. Her plan was to grab her purse and her cell phone, then search the corridors for Ari or anyone who had seen him. But when she got there, he was sitting on her beige sofa, his long legs stretched out in front of him. He was in his white shirt and blue pin dot tie, his jacket folded next to him. He stood.

Dana closed the door behind her and turned to him. They were about eight feet apart, but neither took a step forward.

"Ari," she said, aware that she needed to start. She waited a beat but he said nothing, so she continued. "I didn't mean to hurt you."

"I see. You wanted to break up, with no hard feelings. Neat and easy." His voice was cold, measured, restrained.

"No! I didn't want to break up. You misunderstood."

"Let's just go over the facts," he said, sounding so much like a detective she half expected him to pull a notebook from his pocket and flip it open. "First, you took a new apartment when you knew I wasn't ready for it. My reaction to that couldn't have come as a surprise. So yes, it sure as hell looks like you wanted to push me out the door. It wasn't even subtle, Dana."

"No, I swear. That wasn't my—"

"Let me finish. After I left, I thought there was a small possibility you had merely exercised bad judgment, and hadn't meant to push me away. So I kept my cell phone ringer on, just in case you offered an apology. To be honest, I even got my hopes up. Then you texted." He paused, straining to keep his composure. She could see him swallow. "I had to read it twice to even understand—not even close to an apology. A breakup...in a *text*." He pronounced the word as if it could draw blood.

"Not a breakup!" she pleaded. "Just a time-out. It's not the same thing."

"Please. It's the coward's way of breaking up. If you wanted to see other people, you should have at least been honest about it."

"You think there's someone else?"

"What else am I supposed to think?"

"That's crazy," she said. "My whole world is work and you." Dana studied his face, wondering how he could possibly think she would cheat on him. Her devotion felt as palpable as the very soles of her shoes.

"We both know that's not true."

Dana's hand flew to her heart. "What are you talking about?"

"I know how dedicated you are to that Sweat City group."

"They're my *friends*. You can't honestly be jealous. Most of the men are gay, anyway."

"Not Nathan."

"Nathan is *married*," she said.

He shrugged, as if that wasn't materially important.

"Oh for god's sake, I'm not sleeping with Nathan…or anyone else for that matter." Dana took a step forward, trying to understand. Then she got it. As a cop, he saw the worst in humanity every day, so it was hard for his mind to go elsewhere. "Ari," she said gently, "I was being literal. Honestly. I never wanted to break up with you. I was trying to find a way forward that would solve all our problems…including the ones I created."

Ari folded his arms, but he didn't seem entirely closed off. He was listening.

"I'm sorry I signed the lease," she continued. "It was stupid. But the apartment swept me away, and I felt like I'd regret it if I let the opportunity go. I was already picturing our happily-ever-after in that place—you have to believe me. I thought your promotion would come through any day."

"Then why didn't you apologize that night?"

She threw her hands up. "I thought I was being clever. I thought you could take the lead on the case if we were on a break. And then you'd get your promotion, and we would get back together and… I don't know. It all made perfect sense." She wanted to match his stoicism, but her eyes filled, and she had to blink away tears to focus on his expression. Was he softening? It was so hard to tell.

"I love you," she said, studying his face. It stayed rigid, but she fixed on his eyes, which still weren't giving much away. She tried again. "Ari, *I love you*. And I'm sorry. Can you forgive me?"

He didn't move, but his eyes showed just the tiniest glisten. She hesitated, making sure she saw it, and then charged forward, throwing her arms around him. He returned the embrace, and he felt so good and smelled so much like love and warmth and everything she wanted that Dana couldn't hold back. And then she had to surreptitiously wipe her nose with the back of her hand so she wouldn't dirty his shirt.

They held each other a long time. "I'm so sorry," she repeated.

She felt him draw in a breath, but he said nothing.

"I'll repeat it a hundred times if you want me to," she said.

He kissed the top of her head. "I forgive you," he whispered.

Dana struggled to fill her lungs with a juddering intake of air. She backed up to look into his eyes. "I can't get out of the lease," she said. "I put down a massive deposit."

She worried it might infuriate him, or create an unsolvable impasse. But he nodded to show he understood.

"I mean, I could hire a lawyer to see if I could get out of it, but I don't know if that—"

"Dana, please. Shut up about the damned apartment already. We'll work it out."

"We will?"

He responded by kissing her on the mouth, and it was everything. Forgiveness. Understanding. Love. There was nothing more she could want. Or was there? As their bodies pressed together, the warmth gave way to heat, and the sofa, undersized as it was, yielded to their desperate, breathless frenzy.

We will, his body seemed to say. *We will. We will. We will.* Dana shivered, responding to his desire. It seemed to flume her open, as she softened, then stiffened, then softened again.

"Ari," she breathed. "Ari…"

15

Later, they went back to her apartment and in the morning, when his phone's alarm clock chirped its monstrously cheerful wake-up song, Dana reached for his arm.

"Wait," she pleaded, rolling toward him. She wanted to absorb his smell, his warmth, the smoothness of his touch as his hand ran down the silk of her back. And they made flushed, sleepy love one more time. Afterward, she stayed in bed and fell back into a brief, dreamy sleep, awaking to find him freshly showered and ready to leave.

Dana propped herself on her elbows. "Will you let me know what he says?" she asked, referring to his boss. The night before, they had discussed Ari's strategy for dealing with any possible conflict of interest on the case. He would tell his lieutenant the truth about them, and let him decide if Ari needed to withdraw from the investigation.

"Of course," he said, "but I have to be in court this afternoon for another case, so it might not be until later." Then he gave her a kiss and left.

Dana stayed in bed just a few more minutes, aware that she still had a promise to keep. She needed to track down Eleanor Gratz and see if she could uncover any information on her mysterious visit to the Dennison house. She would have asked Ari if he knew anything about this, but thought it best to let that unfold on its own. If Jamie hadn't told him yet, he would soon.

She dressed and went to the studio an hour early, heading straight to the executive floor. There, she was waylaid by Brenda, the receptionist, who was eager for Dana's speculation on who might have pushed Ivan to his death.

Dana turned the question right around. "Who do *you* think it was?" she asked.

"My money's on Sherry," Brenda said. "But if I was writing it as a screenplay, I'd go with Anna, her significant other—more unexpected."

"And the motive?" Dana asked.

"Easy, looking out for her girlfriend, whose job is on the line."

"Neat twist." Dana rubbed her chin. "What are others saying?"

"What *aren't* they saying?" Brenda corrected. "Honeycutt... Eleanor...the son...even you."

"Me?" Dana wondered what people might have seen that she couldn't remember.

"Personally, I don't think you're the type."

"And why not?" Dana asked, curious about her reputation here. Outside of work—at least among her family members—she was considered impulsive and irresponsible. The very traits that would make her the perfect suspect.

Brenda squinted at her, as if seeing something Dana was trying to hide. "I just don't think this job means that much to you. Certainly not enough to push a guy off the roof for threatening the company."

It was a fair assessment. Sure, Dana liked this gig and wanted to keep it, wanted to see the Shopping Channel succeed. But in the end, it was just a job. Acting was her passion…her calling.

She smiled at Brenda, whom she knew was a fellow trouper. "Are you saying I'd be capable of murder if I had a major role at stake?"

"Wouldn't we all?" Brenda asked.

Dana tapped her desk in appreciation, then went off to see Eleanor Gratz.

This time, there was no hesitation when she knocked on the head buyer's door.

"If that's not Idris Elba in a tuxedo carrying a bouquet of wildflowers, get lost," Eleanor called.

Dana opened the door. Eleanor was dressed lusciously in a navy gabardine dress and statement jewelry. It was, Dana imagined, important to look impeccable when you were dealing with suppliers. Anyone on the other side of the desk needed to know she was fashion-savvy and formidable.

"Do you write these things out beforehand?" Dana asked.

"I compose them on the way to work, clears my head."

She entered the office and sat. "You come up with a new one every day?"

"You want the truth or an entertaining lie?" Eleanor asked.

"I always want the truth."

"Then you're in the wrong business, superwoman. What can I do for you today, other than prostrate myself at your feet?"

Dana smiled. They hadn't spoken since the board meeting, so a debriefing was due. "That was pretty slick, huh?"

"I knew you would charm the board, but I had no idea

you would take them hostage and steal their souls. It was a thing of beauty."

"Glad I could help," Dana said.

"And then you followed it up by having your best show in months. Whatever you're taking, I want some."

"No, you don't." Dana leaned back and crossed her legs. "That's just me under pressure. I don't think we need any more of that around here."

Eleanor agreed. "Trust me, I have my hands full pushing Reluven products into the holiday schedule. We're creating a gift basket with their bath line, which you haven't seen yet. I think it's going to kill, but we have to hustle. The special packaging is being manufactured, and I got the graphics department working on our presentation."

Dana nodded. She knew there was a lot involved in launching a new line on the Shopping Channel. Normally, it took months, not weeks. "You're moving mountains," she said.

"On my back," Eleanor responded, "three times around the globe."

"Anything I can do to help?"

"Yeah, sell the hell out of it." She took off her reading glasses and sat back, pleased. "We might just save this place, you know."

Her eyes were lit like Rockefeller Center at Christmas, and it struck Dana that Eleanor worked pretty well under pressure, too. Now, though, Dana had a tough task. She had to shift the conversation to something which might extinguish that light.

"Have you heard anything from the Dennisons?" she asked. It was intentionally vague. She wanted to test the woman's reaction.

Eleanor's smile went flat. "The Dennisons?" she repeated. "I leave that to Charles Honeycutt and the board of directors." She straightened a pile of papers on her desk as she regained her composure. To Dana, it looked like she was searching for an innocent reason for Dana's question, and thought she found one. "The funeral was private, but there's a memorial service for the public next week out on Long Island. We'll be arranging the schedule here so most senior personnel can make it."

"But you know them, right? The Dennisons?"

The temperature in the room seemed to drop as Eleanor shifted in her chair. "The family?"

"Jamie told me you were out at the house a couple of weeks ago."

Eleanor leaned on her hand, fingers covering her mouth as she considered the statement. "Well, yes. I went to see Ivan about some…business." She avoided eye contact.

"Is that the truth or an entertaining lie?" Dana asked. She said it without malice, but it was too weighty to be taken lightly.

Eleanor's brow tightened. "Why are you asking me this?"

"Listen, I'm not trying to corner you. We're on the same team, right? I just want to help Jamie out. He's concerned about his mom—about the kind of things that might come out about his dad."

Eleanor sat back in her chair, and Dana could sense some internal calculus going on. She was deciding whether to be honest. It took several moments, but at last she leaned forward. "Okay, look—I had an idea of what Dennison was planning, so I reached out to some electronics suppliers and found some dirt on him. I thought I could use it as leverage, get him to back off." She shook her head. "I didn't know what else to do. He was going to destroy everything we built."

"What kind of dirt?" Dana pressed.

Eleanor hesitated for a moment, as if considering what she should divulge. Finally she sighed. "At least one affair and a couple of sexual harassment complaints handled quietly—presumably with settlements."

Dana rubbed her forehead, thinking of the conversation Jamie would need to have with his mother.

"This can't come as a complete surprise to you," Eleanor said. "I saw the way Ivan was all over you at the party."

"It's not that," Dana said. "I just want to understand. Did you threaten to tell his wife?"

"Yeah, that was the idea."

"So what happened?"

"He wouldn't budge."

"But you didn't go through with it," Dana said. It was more of a statement than a question, because she already knew Eleanor left the house without talking to Blair Dennison.

After a moment, Eleanor shrugged.

"Why not?" Dana asked.

"I just…changed my mind."

Dana knew there had to be more to it, but she saw no reason to get contentious. That would be up to the police. For her part, Dana had the information she sought.

After work, Dana went to meet Megan for a quick drink to tell her about the conversation with Eleanor. This time, it was a pub near her studio, and it was jammed. Dana had to push her way through the happy hour crowd to find her friend in a quiet booth she had snagged in the back.

Dana slid in across from her, and Megan signaled the waitress so they could order drinks.

"What happened?" Megan asked, when the waitress left. "Did you talk to Eleanor?"

Dana nodded. "Jamie must be a hell of a reporter, because he got everything right. Eleanor dug up some dirt on Ivan's philandering, and went to the house to threaten to expose him."

"He's sharp as a razor," Megan said, and Dana caught her suppressing a smile.

"You like him," she prodded.

"It's early," Megan said, catching herself, "and a weird way to start a relationship."

"You're allowed to like him," Dana said. "He's smart and cute. And down-to-earth. You'd never know how loaded he is."

Megan waved away the comment. She didn't want to talk about it. "Tell me about Eleanor. I assume she knew about Ivan's plans for the company before she went to see him?"

"Yeah, but she said he wouldn't budge. And for some reason, she decided not to carry through on her threat to tell the wife."

Megan looked thoughtful. "That's curious."

"She was pretty cagey about that part. I think she's hiding something. In fact, if I hadn't confronted her directly—" Dana heard two drunk girls laughing and looked up to see them walking toward her table, leaning on each other for support. When she offered them a small smile, they collapsed into each other, squealing.

"Can I help you?" Megan asked, as the girls stood before them.

The taller one, who had mascara smudges under her eyes, pointed at Dana. "You're that girl from the Shopping Channel. We've seen you on TV."

"We think you're really cute," said the other one, who held a drink that spilled as she spoke.

"I think you're really cute, too," Dana said.

The girls giggled, delighted.

"Can we take a selfie with you?" the tall one asked.

"Sure," Dana said, and stood to pose with the girls for a photo she knew would wind up on social media. That was why it was important to be sweet in public. The tiniest infraction could get her branded a bitch in a post that could go viral in an instant.

"You're so nice," the drink-spilling girl said as she petted Dana's arm.

"You ladies have a great night," she said. "Thanks for saying hi."

"We love you!" they called as they walked away, staring down at the cell-phone image.

"Star power, baby," Megan said, when they were out of earshot.

Dana laughed. "They don't even know my name."

"Patience," Megan said. It was shorthand for all they had discussed about Dana's career. Her plan was for Dana to spend a few years at the Shopping Channel to raise her profile, and then she would have an easier path to the biggest auditions.

A few minutes later, the waitress brought their drinks. Megan stirred hers thoughtfully as she bit her lip. "There's one thing I don't get," she said.

"Matthew McConaughey?" Dana offered. "Me, neither."

"I'm serious," Megan said. "If Eleanor knew what a pig Ivan was, why did she tell you to cozy up to him?"

"She *did* warn me about him."

"But she didn't tell you to keep your distance. She encouraged you to get close to him."

"I guess she thought I could sway him in ways she couldn't."

"Then why wasn't she more up-front about it?" Megan asked. "I mean, if she already knew his plans for the company, she should have told you."

Dana squeezed the lime into her vodka and soda and took a sip. "I can see your wheels spinning."

Megan nodded. "I think she was using you."

"You mean to catch Ivan in the act?"

"Think about it," Megan said. "I bet she thought you'd be the perfect bait—someone Ivan would come on to…but someone strong enough to press sexual harassment charges. He'd be thrown out in a Midtown minute…and his plan along with him."

Dana rubbed her cheek, considering it. The theory sounded pretty logical.

Megan continued, "What else did she say in that first meeting?"

"We just talked about trying to convince Ivan to let us market skin care. And come to think of it…" She trailed off, replaying a conversation from the party.

"What?" Megan pressed.

"He's such a misogynist he actually laughed at me for making a marketing suggestion." She shook her head, thinking about it. "He wouldn't have taken me seriously in a million years. I wonder if Eleanor knew that."

"I bet she did," Megan said. "I bet she knew exactly how sexist he was. She threw you to the wolves, my friend."

Dana leaned back, hurt. She had believed Eleanor was fond of her. "I knew she was driven," Dana said, taking a long sip of her drink, "but I didn't think she was so…ruthless."

"That company means a hell of a lot to her."

"Then why do you think she didn't carry through on her threat to tell Blair Dennison what she knew?" Dana asked.

"Jamie thinks he must have counter-threatened her with something," Megan said. "And it's the only thing that makes sense."

They sat in silence for a few minutes, staring deep into their drinks, as if searching for something. Dana tried to get inside Eleanor's head, the way she would with a character.

She thought about motivation—an intense desire to save her precious fashion empire. And possibly something darker—something Ivan might have been holding over her head. What would someone like that do if the proper opportunity presented itself?

At last, Dana asked the question she assumed they were both mulling.

"Megan," she said, "do you think Eleanor could have killed Ivan Dennison?"

"Do you?" her friend shot back.

She didn't want to. Despite everything, she liked Eleanor. She was a pistol. But when Dana imagined herself in Eleanor's skin, with the opportunity to solve everything with one simple push, it was as plausible as anything she could think of.

16

After meeting with Megan, Dana rushed downtown for Sweat City's first real rehearsal for *Harte of Brooklyn*. They weren't doing much more than blocking the first scene, figuring out where the treadmill would go, and getting a sense of their characters, but Dana could feel the creeping excitement of creating a living, breathing work of art. It started out of nothing—just a spark of an idea in Nathan's head. And soon, characters would transform into people. Lines would morph into emotions. Relationships would be birthed on the stage. And the whole of it would become a performance with the power to delight, engage, move and entertain. It made her heart race.

"I have to say, people," Nathan announced at the end of rehearsal, "from the bottom of my heart, that really sucked."

They laughed, because he was right. It was pretty bad. But it was always bad in the beginning. And since the script had never been performed, it was still a work-in-progress. Nathan had done a bit of rewriting since the read-through, and would probably continue to tweak it as the weeks wore on.

"Let's work on getting off book for scene one so we can start to nail pace. It'll all hinge on that. Now get lost!"

The cast dispersed in good cheer, because they knew it was just a matter of hard work—the kind of work they loved because the payoff was so gratifying.

Dana waited until she was seated on the subway before checking her phone. There was a text from Ari saying he was going home to Brooklyn for clean clothes, and would see her tomorrow. Nothing about the lieutenant's decision on whether Ari could stay on the case. Dana tried to breathe through her anxiety. It felt like everything was dependent on this one factor. If he got a chance to be the lead on this high-profile homicide, he'd be a shoo-in for the promotion. And then they could at least talk about the new apartment.

But tonight, he'd be going back to his place, because her tiny converted studio had so little closet space that Ari never left more than two clean dress shirts there. And even then, they sometimes got so creased from the overcrowding he needed to bring them into the bathroom when he showered so the wrinkles would relax. But that was nothing compared to the problems they had when the two of them needed to get ready simultaneously. The place was just too miniature for two adults moving back and forth between the undersized bathroom and the undersized closet.

So yes, the promotion was critical. Once that happened, Ari would come around and fall in love with the place she found for them. She was sure of it. For now, though, Dana would keep her mouth shut about it. The wound was just too fresh. But in bed alone that night, she drifted to sleep with visions of paint chips and upholstery swatches dancing in her head.

When she got to work the next day, Dana waited in her dressing room for Ari before heading to the makeup department. He had told her he'd be back at the Shopping Channel, reinterviewing staff members about the party. She hoped he also had news about his conversation with the lieutenant.

At last, her assistant poked her head in. "Good mornin'," Ashlee said. "Ari is here. Should I let him in?"

Dana grinned. "Always."

Ari walked in wearing a freshly pressed suit and his usual inscrutable expression. But his face relaxed into a smile when he saw her. He closed the door behind him and extended his arms. They embraced and kissed. He asked how her rehearsal went and she gave him a quick rundown, eager for news from his end.

"I spoke to Covello," he finally said, referring to his lieutenant.

"And?"

Ari paused, and she held her breath.

"He's not taking me off the case."

Dana's sharp inhale felt like a tiny breath of joy. "Wonderful!"

"As long as I don't discuss the investigation with you."

"Not at all?" The joy stopped short of filling Dana's lungs. They already had an off-limits topic—the apartment. And now they couldn't discuss his work. Of course, there were other things they could talk about, but this could create a lot of strain on a relationship that just regained its footing.

"Well, obviously I can discuss things that directly involve you."

"Like my drug test," she offered.

He nodded. "In fact, the lab report came in this morning." He paused and put his hands on her shoulders, as if bracing her for the news. "There were traces of a date rape drug in your system—Rohypnol."

She could see him searching her face, concerned with how she would take this news. It was, of course, exactly what she expected to hear. But the reality of it still jolted her. And Ari—more sensitive than most people could possibly guess—had somehow intuited this.

She swallowed.

"Are you okay?" he asked.

Dana nodded, trying to find her voice. It was real. Someone had slipped a drug into her drink with the intention of assaulting her. It was only by chance that she had managed to stay safe. Perhaps Ivan's death had saved her.

"Do you know who did it?" she asked.

"Not yet. But we'll find out."

"And you'll be allowed to tell me that much at least?" she asked.

He put his hand to his heart. "I promise."

Later, when Dana was in the makeup chair, she gently goaded Jo and Felicia into spilling the latest gossip about Ivan's murder.

"Did you hear he came on to Sherry's girlfriend?" Jo asked, as she pushed Dana's cuticles with a tapered wooden stick.

"Um… I'm not sure," Dana equivocated. Better to hear what people were saying than to lead the witness with what she knew.

"You know Micaela?" Jo asked. "With the blond bangs?"

"Robért's assistant?" Dana asked, as she was pretty sure the girl worked for the in-house hairdresser.

"That's her," Jo said. "She told us that one of the girls from accounting overheard Ivan making a pass at Anna, right in front of Sherry."

"And she said Sherry was *pissed*," Felicia added, as she smoothed foundation onto Dana's face with a sponge.

"Why wouldn't she be?" Dana asked, thinking about the receptionist's speculation that Sherry was the murderer. But Brenda's conclusion was based on Sherry's devotion to her career, not on jealousy. It was hard to imagine Sherry with that much passion.

"The thing is," Felicia said, "they were right by the railing when this happened."

Dana could picture it. That seemed to be Ivan's modus operandi—cornering his prey.

"You know what *I* think?" Jo said.

Dana nodded. "I think I do."

Jo ignored her and continued. "I think Sherry pushed Ivan off the roof in a jealous rage!" She seemed utterly pleased with herself for articulating the soap opera scenario.

"Don't you think that's a little far-fetched?" Dana asked.

"Hey, *somebody* killed him," Jo said. "And you know what a bitch Sherry is."

Too well, Dana thought. But she said, "She's not out-of-control, though. It's hard to picture her exploding in rage like that."

Felicia harrumphed. "People are different when it comes to love. And I just bet she's the jealous type."

"Anyway," Jo added, "I think we'll know soon enough. That Detective Marks doesn't let nothing get by him."

Dana's phone pinged and she looked down to see a text from Megan.

You up for a visit after your segment? I'm with Jamie and we want to stop by.

Dana assumed there was something important they wanted to discuss. She texted back a thumbs-up and typed: CU soon.

It was officially holiday selling season, so Dana's show that day featured a line of jewelry from Quentin Daye, a designer who was a favorite among Shopping Channel viewers. Dana had a long vocabulary of adjectives at her disposal for all things sparkly, so she knew it would be fun, showcasing the gemstone pieces embellished with cubic zirconia. And she had Quentin at her side, which meant she had someone to banter with. Even better—Jessalyn told Dana they would open the phone lines so viewers could call in. She didn't do this very often, because saving it for special occasions made the merchandise seem that much more special.

Dana enjoyed chatting with the viewers, even though it meant standing on the set and having a conversation with the disembodied voice of someone looking right at her. There were five excited callers that day—three were first-timers, and two were superfans who rushed to the phone every time they got the opportunity. One of them was Dana's favorite— a woman named Mary from Sacramento, who sounded at least a hundred years old. She was funny as hell and easy to talk to, especially when she'd been hitting the sauce. Dana liked to imagine her sitting in a cluttered living room, a box of wine on a tray table next to her. That day, Mary bought a marquise-cut blue tanzanite pendant on a gold chain, and matching earrings. Dana hoped the old bird had someplace wonderful to wear them to. And if not, she hoped she would enjoy sparkling all the way to Walmart or her bingo club.

"You made a good choice, Mary," Quentin said into the camera. Like Dana, he had been trained to call the viewers by name. "I hope you enjoy it."

"Oh, honey," she said. "I enjoy everything."

Dana laughed. "We love you, Mary!" she said, and at that moment, she meant it.

Viewers responded to the warmth by flooding the phone lines, and soon enough, it was time to wrap up.

Megan and Jamie emerged from the control booth as Lorenzo unclipped Dana's mike.

"That was impressive," Jamie said. "I've watched on TV a few times, but seeing it up close really drives home your skills."

"I told you she was good." Megan beamed.

"You really seemed to be enjoying yourself out there." Jamie sounded amazed that she had pulled it off.

"I *was*," Dana said. "And that may be the secret of my success. If you're faking it, the viewers can tell."

She went over the day's sales figures with Jessalyn, and then took Megan and Jamie back to her dressing room for a private chat. On the way, she filled Megan in on what Ari had told her about confirming the date-rape drug in her system. Megan wasn't surprised, but she gave Dana a reassuring hug.

When they reached her dressing room, Dana asked Jamie how his mother was holding up.

"A little worse every day," he said. "It's difficult to watch."

Dana studied him. He seemed to be on full output mode, more focused on projecting his thoughts than letting anything touch him. Dana couldn't even find a keyhole view of what was in his heart. But maybe that was his training as a journalist. It was all about telling the story, not about what he felt.

"I'm sorry," she said.

"I haven't yet made a decision on what I'm going to tell her about my dad."

"Does she seem ready to hear it?"

He shook his head. "I don't think she'll ever be ready to hear something like that."

His expression remained even, but Dana gave his arm a

sympathetic squeeze, and excused herself into the alcove so she could change.

"I passed along your debriefing about Eleanor," Megan called.

"So I guessed," Dana said, as she pulled off the red dress the wardrobe supervisor had chosen for today's show. She slipped into her own shirt and yanked on her jeans, feeling like she was settling back into the person she had been before she ever dreamed of a Shopping Channel gig. She came back into the main part of the room and took a chair opposite Megan and Jamie as she pulled on her socks and boots.

"I wish there was more I could do to help," she said to Jamie. "I told Megan everything I know."

"I appreciate that," Jamie said. "The thing is, I'm trying to figure out what my dad might have had on Eleanor."

"Is that important?" Dana asked. "To your mom, I mean."

Jamie shrugged. "If it's important to the investigation, it'll be important to my mom. She wants to know who killed him."

"Of course," Dana said.

Megan leaned forward. "He did some sleuthing."

"Sleuthing?" Dana asked.

"I got into my dad's laptop and accessed his email. I wanted to see if there was anything that might shed light on his interaction with Eleanor Gratz."

"Find anything?"

"Sort of. There was an email he sent her. It was pretty cryptic, but he warned her to stay away from his family, and said something about 'the file.'"

"Like a computer file?" Dana asked.

"I don't think so, because he also mentioned something about a paper trail. I believe that was literal."

"So you think there's an actual folder that exposes whatever dirt he had on Eleanor?"

"Possibly. But I looked through every inch of his home office and couldn't find it."

"We think it might be here, at his office upstairs," Megan said.

Dana gave a thoughtful nod as she imagined the thoroughness of the investigation. "I'm sure the police already looked through those files."

"I'm sure they *didn't*," Jamie said.

Dana raised an eyebrow, and Jamie responded by holding up a set of keys.

"What's that?" she asked.

"The keys to his office cabinets. The detectives asked me if I knew where they were, and I promised I would look for them."

"I assume you also promised you would turn them over?"

"And I will," he said. "Just not yet."

Dana paused, looking from Megan to Jamie. They stared at her expectantly. "Is that why you came?" she asked. "You want to search through his office?"

"I'm his son," Jamie said. "I think I have a right." His tone was friendly but determined.

Dana sighed. She didn't want to fight with him. He did have a right, after all. But there was a murder investigation going on.

"You need to tell Ari all this," she said. "Let the police look for it."

"It's not that I plan on keeping it from them," Jamie explained. "It's just that I'd like to know what my dad was up to before it blows up in my mom's face. You understand, don't you? She's so fragile. It's my responsibility now."

"Did you ask Beecham if he'd let you have access to the office?" Dana asked, referring to the building's head of security.

Jamie frowned. "Pretty sure he'd say no."

"So that's why you're here," Dana mused. "You want me to bring you upstairs."

Megan looked at her watch. "It's after five," she said. "In a little while, all the office workers upstairs will empty out. I figured you could use your RFID card to open the door and let us in."

Dana leaned back as she considered it. She hated saying no to Jamie, but knew that Ari would be troubled by this kind of meddling in the evidence. This was police work. On the other hand, she burned with curiosity about what the hell Ivan could possibly have on Eleanor, and knew it was information Ari wasn't at liberty to share with her.

"You wouldn't even need to come with us," Megan said. "Just let us in. If anyone asks, you can just say Jamie wanted to get some of his dad's personal things."

"No way," Dana said.

Megan looked surprised. "What?"

"If you're going to be snooping around for that file, I want to be there."

17

"Need anything else today?" Ashlee asked. She stood in the doorway of Dana's dressing room, as blonde and statuesque as a supersized Charlize Theron, her coat draped over her arm.

"Just one little thing. When you're on your way out, check and see if Beecham is still there," Dana said. "Then send me a text with the answer."

"Do I want to know why?"

"You do not."

The fact was, Dana knew that Beecham checked the entryway security cams, scrutinized the day's visitors' logs and did one last walkthrough of the building before leaving for the night. His replacement was a young guy whose dedication to the job went about as far as his paycheck.

A few minutes later, Dana's phone pinged with a text from Ashlee:

He's still here, but looks like he's wrapping up.

"What should we do?" Megan asked.

"I'm sure he'll be gone in five minutes," Dana said. "But let's give it twenty, just to be safe."

And they did, staying in Dana's dressing room until she felt it was all clear. Then she led them to the elevator and up to the executive floor, where they waltzed by the empty reception desk. Dana waved her ID card over the electronic sensor and pushed open the door to the main corridor, letting it lock behind them. They walked down the long carpeted hallway to the massive corner office Ivan had occupied.

The décor was plain compared to Eleanor's and Sherry's offices. The windows had tan slatted blinds, and the walls were painted a dull beige. They held framed prints of extreme close-up photography from the natural world—kiwi fruit, a bee on a petal, a snowflake, the nose of a dog, the eyeball of a human. The effect, Dana thought, was for Ivan's guests to feel as if they were under a microscope. She also detected just a faint whiff of his aftershave, as if part of Ivan Dennison still lingered. Dana sneaked a glance at Jamie to see if it brought anything up for him, but his face looked more tense and determined than pained.

She noticed there was an oddly placed cross, very high up on the wall, facing the visitors' chairs. Dana could imagine Ivan calling maintenance and telling them to bring a ladder. But she couldn't discern why he wanted it so high. Closer to God? Harder to remove?

The king of the room was the massive black desk, which had several piles of paper neatly stacked. There was no computer, and Dana assumed the detectives had already confiscated it to do a deep dive into Ivan's background, looking for clues on who might want him dead. That, she knew, could yield a long list, as nearly everyone at that party had a reason to despise the man.

At the corner of the desk, in a heavy silver frame, there was a wedding photo of Ivan and Blair looking young and healthy. Next to it was a picture of a grinning boy of about ten, holding a cheesy tennis trophy. He wore glasses, but Dana knew immediately it wasn't Jamie. The kernel-sized teeth gave away that it was a young Ivan, pre-contact lenses. What kind of egomaniac kept their own picture on their desk? At least it was balanced by a picture of Blair as a young mother, flanked by two little boys, the smaller of whom was clearly Jamie.

Jamie made quick work of unlocking the drawers and file cabinets, and they began their hunt.

Dana and Megan went to work on the file cabinets, rifling through the folders, while Jamie rummaged through everything that didn't hold files—cabinets, shelves and desk drawers.

As far as Dana could see, all the folders held budget reports. It was just numbers and more numbers. Still, she was careful to check every file, just in case.

She was just finishing up the first drawer when she heard Jamie cry out. Dana turned to see him holding a blue file folder that seemed to be filled with two or three magazines.

"What's the matter?" Megan asked.

Jamie dropped the file on the desk and backed up, as if it were radioactive. "Porn," he said, his face contorting in disgust. "My dad has a porn stash...in his *office*." At that moment, his journalistic guard was down. He was just a son horrified by his father's vulgar habits.

"Why can't he just go online like a normal person?" Megan asked. It wasn't rhetorical—she seemed genuinely curious.

Jamie lowered himself into the leather swivel chair behind the desk, as if he needed a moment to recover. He pushed the file farther away from him and answered. "For a guy who made his living in electronics, my father was incredibly unschooled in cyberspace. He knew just enough to understand that his internet searches could be traced, but he didn't know how to hide his ISP or delete his browsing history without calling in an IT guy."

Dana and Megan approached the desk and stared down at the folder.

Megan slowly lifted the corner. "Anything especially pervy in here?"

"I don't even want to know," Jamie said.

"You look a little ashen," Dana observed.

Jamie made a face like he just got wind of something putrid. "How would you feel if you found *your* father's porn stash?"

Now that's *a rhetorical question,* Dana thought, and her only response was an involuntary shudder.

Megan grabbed the top magazine and opened to a random page, which showed a close-up of a woman's lipsticked mouth on an impossibly thick shaft.

"Pretty old-school," she observed, cocking her head for a better view.

"Just set it down," Jamie said. "I'm begging you."

Megan returned it to the folder and tried to hand it to Jamie. "Put it back in his drawer," she said.

"You don't think I should throw it out?"

"It might be evidence or something." Megan waved the folder at him to indicate that he should take it.

"I agree," Dana said. "You don't want to tamper with anything. Just in case." She didn't want to get too specific with Jamie, but if his father's sexual proclivities wound up being relevant to the case, the police would want every bit of evidence.

Jamie shook his head. "I don't want to touch it."

Megan tsked. "I'll put it back," she said, and walked around the massive desk to the drawers in the front. Jamie rolled back his chair.

"This where you found it?" she asked.

He nodded and she slipped the file back in the drawer and began sorting through the rest of it. "You know, he's got several porn files. They're just labeled *A* through *M*. Looks like *D* was his favorite." She pulled out the file and began looking through the magazines. She took one out and held it toward Dana. It was well worn, with a title font that looked like something from the seventies or eighties. In bubble-shaped letters, across the cleavage of a very large woman, were the words *Big Fat Tits*.

"Subtle," Dana said.

"Kind of makes me wonder what he saw in you," Megan teased her.

Jamie held his head in his hands. "Make it stop."

Megan took out another publication and held it toward him. "The man had eclectic tastes, at least." She turned the magazine toward Dana. It showed another large woman, but from the other end of her anatomy.

Jamie said, "It's all fun and games until the young son of the deceased has a heart attack in the middle of his office."

"Okay, I'll stop," Megan said. "But you'll laugh about this later."

She put the folder back and continued looking through the drawer. She pulled out another file.

"Have mercy," Jamie said.

Megan shook her head. "This isn't porn."

"What is it?"

"It's labeled with the letter *G*, but it doesn't have magazines inside."

A secret folder hidden among his secret porn? Now Dana was intrigued. "What's in it?" she asked.

Megan opened it and studied the top page. "Looks like some kind of a purchase order signed by Eleanor Gratz. It's dated December 12, 1999."

Jamie sat up. "Why would he have something that old?"

Megan put the folder on the desk and the three of them stared down at the page, which seemed to be an agreement with a skin care company called Maria Faye. It contained a lot of legalese about delivery and payment, most of which seemed boilerplate. Megan flipped the page to expose an invoice to the Shopping Channel for $227,000, minus a sum of $15,000 paid to a company called Hartsdale Marketing. Someone had drawn a circle around the amount and the company name. Dana reached over and flipped the page to find a photocopy of an article of incorporation for Hartsdale Marketing. The principal owner of the company, according to the filing, was Philip M. Wagoner.

The name was familiar, and it took another second for Dana to make the connection. She felt a chill prickling her shoulders. "Oh shit," she whispered.

"What does it mean?" Megan asked.

"Philip Wagoner is Eleanor's husband," Dana said. "And he's not in marketing. He's a middle school teacher."

Megan looked confused. "I don't understand."

Dana went back to the page showing a payment of $15,000 to Hartsdale Marketing. "I think this is a kickback," she said. "Eleanor signed the order, meaning she bought these products for the Shopping Channel from this Maria Faye company. Then they kicked back money to her husband's company...or rather, a shell company set up by her husband."

Jamie stared down at the page for several seconds, concentrating. "I think you're right," he said.

Megan whistled, impressed. "Since when did you become a forensic accountant?" she said to Dana.

"It's all right there. And honestly, a year ago this would have been meaningless to me. But when I first came on board,

Sherry made me spend so much time studying those spreadsheets that some of it seeped in."

"Now all the pieces fit together," Jamie said. "Eleanor threatened to go to my mother with dirt on my dad. And then he threatened to expose her for this twenty-year-old kickback."

"This is sickening," Dana said. "I just didn't think Eleanor was a grifter."

"If it makes you feel any better," Jamie said, "it looks like he had to go back a long time to find any dirt on her. My guess is that she's been clean ever since, or he would have used something more recent."

"So what now?" Megan asked. "Do we show this to the police?"

"No!" Dana said sharply. "No one can know I let you in here. I could get fired."

Jamie pulled out his cell phone and took pictures of the pages. Then he closed the file and put it back in the drawer. "It's okay. I'll tell the police what I saw at my house, and what I suspect. I'll even tell them about the email I found. They'll search the office and find this on their own."

"How can you be so sure?" Megan asked.

Dana thought about all the stories she heard from Ari about the depths of his investigations, and knew they'd comb the office and uncover this file. Nothing got past these guys. "I'm sure," she said.

Megan paused, as if weighing Dana's words, and deciding to trust them. She let out a breath. "Then let's get out of here," she said.

Jamie took out his keys and relocked all the drawers. Then he led them down the hall toward the exit door.

"Wait up," Dana said. "I need my ID card to get us out."

She flashed her card across the sensor. The light stayed red. She tried the door. Locked. She tried her card again. Nothing.

"What's the matter?" Megan asked.

"Oh god," Dana said. "What time is it?"

Jamie looked at his phone. "Six thirty-six. Why?"

"I forgot that I don't have twenty-four-hour clearance anymore," Dana said. "It never came up before, but my card only works until six thirty."

"How is that possible?" Megan asked.

"It's one of Beecham's new security measures," Dana said. "Most employees no longer have twenty-four-hour access. My card works only during specific hours in specific areas of the building."

Megan tried the door, as if she might have the magic touch. "What are we going to do?"

Dana thought about the young security guy downstairs. She could call him and they would be out in minutes. But he would ask what they were doing up here, and no matter what she said, he would tell Beecham. That was his job. And Beecham would report her to Honeycutt. She turned to Megan.

"What would happen to me if Honeycutt found out I'd let you in?"

"We can come up with a sympathetic story," Jamie said. "I can say I wanted a picture from my dad's desk and that I was so grief-stricken I convinced you to let me in."

"Beecham isn't an idiot," Dana said. "He'd want to know why you couldn't ask the security guard to take you up here, and why it was such an emergency."

Jamie turned to Megan. "Dana's their star host right now. They're not going to fire her, are they?"

Megan sighed. "The problem is that the company is still shaky. If it doesn't turn around, they're going to look for excuses to break contracts."

Jamie looked back at Dana. "Is there anyone you can call? A friend in the company who has a twenty-four-hour ID card?"

It was an excellent question, and Dana ran down the short list of people she knew who might have round-the-clock security clearance. Most of them were executives, and possibly their assistants. Dana had cordial relationships with all of them, but close friendships with none.

Then she realized there was someone who might be able to help. Ashlee. The girl was a walking friend magnet. Maybe she could finagle an ID card from a sympathetic pal. Dana whipped out her phone to call her assistant. When she finished explaining the situation, there was a pause, and she worried Ashlee might clutch her Southern pearls in horror.

"Can you help?" Dana pleaded.

As she heard Ashlee inhale, Dana prepared herself for a *no*. Of course Ashlee wouldn't help. Why should she? The girl had nothing to gain and everything to lose. Dana went through her mental checklist again, looking for anyone else who might come to her rescue. But there was no one. There would be nothing left to do but try to convince Beecham to keep their secret—which she knew would never work. She was ready to hang up the phone in resignation when Ashlee finally spoke.

"Of course, you silly goose," she said. "I'll be right there."

Sure enough, less than twenty minutes later, they heard the ding of the elevator and then the soft click of the door unlocking. It swung open and there stood Ashlee St. Pierre, like a goddess in a white faux shearling jacket and a proud grin.

Dana was stunned. "How did you manage this?"

"Nothing to it," she said, as if people asked her to do things like this all the time.

"I thought it might take hours, at best," Dana said.

"I was at a bar nearby when you called. So I ambled back into the building and flirted with that cute boy at the desk, tellin' him I forgot my hat upstairs. Played it real cute. He's a nice kid, but so dumb he could throw himself on the ground and miss. While he was looking at my chest, I swiped one of the other security guards' ID cards from the desk. Easy as cherry pie."

"I knew you had talent," Dana gushed, "but I'm still impressed."

Ashlee brushed it off. "A little Southern charm, a little method acting. Nothin' to it."

They were all silent for a moment, in shock that she had pulled it off so neatly, looking for adequate words to thank her.

At last Megan said, "Any chance you're looking for a manager?"

18

By Sunday's rehearsal, the Sweat City Company was making actual progress with the production. The rhythm was making sense to the actors. Sometimes they even got a sense of when they would need to pause for laughter. But for Dana, there was lingering anxiety. She felt she was struggling with the character, whose earnestness seemed to override her common sense. She couldn't figure out how to play her without going broad. It got laughs from her fellow cast members, but she knew it wasn't quite right.

"I thought I got her, but now I'm not so sure," she complained to Nathan after everyone else had left.

Despite being in his late thirties, he still had a boyishness to his face, with full cheeks, small eyes and naturally blond hair that was just beginning to recede. They were backstage, in the space they called their greenroom. It was actually a black-painted alcove, separated from the rest of the backstage area by an ancient velvet curtain that had been retired from use. The furnishings were also scenery castoffs.

"You will," he said.

She studied his face, trying to read it for sincerity. She feared he would regret casting her for the role. He seemed to read her mind.

"Dana," he said, putting his hands on her shoulders and bringing his face right up to hers. "I wrote this part for you."

"You did?" It was a surprising revelation. She knew Nathan admired her talent, but he felt that way about everyone in the company. So why her?

He stood so close she felt his breath on her face, and another thought flashed through her mind. She hoped it was wrong. Nathan was like a big brother to her. And he was a married guy. But for minute, it felt like he was going to lean in and kiss her. She tensed.

He released her and backed up. Now she wondered if she had misread the situation. Maybe Ari's jealousy had planted the seed in her brain. She decided that had to be it. Nathan had simply seen her as right for the part. She gave him a cheerful thanks, and hurried toward home.

On the way, her cell phone rang. It was Chelsea.

"In a little while, you're going to get a call from Jennifer inviting you for dinner tomorrow," her sister said, referring to the cardiologist her father had married over the summer.

"Suddenly you can see the future and *that's* your heads-up?" Dana said. "How about a stock tip?"

Chelsea ignored the joke. "I want you to say yes."

"Can't. I have rehearsals." Dana hitched her purse up on her shoulder and hurried her pace. She was almost at her apartment building, and a night chill was descending.

"Reschedule it," Chelsea pleaded. "I need you."

"You're not the boss of me," Dana joked. It had been their most heated phrase as kids—the one that always preceded a fight.

"This isn't funny."

Dana sighed. "You can't reschedule rehearsals," she said. "Anyway, why do you *need* me?"

"We're going to be telling them about the pregnancy. But we're bringing Wesley and I need someone to distract him while we're sharing the news. I just don't want him to know yet. It's so far off he won't understand."

And you're still afraid you might miscarry, Dana thought. "How about if I meet up with you after rehearsals?" she said. "Around 8:30."

"Are you kidding? We'll be leaving by then. We have to get him home to bed. It's an early dinner."

"You want me to miss rehearsals?"

"Please."

"That's a big ask, Chelsea. What about Rachel?" she said, referring to her sister's live-in babysitter.

"She had to rush back to Missouri. Her mom is sick. And anyway, Dad and Jennifer want to see Wesley. They want to see you, too."

Dana's eyes rolled so far back in her head she was afraid they'd get stuck. "Yeah, I'm sure," she said.

"Stop it."

"Can I let you know?" Dana said, struggling to find a way to wriggle out of this.

"How often do I ask for a favor?"

Never, Dana thought, and felt a rock of guilt drop in her belly as she recalled the money Chelsea and Brandon had given her when she was unemployed and couldn't make rent. That was after she got fired as a waitress and before she got hired and then fired as a Hot Topic cashier. They never made her feel guilty, never asked her to pay it back. Hell, they even wired the money right into her account so she could have it immediately.

"But I have a *commitment*," Dana pleaded. People who weren't in the theater didn't seemed to understand its importance, how you had an obligation to the rest of the cast. They seemed to think it was just a bunch of adults having a playdate.

"It's not like you're an indentured servant," Chelsea said. "Tell them you have a family emergency. Even people in the theater have family emergencies, don't they?"

Dana thought about all the people she knew who went onstage in the midst of crushing family crises. The show must go on, and all that. Then again, this *was* just a rehearsal, not a performance, and she guessed she could ask Nathan if they could do without her for one night. The timing sucked though, because he might think her request had something to do with the weird moment they just shared.

"Come on, Dana. Please. It's just this one night. I wouldn't ask if it wasn't important."

Dana sighed. "Let me call you back," she said, and then rehearsed a little speech for Nathan—something compelling and not-at-all-weird. She would take him into her confidence so he wouldn't feel like she was simply wigging out after their exchange.

It worked, of course, and he said they would rehearse scene two, which she wasn't in. Then Dana called her sister back and told her she'd be there.

"You promise?" Chelsea asked.

"Of course."

Her sister paused, as if she didn't quite believe her. But at last she said, "I'm counting on you."

Monday's show was another holiday push, divided between sweaters (which sold well in the northeast), and chenille bathrobes (which were strongest in the Midwest). It wasn't a particularly challenging sell-through, but the pressure was on for high volume. Even in the best of times, the holiday season could make or break their whole year. Fortunately, Dana found the energy to gush and coo over every color and style, and orders were strong.

Afterward, she went back into her dressing room to change into her street clothes, so she could scurry over to Dad and Jennifer's apartment on the East Side. Ari was meeting her there, and had been briefed on their mission to distract Wesley.

She had just slipped on her jacket and was freshening up her lipstick when Ashlee knocked on her door.

"You've been summoned to a meeting in Mr. Honeycutt's office," she said.

"Now?"

"Sherry said I should tell you it's important."

If it was anyone but Sherry, Dana would take that as an ominous request. But it was probably nothing. At least she hoped it was, because she simply couldn't blow off her sister.

"I have a previous engagement," she said. "Can't it wait until tomorrow?"

"I'm sure I don't know," Ashlee said. "But Sherry looked like she was fixin' to cream somebody's corn."

Dana had never heard the expression, but the context made it an easy translation. "Doesn't Sherry always look like that?"

"Not this bad. She didn't say so precisely, but I got a dark sense. Like you were in some kind of trouble."

"Trouble?" Dana said, tightening the belt on her coat, as if the sudden chill she felt came from the outside and not the inside, where her blood temperature dropped.

"I could be readin' it wrong, but I don't think so."

Dana wondered what Sherry could be so mad about she

would want to involve Honeycutt. It couldn't be her sales figures, which had been right on target that day.

"Ashlee, I have to ask—did you tell anybody about the other night?"

"No ma'am! Not a soul." She held up her hand in solemn oath and Dana could tell she was genuine.

Dana considered dashing upstairs and trying to make quick business of whatever they needed from her, then arriving at dinner just a bit late. But she didn't think that would be possible. If something serious was going on, it would require a long meeting. Besides, if she were really in some kind of trouble, she would want Megan there.

She shook her head. "I can't do it, Ashlee. I have to leave."

"Want me to say I couldn't catch you?"

"No," Dana said quickly. She didn't think it was fair to ask Ashlee to lie for her on top of what she had already done. "Just tell them I had a previous appointment and I'll see them tomorrow."

"You sure?" Ashlee said. She didn't seem convinced it was the best course of action.

"Not even a little," Dana said, but she grabbed her purse, and left.

19

Though only a few minutes late, Dana was the last to arrive. She knew this before she even stepped off the elevator, because her sister had texted to say: Everyone is here. Where are you?

She pressed the buzzer on apartment 7F and the door seemed to swing open on its own. Then she looked down and saw her four-year-old nephew.

"Well hello, Dad," she said to the boy.

"I'm *Wesley*."

Dana crouched to give him a hug. He smelled like peanut butter and crayons. "I always get you guys mixed up," she said.

"Guess what we're eating," he said.

"Reese's Pieces?"

"Nope."

She put her finger to her chin. "Green beans?"

"Ghost cheese!" he proudly pronounced. Then he curved his little hands and held them up in approximation of a terrifying spirit.

"Goat cheese," his father, Brandon, corrected from the living room.

Dana entered the apartment and shut the door behind her. "Sorry I'm late," she announced.

"They make cheese from goats?" the boy asked, incredulous.

"From goat's *milk*," Brandon explained.

Wesley frowned. "Why do they take milk from goats? Can't they buy their own?"

As Brandon launched into an explanation of how all mammals produce milk—a lesson that would no doubt come in handy once the baby was born—Dana shrugged off her coat and hung it on a rack near the door.

Ari rose from the couch and came to hug her. She held tight and breathed him in. He smelled even better than peanut butter and crayons.

"How was work?" he asked.

"I'll know more tomorrow."

He backed up to look at her. "What does that mean?"

She glanced over her shoulder at her father, who was in the brown leather easy chair listening to the conversation.

"Nothing," she said to Ari, and they exchanged a look. He nodded, understanding that the conversation would be continued in private.

Dana said hello to everyone in the room, and took a seat on the couch with Ari. Wesley picked up a cracker with cheese and handed it to her.

"It's made from the *milk* of *goats*," he explained, proud of his new expertise.

"Can I get you something to drink?" Jennifer asked her. "White wine?"

Dana agreed, then turned her attention to her father, who leaned back in his chair as he sipped what looked like scotch.

"Ari was telling us about the murder investigation," he said.

Dana turned to her boyfriend, surprised. "You were?"

"Just that it's in full swing," Ari explained, "and that we're following a number of leads."

"What do the people in your company think?" Jennifer asked, handing Dana her wine.

"The same thing the police think—that nearly everyone's a suspect. But Ari and I really aren't allowed to talk about it."

"Why not?" her father asked, his brow tightening. "Are you a murder suspect?"

Wesley looked at his mom, excited. "Did Aunt Dana kill somebody?"

"No, sweetheart."

Dana inhaled, trying to figure out how to explain to her father why she and Ari couldn't talk about it. The last thing she wanted to do was tell him she had no memory of the night because someone has slipped her a date rape drug. Before she got a word out, Ari stepped in, intuiting her discomfort.

"It's just that she was at the party," he said, "and I don't want to taint the investigation by discussing it."

Kenneth gave a nod, as if no one could understand the complexity of a police investigation better than he. As Dana watched him, she tried to wrap her mind around the thought that her father had come to accept and even admire Ari. When they first started dating, he couldn't understand why she would choose a cop when there were single neurologists and cardiologists available. Even an internist would have been acceptable. But a cop? Preposterous.

Funny thing is that until she met Ari, Dana, too, thought dating a cop was preposterous. She just didn't think rule followers were hot. Guys with a little edge were the ones that rocked her world. Then in walked this man. This too-tall grown-up man with his serious face and his serious suit. A man whose job was catching the bad guys. It all seemed so very wrong. She had resented him immediately, but couldn't stop thinking about him. Eventually, her head caught up to her heart.

"Maybe we should change the subject," Chelsea said.

Dana agreed, looking around. "Did you repaint this room?" she asked, noting that the walls, previously a pale cream, were now a light golden beige. The apartment had been Jennifer's before they married over the summer, at which point Kenneth sold his house and moved in.

"Your father picked the color," Jennifer said.

Dana tried to imagine Dr. Kenneth Barry, MD, examining paint chips, and couldn't. Her father had been so completely removed from the domestic affairs of her childhood that he often seemed more like a boarder in the house than a member of the family. She could still hear her mother trying to involve him in a decision on kitchen cabinetry or carpeting. "Rhonda, please," he would say, exasperated, as if insulted that she would try to lower him to such trivial matters. Then it would fall to Chelsea and Dana—who were sensitive enough to intuit their mother's hurt feelings—to jump in with opinions.

And now, her father was examining paint chips in different shades of vanilla? It almost didn't seem fair.

"It's lovely, Dad," Chelsea said.

Dana popped a cracker into her mouth and grunted.

"I understand *you're* moving into a new apartment," Kenneth said, turning to her.

Dana nearly choked. "Where did you hear that?" She glared at Chelsea, who wasn't supposed to say anything about the apartment in front of Ari.

"My fault," Brandon chimed in. "I didn't know it was a secret."

"Why should it be a secret?" Kenneth said.

"It's *not* a secret. It's just…it's sort of a sore point right now. Can we talk about something else, like—" she looked around, picked up a cardiology journal from the side table and read from the cover "—*trends in surgical and transcatheter mitral valve repair?*"

"A sore point?" Kenneth asked. "With whom? Ari?"

"*Dad*," Dana pleaded.

"It's okay," Ari said. "You can talk about it."

She looked at him. "You sure?"

"Why not?" he said, and gave her hand a reassuring squeeze.

Dana sighed, relenting. "I signed a lease on an apartment for Ari and me. But I didn't check with him first. I got carried away. So I'll be taking the place on my own."

Ari laughed.

"What's so funny?" she asked.

His hands went up in good-natured surrender. "I meant you could talk about the apartment itself. But if you want to talk about this part, that's fine, too."

Dana groaned. "Oh god. I can't stop putting my foot in my mouth."

Wesley, who was on the floor, looking from one grown-up to the other, raised his shoed foot toward his open mouth.

"Wesley, no!" Chelsea said.

"Aunt Dana did it."

"She didn't, sweetheart. It's just an expression."

"So can we hear about the apartment?" Jennifer asked. "Unless you don't want to—"

"No, it's fine," Dana said, and took out her phone. She scrolled to the pictures of the apartment and handed it to Jennifer.

"Oh!" she said, swiping through. "Look at those windows. And floors. It's beautiful. One bedroom?"

"Two," Dana said.

Kenneth's brow tightened. "Can you afford that?"

"Yes, Dad," she said, and braced herself.

"A two-bedroom on the West Side?" he asked, dubious.

"I just said yes, didn't I?"

Kenneth took the phone from Jennifer and swiped through the pictures. "This looks prohibitively expensive."

"Would it kill you to have an ounce of faith in my judgment?" Dana asked.

"You just said you got carried away. I just want to make sure you didn't get yourself in over your head."

"Trust me, I got a bargain."

Kenneth looked from Dana to Ari and back to Dana. "But you're going to be paying the rent on your own?"

"Not that it's any of your business, but yes."

"In one of those articles about the murder, it said the Shopping Channel is having financial difficulties."

Dana sighed, exasperated. "Can you please let me worry about my own finances?"

"I'm just saying this might not be the right time to take on such an expense. I'm sure your current apartment is adequate for a single woman."

Dana's jaw went so tight she had to unhinge it to speak. "You've never even *seen* my apartment." *Despite the many times I invited you up*, she thought.

"Irrelevant. I know that it's a one-bedroom, and that Manhattan is among the most expensive places to live."

"It's not even a real one-bedroom," Dana said. "It's a studio with an alcove I turned into a bedroom. It's miniscule, and I'm done with it. Besides, I can afford a bigger place."

"Well," Kenneth said, "if Ari's not moving in with you, perhaps you should get a roommate. That would help with the rent."

This, Dana thought, was the perfect time to take a breather

with Wesley. She stood, hoping it would equalize the pressure in her brain and keep it from exploding. "I think I'm going to get some air," she said. "Wesley, would you like to go out for a walk with Ari and me?"

"You're here for dinner," Kenneth said. "You can go for a walk on your own time."

"I'm sure Jennifer wouldn't mind if they went out for a bit," Chelsea said. "Would you?"

Jennifer said it was fine, and that they would be eating in about half an hour. So Dana, Ari and Wesley put on their jackets, and left.

They headed west and then walked up Fifth Avenue, with Wesley in the middle—his tiny hands held by the grown-ups.

"Do you like New York City?" Wesley asked, looking up at his aunt.

"Sure I do," she said. "Don't you?"

"It's okay."

Dana studied his sweet little face, so painfully earnest. "You like Roslyn better?" she asked.

Wesley nodded decisively.

"And why's that?" Ari pressed.

Wesley looked around. "Where do kids play?"

"There are plenty of parks," Dana explained. "And a great big one right in the middle of the city. But your point is well taken—it's mostly a playground for grown-ups."

"Harper lives in Roslyn," Wesley said.

"Is that your best friend?" Dana asked.

"She has red hair *and* she has a popcorn machine."

"Is she single?" Ari said.

They continued walking up Fifth Avenue, occasionally swinging Wesley forward by his arms. He cried "More!" every time, but they had to wait for a break in the pedestrian traffic before they could accommodate him.

At last, they reached the fountain in front of the Plaza Hotel, and Wesley was intrigued.

"Can I make a wish?" he asked.

Ari dug into his pocket, pulled out a penny and handed it to the boy. Wesley closed his eyes tight, waited a beat and threw his coin overhand into the water.

"What did you wish for?" Dana asked.

"Brownies with frosting."

"That's a good wish," she said.

Ari pressed a penny into Dana's palm. "Your turn."

She closed her eyes, and faced the dilemma that always presented itself when she had the opportunity to wish. What were the rules? Could you wish for more than one thing, or was that cheating?

At last, she decided it was probably okay to break the single-wish rule, and came up with a list that included her career and Ari's, their happily-ever-after, a healthy baby for her sister, and more. She could have gone on, but sensed that Ari and Wesley were anxiously waiting for her to finish, so Dana tossed her penny into the fountain.

"What did you wish for, Aunt Dana?" Wesley asked.

"Brownies with chocolate chips," she said.

Ari fished another coin from his pocket and threw it so quickly it looked like he was trying to nail a runner at first base.

Dana laughed. "A man who knows what he wants."

He stared at her so pointedly she knew his wish had been about her. She felt like her heart might melt out of her body and dribble into her shoes. She took his hand.

"Thank you for not making it weird in there when we talked about the apartment," she said.

"Your father has that market cornered."

"I'm glad we can talk about it," she said, "because I'm going to have to get busy soon—buying furniture and hiring movers. If I had to do all that in secret—"

"Why don't we do it together?" he said.

Dana took a sharp breath, trying to keep a shiver of hope from spreading too far. "What are you saying?" she asked, examining his face.

"I'm saying let's do this, even if the promotion doesn't come through."

"Are you serious?"

"Think of all the chances I'll get to make you feel guilty for keeping me out of the loop. How can I pass that up?"

"Oh, Ari!" she said, and threw her arms around him.

"What's going on, you guys?" Wesley asked.

"I just got my wish," Dana said.

"You said you wished for brownies," the boy insisted.

Dana assured Wesley they could pick some up on their way back, and the three of them headed downtown, making a brief side trip to a bakery Ari knew on East Fifty-Sixth Street. Wesley was thrilled they had frosted brownies, but chagrined to learn they had no chocolate chips.

"What about your wish?" he said to his aunt.

Ari assured him he would get Aunt Dana all the chocolate chip brownies she wanted.

When they got back to the apartment, Dana was eager to salvage this difficult visit by telling her father that Ari would be moving in with her after all. First, though, she checked in with her sister.

"Everything okay?" she asked, cryptically.

Chelsea rested a hand on her stomach. "Mission accomplished."

Jennifer cozied up to the sisters and whispered to Dana, "We're so happy for them...and for *us!*"

"Guess what?" Wesley announced to the group. "We made wishes and mine came true!"

"Yup," Dana said, pointing to the box Wesley held. "We got brownies."

Wesley opened the box and made sure all the grown-ups got to see what was inside. They made appropriately enthusiastic noises over the chocolatey dessert.

"Only Aunt Dana didn't get her wish yet," Wesley announced.

"Oh, I got one of them," she said, and turned to her father. "We talked about it, and Ari's going to be moving in with me after all."

She waited expectantly for her father's reaction. He nodded but didn't look up at her, as he was still staring into the box of brownies. "No nuts?" he said.

20

That night, before Ari and Dana went to sleep in her tiny, soon-to-be-former apartment, she turned on the small lamp by the bed and spent an hour studying her script. By the time she was done, Ari was locked in the deep breathing of sleep. She set the pages aside, clicked off the lamp and picked up her phone for one last look at her email. A message from Sherry gave her a jolt. The subject line: Urgent. She opened it to see that Charles Honeycutt had been cc-ed. The message read: Meeting tomorrow morning in conference room 3 at 9:15. Your attendance is required.

"Uh-oh," Dana whispered.

Ari stirred. "What's wrong?"

"Sorry. Didn't mean to wake you."

He turned toward her. "It's okay. I was up."

She leaned over and kissed his forehead. This guy. It was moments like this that made Dana wonder why she had spent so many years falling for selfish men.

"I think I'm in some deep shit at work," she said.

"Over what?"

"I don't know," Dana said, and she meant it, though she suspected it had something to do with the after-hours visit to Ivan's office. She just couldn't understand how they had found out. Still, this wasn't something she could discuss with Ari, so she told him to go back to sleep. Then she sent a text to Megan to explain what had happened, and they arranged to meet up at the office so that her friend and manager could help get her out of whatever trouble she was in.

Dana put down her phone and went to sleep. Or tried to. After tossing and turning for an hour, going back and forth on whether she should do something to mellow her—like pour a glass of wine or take a hit off a joint—she finally opted for the latter. She went into the living room area so she wouldn't wake Ari again. But about a minute after she lit the joint, he was standing in the doorway, shirtless in the doggy print pajama pants she had bought him.

"You alright?" he asked, because he knew she wouldn't be sitting up at the tiny bistro table where she ate her meals, holding a lungful of smoke deep in her chest, if she wasn't in dire need of chilling out.

She exhaled. "Couldn't sleep."

"Nasty habit," he said, walking toward her.

It was an inside joke. As a cop, he gave lip service to the notion that it was still an illegal substance, while reminding Dana that he was murder police, not a narc.

She caught his drift and passed him the joint. He took two quick tokes and handed it back. As she was snuffing it out in the ashtray, he ran his hand down her shoulder and she understood that signal, too. He had an idea that would help both of them relax.

★ ★ ★

The next morning, Dana met Megan in her dressing room, where they had a hushed discussion before going upstairs. They needed to decide what they would say if confronted with evidence about sneaking into Ivan's office.

"I think we should go with Jamie's suggestion," Megan said, as she sipped a Starbucks coffee. She had brought one for Dana, too. "We'll just insist he was deep in grief and wanted a certain memento from his father's office."

"Might be more believable if we bring his mom into it," Dana said. "Maybe we can say he needed something to help with *her* grief."

Megan nodded as she thought about it. "That's closer to the truth."

Dana studied her friend's face. She looked uneasy, and Dana wondered if she was troubled that Jamie wasn't wracked with grief. After all, their relationship was moving forward at the warp speed of a summer camp romance, and Megan could be second-guessing herself.

"I get the sense his father's death hasn't really hit him," Dana said. It was meant to be comforting, and also provide an opening in case Megan wanted to talk about it.

"I don't know if he'll ever shed a tear for that man," she said. "He's so angry with him."

"It's still his father," Dana said. "Sooner or later, he's going to feel it."

Megan shrugged. "I don't think he can forgive him for cheating on Blair. He's very protective of her."

Dana thought back to when her mother's sister died in a car accident. It was a terrible shock. And yes, her mother cried, but all her sorrow was directed toward Aunt Joan's sons. *Those poor children*, she kept saying. *My heart.* And even though Dana was only thirteen at the time, she understood that her mother needed to focus on the children's grief because her own was too much to bear.

"Maybe," Dana said. "But I think sometimes it's just easier to focus on someone else's pain than your own, you know?"

"He doesn't often vent," Megan said. "I think he's holding it all in and will let loose once he knows who murdered his father." She put her coffee down, finished with the discussion. "I think it's time to go upstairs. You all set on our story?"

Dana hesitated. "What if they ask why Jamie's request was such an emergency that it couldn't wait until normal business hours?"

Megan swept away the concern, indicating she had already thought of that. "We'll attribute it to your soft heart. You can say Jamie was beside himself with grief and you couldn't disappoint him."

"You think they'll buy that?"

"Got any better ideas?" Megan said.

Dana thought about it for a minute, and realized it was their best option. She hoped it would work, because telling the truth would be a disaster—professionally and personally. She closed her eyes and took several cleansing breaths as she tried to concentrate.

"What are you doing?" Megan asked.

"Getting into character."

Megan didn't scoff. She had been an actor, too, and understood that everyone had their process. She gave Dana a few quiet minutes, and by the time they got to the elevator, Dana had practically convinced herself the story was true.

Conference room 3 was like a smaller version of the space where Dana had performed for the board of directors. And walking in, she got the same foreboding vibe—only instead of a group of powerful strangers prepared to decide the fate of the whole company, there was one underweight woman prepared to decide of fate of Dana Barry.

Sherry Zidel was in one of the black leather swivel chairs, legs tightly crossed, arms folded over her print blouse. She looked down at her watch as if they were late, and Dana glanced at the large wall clock. They were five minutes early.

"Have a seat," Sherry said.

"Will Charles Honeycutt be joining us?" Megan asked, as she and Dana pulled out chairs and sat, their backs to the door.

"Soon."

Megan got right to business. "What is this meeting about?"

Sherry cleared her throat self-consciously. "I didn't know Dana was bringing representation."

It wasn't like Sherry to be uncomfortable, and that set off alarm bells. Why was the prickly supervising producer so unnerved?

Whatever it is, Dana coached herself, *you can deal with it. Besides, you have a contract. And Megan.* She slowed her breathing. She knew she could sell the lie if she wasn't nervous or defensive. She had to own it.

"You said it was urgent," Megan said, "so here I am. Tell us what's going on."

Sherry cleared her throat again. Recrossed her legs. Dana felt like she was looking at a seat full of sharp angles. Bony shoulders, bony elbows, bony knees. It was as if any part of her could impale her opponent.

"I was forced to tell Charles that Ivan had relieved me of the responsibility of approving any extracurricular opportunities for Dana," she announced.

Dana's face flushed hot. This wasn't what she had expected— it was worse. It meant Sherry had spilled the beans on Kayla Bean, Dana's Sweat City alter ego. How could she! Dana felt sick. She closed her eyes and could practically smell the dusty stage of her precious theater, feel the electricity of opening night. She thought of her friends in the group, and how much she loved each one. And now Sherry would be telling her she had to abandon them. To abandon all of it.

"What do you mean you were 'forced to'?" she seethed.

"Goddamn it, Sherry," Megan said. "We discussed this. What, exactly, did you tell him?"

"What did you expect me to do?" Sherry said, standing. "Put my fucking job on the line? Charles and I had a meeting about all the loose odds and ends Ivan left behind, and I had to tell him. Otherwise, I would have been the one in deep shit."

"Would it have killed you to keep your mouth shut?" Dana asked. This wasn't just anger, it was righteous indignation.

Sherry pointed at Dana's face. "It was a hell of a position you put me in!"

"Okay, everybody calm down," Megan said. "Explain what happened. Did you tell him everything?"

"I had to."

"So he knows we came to you asking permission for Dana to perform in a play?"

Sherry sat back down. "He does."

"Fuck," Dana said, covering her face. She couldn't see a way out of this.

Megan's voice got preternaturally calm. "Tell me what he said. Was he angry?"

Sherry shook her head, and Dana thought she detected a hint of remorse. But that didn't mean Sherry was actually sorry for what she had done, just vexed to admit it.

"It wasn't like that. I told him that since I no longer had the authority to make the determination, it fell to him."

"And how did he respond?"

"He told me he'd think about it and get back to me."

"And that's the purpose of this meeting?" Megan asked. "He's going to tell us his decision?"

"No." Sherry sat back and exhaled, as if relieved to have unburdened herself. "He reached out later in the afternoon and said he was returning the authority to me."

Megan and Dana went quiet as they took this in. Dana was new to the corporate world, and hadn't really seen this kind of passing-the-buck in person. She stared at Sherry, wondering how it felt to have the authority taken away and then given back. But mostly, she was comforted, because she knew Sherry wouldn't withhold her permission. There was simply too much history for her to take that chance.

Dana sat back, too. "So we're cool, then," she said, wondering why Sherry hadn't led the meeting with this news instead of putting her through such torture.

"Sure," Sherry said, "as long as you don't do that play."

Dana's mouth opened. "You can't be serious."

"Goddamn it, Sherry," Megan said, "we had an agreement!"

"That was then, this is now," Sherry said. "You want to rat me out for what I did last year, have at it. No one's going to give a shit at this point. And it won't get Dana any closer to what she wants."

"But why would you do this?" Megan demanded. "Why would you deny her this opportunity?"

"Because I have a business to run here! And Dana is fucking important to its success. I can't have her focus divided between the Shopping Channel and her little theater group. I need her one hundred percent in the game."

"Oh, c'mon, Sherry," Dana said. "You *know* I can do both. You saw me in action."

"The stakes are higher now."

"This is ridiculous," Dana mumbled. "I'm not giving up my play."

"You really want to risk being in breach of contract?" Sherry said. "I wouldn't suggest it. The board might have been impressed with you, but one dip in the numbers is all it takes for them to turn."

"I see what's going on here," Megan said. "You're covering your ass. If Dana has a bad day and you've given her permission to do her play, you'll have to answer for it."

"Damn straight I'll have to answer for it!" Sherry said. "Because that's *my job.* You know how many people would be unemployed if it weren't for me?"

"Oh, please," Dana said. "You don't care about anyone but yourself."

Sherry pounded the table. "I care about everyone in this company!"

"Yeah?" Dana said. "Well, half of them think you pushed Ivan off the roof! How do you like that?"

"What?" Sherry seethed, her eyes dark and furious.

"Everyone knows about your temper, and everyone knows Ivan came on to Anna right in front of you. So when they tell me they think you could be the murderer, I can't even argue with them!" Of course, she didn't actually believe Sherry was a murderer, but she was in such a rage she wanted to thrust the knife as deep as it would go.

"At least I didn't have a shouting match with him just minutes before he died," Sherry said.

"What are you talking about?" Dana demanded.

"You!" Sherry said. "I'm talking about *you.*"

Dana searched her memory. Surely she would remember something like that…wouldn't she?

"I didn't have a shouting match with Ivan," she insisted.

"You sure as hell did."

"You're making this up."

Sherry folded her arms again. "Anna heard it, too. You told him to get his fucking hands off you or he'd regret it."

Dana laughed, derisively. "Anna! Well, that's convenient, isn't it?"

"If there's no one else who can corroborate this—" Megan said.

"There is!" Sherry said, her nostrils flaring. "That woman bartender. She was standing right there. She heard the whole thing. So if anyone is under suspicion for killing Ivan in a fit of anger, it's *you*."

At that, the door opened and Charles Honeycutt appeared. They all fell silent as the familiar scent of his expensive cologne wafted into the room.

"So," he said, "did you ladies get everything squared away?"

21

Dana slammed the door of her dressing room. "Could it be true?" she said to Megan. "Do you really think I said that to Ivan?"

"It doesn't matter. You didn't kill him."

"How do I know that?"

"Dana, please."

She paced the dressing room, barely connected to her own body. It was as if some invisible force propelled her forward and back.

"What am I going to tell Ari?"

"You don't have to tell him anything," Megan said. "Just accept that Sherry probably made up the whole thing to piss you off."

"What about the bartender? If Sherry is telling the truth, she heard me tell Ivan if he didn't get his hands off me he'd regret it. Maybe she even saw me push him."

Megan grabbed her roughly by the shoulders, stood on her

toes and brought her face right up to Dana's. "Listen. To. Me. You did not kill Ivan Dennison."

"How do you know?"

"Because I know you, and I know you wouldn't kill someone. Even drugged, you wouldn't do it. It's not who you are."

"You really think so?"

"I know so."

Dana dropped into a cushioned chair, and tried once again to remember what happened at the party. She couldn't recall any conversations with Ivan after she sipped that drink. There was one hazy memory of a man grabbing her arm. Could that have been Ivan? Maybe. But her sense was that someone else was right there, aiding her. The specifics were like vapor, but the emotional memory felt solid. She had been rescued. Maybe that was the fight Sherry overheard. And if that were true, Dana couldn't have pushed Ivan, because someone pulled her away.

"I didn't kill Ivan," she said, looking into her friend's dark eyes for confirmation.

"Of course not."

"What am I going to do?"

"You're not going to do anything. You're just going to trust Ari to solve the case and find out who the real killer is."

"But what if he doesn't? Do you know how many cold cases there are in New York? Not every murder gets solved." Dana thought she might go crazy, spending her whole life wondering if she could have done it.

"This one will," Megan assured her. "There were dozens of people at that party. Even with the lights out, somebody saw something. I wouldn't even be surprised if Ari already knows who did it."

Dana nodded. She understood this could be true. If Ari knew who the killer was, he would likely be playing his cards close to the vest until he had enough evidence to indict, and maybe even get a confession.

Then again, he might still be following several leads...one of which could bring him straight to her.

"He'd better solve this soon," Dana said. "If he doesn't, I'll lose my mind."

"Concentrate on your Shopping Channel show," Megan said. "It'll help keep you centered."

The thought of it brought Dana back to what Sherry had said about needing her to focus, as if her involvement in Sweat City could compromise her Shopping Channel efforts.

"Can you believe that bitch tried to use my work ethic to justify her bullshit decision? As if I ever gave less than one hundred percent!" She felt her blood pressure rising with anger, and Megan sensed it.

"I know you're mad," she said. "But you'll need to put it on hold. You have purses to sell today."

"She knows damned well I can do this!" Dana said, thinking about all the effort she had put into making her Shopping Channel show a success. She got up and resumed pacing. "I've never been anything but professional here."

"Of course," Megan said. She went to the counter and opened the spigot on the Poland Spring jug to fill a glass of water. She held it toward Dana, who ignored it.

"And she dragged Honeycutt into it! So now I'll be under a microscope. Every time I leave at a reasonable hour to make rehearsals, I'll be scrutinized."

Megan put down the glass. "Wait a second," she said. "You're not still considering doing the play?"

Dana stopped pacing and stared at her. "Of course I am."

"But you *can't*."

Dana's heart went cold and brittle. She couldn't believe what she was hearing. "You're supposed to be on my side."

"My friend, it's game over. You asked permission, it was denied. If you do the play, it's a clear breach of contract."

"Oh, come on. If I'm their best-selling host—they wouldn't dare fire me."

"And what if you're *not*?" Megan said.

"You've seen the way I've been selling," Dana said. "I can't believe I have to defend myself to you."

"Everyone has an off day once in a while, even you. And sometimes it's not even your fault. What if they saddle you with some shit no one will buy? If Sherry decides to scapegoat you—and trust me, she'd do it in a heartbeat—I cannot protect you."

"Maybe I'm willing to take that chance."

"You just signed a new lease," Megan said, her voice rising. "If you lost this job, what would you do?"

"I thought you believed in me."

"Oh, don't go there. You know damned well what I think of your talents. But we have to be pragmatic. This is your life."

"You need to support me on this!" Dana could feel herself shattering. There was so little to hold her together now.

"Dana, be reasonable."

"You *know* what Sweat City means to me." Dana tried to hold back tears, to stem the flow that would fill her face with mucus, swell her nose and cheeks, make her eyes look like little red slits on the air.

"Of course I do," Megan said. She grabbed the tissue box and held it toward Dana.

"You really think they would fire me?" she said, taking a tissue.

"It's a ruthless business."

Dana lowered herself onto the couch and blew her nose. Megan sat next to her.

"I know I'm making this hard for you," Dana said, wishing she didn't have to drag Megan down with her.

Her friend waved it away. "It's not about me."

"Sherry is such a bitch."

"Of course she is," Megan agreed.

They sat in silence for a few moments, and there was a knock at the door. Ashlee poked her head in.

"They're ready for you in makeup."

"I'll be right there," Dana said, dismissing her. When the door closed she turned back to Megan. "I have to get ready for my show."

"Are you okay?"

Dana shook her head.

"I'll stick around if you like," Megan said.

"I'll be fine," she lied.

Megan leaned in and hugged her. "I know this is a bitter pill, but there will be other plays."

Dana wiped her nose and stared at her friend. "I don't think you understand," she said. "I'm doing the play."

22

"Sit still," Jo said, as she slapped Dana's fingers. "And relax your hands."

Dana tried telling herself she wasn't rattled by either of Sherry's revelations, but here she was in the makeup chair, still struggling to get herself into the right frame of mind for her show.

"What did you do to yourself?" Felicia said as she stared into Dana's face. "Everything is swollen."

"I'm an ugly crier."

Felicia thought for a moment, then disappeared into the bathroom. She returned holding a wet washcloth. "Lean back," she ordered.

Dana did as she asked, expecting a warm, soothing compress that would help her relax. Instead, she was assaulted with an ice-water-drenched cloth.

"What the hell!"

"We need to get down the swelling," Felicia insisted.

"What were you crying about, anyway?" Jo asked.

Dana wanted to rip the torturous rag off her face, but she knew she looked like a grown-up Cabbage Patch doll, so she balled her fists to help withstand the cold. "Doesn't matter," she muttered into the damp terry cloth.

"What did she say?" Felicia asked.

"I have no idea," Jo said. "But if Ari broke up with her, I'm available."

"It's not about Ari," Dana said.

"What?" Jo asked.

"I think she said she's going to a party," Felicia translated.

"A party?" Jo said. "What party? The Christmas party?"

"That's not until next month," Felicia said.

Jo clucked. "I heard they was going to cancel it because of…you know, Ivan."

"No, they're just moving it to Studio E. No more rooftop parties—at least for a while."

"Is that what you was talking about?" Jo asked Dana. "The Christmas party?"

Dana took the towel off her face. "I didn't say anything about a party. I said it's not about *Ari*."

Felicia looked thoughtful as she took that in. "Well, thank god," she finally said. "But do me a favor—don't do no more crying, at least until after the show. I'm going to have a hell of a job making you presentable."

"The swelling usually goes down pretty fast," Dana said.

"Not fast enough," Felicia said, frowning. "It'll probably go away while you're on the air. And you know what'll happen? The foundation will stick into the fine lines on your face and make you look like a hag."

"Fine lines?" Dana said. She was aware she had them— everybody did. But she didn't think hers would be an issue for several years.

"High-def can be a nightmare. But don't worry. I know what to do. I'll airbrush your makeup today. It's a lighter coating and will give us less problems when your normal face comes back."

For the next few minutes, Dana held still while Felicia applied a fine mist of foundation to her face. When she was done, the two experts stood back and assessed her.

"What do you think?" Felicia asked.

"Not too bad," Jo said.

Felicia clucked. "But not great."

"Can I see?" Dana asked.

"Shh, don't talk," Felicia said. "And don't open your eyes for a few minutes. I need it to set."

While Dana was waiting for her face to dry, the women launched into the latest company gossip, starting with the morning host's new Botox treatment, and circling back to Ivan's murder.

"For what it's worth," Jo said, "I don't think it was Honeycutt that pushed him."

"I don't think it was Honeycutt neither."

"Last week you said you thought it was Honeycutt."

Felicia tsked. "Well, I don't think that no more. I'm allowed to change my mind, aren't I? He's just too mellow. And he's got those cute girls. The little one is to die for. He wouldn't risk that."

"You seen Sherry Zidel this morning? She looked like she could kill somebody for breathing wrong."

"She always looks like that," Felicia said.

The women went quiet for a few moments as they worked on Dana's face and nails.

"I keep staring at that picture on my phone," Jo said, "looking for a clue."

At that, Dana could no longer contain herself. *Pictures.* She hadn't considered that anyone had taken a photo she could examine.

"Can I talk yet?" she asked.

"Yeah, you're good," Felicia said with a nod.

Dana turned to Jo, who was running a buffer across one of her nails. "You said you have a picture?"

"Took it with my phone." She laughed. "It wasn't like he was going nowhere."

"You mean you have a picture of the body?" Dana asked.

"You want to see?"

"Hell, yes."

Jo put down the instrument and began rummaging through her oversized purse, an activity that took far too long. At last she extracted a phone in a glittery rose gold case, and scrolled to an image. She handed it to Dana.

A few people had described the scene to her, but Dana still wasn't prepared for what she saw. It was so real—Ivan's lifeless body illuminated by a streetlamp. His torso seemed to be bent in half. Only one leg was visible; the other must have been under his body at a strange angle. His arms were over his head and his suit jacket was splayed open. His red striped tie pointed away from his body, as if it were trying to get away. She put her fingers on the picture and spread them open to get a closer look at his face, and was horrified to discover that his eyes were open. Worst of all, she was able to see a pool of dark blood running over the sidewalk from the back of his head, and a gray oozing mass near his skull. She put her finger on the screen to move the picture around, searching for clues. His shoe was off, but that probably meant nothing. There was something silver near his head—a piece of metal or possibly a broken mirror. On the right, near his hand, there was something whitish. Hard to tell if he was holding it, or if it was sidewalk debris. She showed it to the girls.

"I think that's just litter," Felicia said.

"A strip of fabric or something," Jo offered. "It looks like he's holding it."

She pointed out the triangle of silver near his head, and they couldn't agree on that, either. Dana asked Jo to forward her the picture so she could study it. If any of these things were clues, she damned well wanted to know what they were. In the meantime, she would try to track down Margaux, the dancer/bartender, who might be able to tell Dana that she had been nowhere near Ivan when the lights went out.

When Dana got to the set and stood behind a display of Barlow and Ricci pebble leather tassel totes, she had to call upon all her training to focus. She was not going to let Sherry's cruelty get under her skin.

Everything is going to be fine, she told herself. *You will do your play, you will not get in trouble. You'll perform under the name Kayla Bean and no one will find out.*

You did not kill Ivan Dennison.

The last bit rattled her so badly that that when the camera light came on, Dana froze. She'd been far away, trying to recapture that memory from the roof. For a split second, she didn't even know where she was. And then, there was Jessalyn's voice in her ear: *Dana! You're on the air!*

And just like that, she snapped out of it. "Welcome!" she gushed, her carefully honed skills kicking in. "You're just in time for this newest line of impeccable, scratch-resistant leather totes from my favorite handbag designer!"

She went right into the zone, marveling at the workmanship, the quality of the leather, the convenience of the interior, the stylishness of the hardware, the comfort of the straps and the beauty of the colors. Oh, the colors! Dana displayed them one by one, falling more in love with each selection: midnight blue, caramel, charcoal, rose blush, tobacco, dove gray, warm red, sky blue and classic black. Her delight was breathless, excited, nearly sexual, and the viewers reacted by going crazy with orders. And then the first style was sold out, and she moved on to the next and then the next. She was on the final product and almost done with her show when a narrow figure appeared on set and moved into her field of vision. It was Sherry. Damn her. She almost never came down during airtime, and it knocked Dana off her game.

Jessalyn whispered something into Dana's earpiece about the dove gray, and she panicked. Was her concentration so interrupted she had left out a color? She looked down at the current display. They were structured satchels with a detachable shoulder strap, and she had her hands on the warm red. She put it down and picked up the dove gray.

"Of course, the dove gray is great with basic black," she said, "but I personally *love* it with denim." She punched the word *love* like her tongue had never tasted anything so intensely satisfying.

No, no! Jessalyn whispered. *I said the dove gray is sold out.*

Shit! Dana exhaled and tried to regain her footing.

"Oh! I just got word this one's gone," she chirped, and tucked it under the table. "But the sky blue is a crisp choice for any denim shade."

She was rattled, but the show was winding down, and she managed to get through the final moments—cooing that any woman would love getting this handbag as a holiday gift—without another screw-up. She introduced the next host, Vanessa Valdes, and waited for the camera light to go dark. She took a glance at the monitor to make sure she was off the air, and pulled out her earpiece.

"What the hell happened with the dove gray?" Sherry demanded, storming toward her.

"Since when do you walk around on set during airtime?" Dana asked.

"That's not an answer."

"You threw me for a loop," Dana said. "I can't concentrate with you pacing the floor."

"Do I need to remind you that concentration is your job?"

"Talk to Jessalyn about my numbers today, and you'll get a good idea of my concentration." She unclipped her mike and started to walk away.

"Where are you going?" Sherry demanded.

Dana knew what she was getting at. Sherry wanted to make sure Dana wasn't rushing off to rehearsals. In fact, that was probably the reason for her unexpected visit.

"To my dressing room," Dana said.

"Well, don't be in such a hurry. Let's have a sit-down with Jessalyn and go over your sales figures."

Dana whirled around and stared into Sherry's face. Sherry stared back. It felt like a standoff. The producer either knew or suspected Dana was about to run off to the Sweat City theater, and she wanted to get in her way. Now Dana had a decision to make: acquiesce, and be late for rehearsals, or make up some lie about a previous engagement.

"Unless you have someplace to be?" Sherry asked, folding her arms.

"No," Dana seethed. "I have no place to be." She hated being late for rehearsals, but this felt like her only move, and she resented the hell out of Sherry for forcing it.

They went into the control booth and met with Jessalyn, and Sherry insisted on discussing every number in painstaking detail, assuring that a ten-minute meeting stretched out to thirty. When they were done, Dana ambled out slowly, as if she had all the time in the world. But as soon as she was out of sight, she ran to her dressing room, changed, dashed out the door and hopped on a subway downtown to rehearse *Harte of Brooklyn*.

★ ★ ★

"Nice of you to show up," Nathan said, when she reached the theater. Everyone was still in the greenroom, going over some notes before beginning rehearsals. Dana felt herself flush as they all turned to her. Lateness wasn't just inexcusable. It was rude. Thoughtless. Selfish. Especially for someone who had skipped yesterday's entire rehearsal.

"I'm sorry!" Dana cried. "It won't happen again."

Nathan gave her a look so loaded she wished life offered second takes so that she could go back and tell Sherry to fuck herself. Because nothing was worth the disappointment in his eyes. They seemed to say, *You're taking advantage—you of all people. I never should have opened up to you.* And she couldn't explain to him that she'd tried, but her boss was being a pain in the ass. Because if she told him rehearsals would continue being a challenge for her, he'd probably make her switch roles with Carolyn. And she couldn't let that happen, not after she did so much digging into the role and finally discovered what made Penny tick. It took a long time, but she had an epiphany—she couldn't play it for laughs. That was the trick. She had to approach the role in the exact same way she approached dramatic parts. Once she did that, Dana was able to tap into an earnestness at the center of her own being, and find a way to push it front and center for this character. She couldn't wait for rehearsals to get started so that she could show them what she'd unearthed.

Nathan went back to his notes, explaining some changes and tweaks he expected from his actors.

"Does anybody have any questions?" he asked.

Tyrel expressed some confusion about the prop in scene four, and Nathan said they'd work it out onstage.

"Anything else?" he asked.

Dana knew it wasn't the best time to call attention to herself, but there was a burning question that only her actor friends could help her with, and so she raised her hand. "I do have one thing, but it's not relevant to the play. Is that okay?"

Nathan sighed. "Out with it."

"I was just wondering if anybody knows a dancer named Margaux who works for a caterer."

They all looked at her blankly.

"Small nose, pointy widow's peak? Spells her name with an *X*?" she said.

There were some shrugs and head shakes.

Nathan folded his arms. "Okay with you if we move on?"

"Please," she said, and took some deep breaths to get into character. She would impress them if it killed her.

23

The next morning was Ivan Dennison's memorial service. The family had held a small private funeral the week before, which Megan described as "brutally grim." The public event, by contrast, was planned as a celebration of his life, and the family invited a wide circle of friends and business associates.

The Shopping Channel provided a luxury bus from its West Side address to the church out on Long Island. Megan had special permission to ride with the staff, and she climbed onboard with Dana. She gave a low whistle when she saw the plush leather reclining chairs with armrests.

"Like flying first class," Dana replied. "But with potholes."

When they sat across from Eleanor Gratz and her husband, Philip Wagoner, Megan elbowed Dana conspiratorially. The message was clear: *We may be sitting right beside Ivan's killers.* Dana was still skeptical. Yes, the evidence was pretty damning, but it was hard to imagine Eleanor as a murderer. Still, she was committed to paying close attention to anything that might provide a clue, as she had a personal stake in this now. Dana needed to know the culprit was anyone but her. For now, though, all the two friends could do was act as if they knew nothing about the twenty-year-old kickback and Ivan's apparent threat to expose it.

Dana settled into her seat and watched as her coworkers filed onto the bus with carefully suppressed enthusiasm. This was a memorial service, after all, and they were trying to show respect. But soon enough, the stoicism melted away, and the atmosphere on the bus went from forced solemnity to relaxed camaraderie and, finally, to excitement. They were going on a field trip!

Eleanor leaned across the aisle to talk business with Dana, filling her in on the status of the Reluven gift basket she would soon be selling on the air. Eleanor's passion was contagious, and Dana's enthusiasm rose to match it.

Then Eleanor turned her attention to Megan. "Were you at the funeral?" she asked.

At that, Dana knew Eleanor had connected the dots linking Megan to Jamie. Why else would she have even considered that Megan might be there? Dana wondered if the whole company knew Jamie and Megan were an item.

"It was nearly unbearable," Megan said.

"I heard Blair was practically catatonic," Eleanor offered, and Dana tried to imagine who might have told her that, as the funeral was almost exclusively confined to family.

"It's very hard on her," Megan said.

"The poor thing. She has to be so careful—stress can really trigger a flare-up."

Now that was curious. Eleanor seemed to know a lot about Blair Dennison's condition. In fact, she used almost the exact same phrase Jamie had used. It might mean absolutely nothing, of course, but Dana was collecting every impression.

There was a hissing sound as the bus door closed, and then a small lurch as the driver put it into gear and they headed on their way, going straight across town and heading over the Fifty-Ninth Street Bridge.

People talked and laughed throughout the journey, and Dana tried to listen through the chatter for any mention of Ivan. But the Shopping Channel employees barely knew him, and the snippets of conversation Dana could overhear included references to binge-watching a new Amazon sci-fi series, something about football, a bit of cooing over a cute baby picture, a question about the company's upcoming Christmas party and a discussion of appropriate attire for a memorial service, which devolved into a smackdown of someone's red patent leather pumps.

At last the bus pulled into the parking lot of an old stone church designed to look practically medieval. It was a sunny autumn day, the air crisp and chill as they piled out of the bus and walked up the stone path to the cathedral-like doorway. Inside, they proceeded to the high-ceilinged sanctuary, which had a tall stained glass window behind the altar. In front of it, lining the steps, were dozens of baskets of white flowers, filling the place with enough floral scent to nearly mask the smell of musty wood and lemon furniture polish. There was a poster-sized blowup of Ivan's business portrait propped on an easel to the left of the altar. On the right, there was a blurrier poster of him, obviously enlarged from an older snapshot. It showed a younger, handsomer Ivan in a casual polo shirt, smiling into the sun.

Dana took a moment to study the photographs, trying to tap into some sympathy. It didn't take her long, since her training as an actor created pathways to her own pathos, and Dana found herself imagining the news of her own father's death. Her love for him was buried so deeply beneath her disdain and hurt feelings that it didn't often surface. But now, imagining how it would feel to lose him, it welled right up to the surface. Sure, he could be insensitive, judgmental, rude, a total asshat. But he was *her* asshat.

"Too bad there's no open bar," Megan said.

"Why?" Dana asked.

"Because you look like you could use a drink."

Dana sighed. "Just having a moment."

She peered around the sanctuary. Jamie and his mother were already seated in the front row, along with several other people, including a man Dana presumed to be the older son. The Shopping Channel people slid into the wooden pews, making room for one another, and the church brimmed with the loud hum of people trying to be respectful.

They sat there for quite some time, waiting for the sanctuary to fill. Every few minutes Jamie and his brother turned toward the back of the church to see who was coming in. It looked like they were reporting the details to their mother, and Dana wondered if there was someone specific they were waiting for. At one point, Jamie stood and waved to an older couple with a yacht-club air about them—they looked tanned, relaxed, and impossibly wealthy. Dana couldn't see the husband's socks, but she would have bet money they were...*interesting*. That is, if he were wearing socks at all. Based on the wife's cheekbones, Dana pegged them as relatives of Blair's. And sure enough, they approached the front row, bent to kiss her, and took seats with the family.

Eleanor was keeping a careful eye on the entrance, turning toward it every few minutes. Dana watched the doorway, too, as she knew Ari and his partner, Kevin Lee, would be attending the service. Ostensibly, it was to pay their respects, but Dana understood they would be watching and studying every attendee.

At last she saw them enter, and Ari caught her eye almost immediately. He gave a quiet nod, but didn't approach. They had already discussed the protocol. Ari needed to look professional and keep his distance. He and Detective Lee remained standing, surveying the crowd like sentries.

When the arriving guests slowed to a trickle, Dana assumed the service was about to begin. She glanced back at Jamie, who was still checking out the crowd. He must have seen something that alarmed him, because he shook his brother's shoulder and they both turned and stared. Jamie stood, as if deciding whether to do something.

Dana pivoted around to see who they were watching, and observed two women who seemed to be mother and daughter. The older woman was slim, with dark loose curls and a carefully tailored suit. The younger woman looked college-aged, and had her hands tucked into the pockets of her navy peacoat. She wore glasses, and her long hair—probably naturally curly—had been blown straight and was admirably lustrous. Beyond those superficialities, they looked very much alike.

Dana watched, wondering if they would join the family at the front of the church, but they took a seat in the rear. Jamie and his brother had a whispered conversation, and then the brother rose and walked to the back of the church to talk to the latecomers. It was impossible for Dana to catch any drift of the exchange, but she noticed that Eleanor seemed especially interested in it, as she didn't take her eyes off them, even as she put her hand over her mouth and whispered something to her husband.

Dana glanced back at Ari to see if he noticed the exchange, and of course he was paying close attention.

When the brother finally finished his conversation, he walked briskly toward the front of the church, his face reddening the same way Ivan's sometimes did. Dana burned with curiosity.

"Do you have any idea who that is?" she asked Megan.

"Some estranged relative, I would guess," Megan said.

"You think he was asking her to leave?"

"That would be some hell of a feud, wouldn't it? Kind of thing that would happen with *my* family."

Dana nodded. Megan's family was notorious for long grudges. She had aunts, uncles and cousins who hadn't spoken to one another in twenty years. The Silvestri family weddings weren't so much planned as brokered, like ceasefires.

The rest of the service seemed carefully arranged, with a succession of speakers who made Ivan Dennison seem like a cross between Warren Buffett, Steve Jobs, Roger Federer and the Dalai Lama. The minister opened, discussing Ivan's firm commitment to his faith. Dana tried to hold very still, but when he mentioned Ivan's servitude to God, she couldn't resist giving Megan the side-eye. An old high school friend talked about his tireless dedication to tennis, and how he had nearly gone pro. A college buddy made some cute asides about their fraternity parties, but kept most of his focus on Ivan's popularity and his position on the crew team. A man who worked with him at the electronics giant discussed Ivan's unprecedented success, and joked about how jealous they all were when he was recruited by the Shopping Channel. Charles Honeycutt made some brief but respectful remarks about their first encounters and how much Ivan had impressed the notoriously impossible-to-please board of directors. Not one woman had been invited to speak, which Dana presumed had been a conscious choice to keep any whispers from circulating.

The service concluded with speeches by Ivan's sons, Jamie and Brock, and their uncle, Everett Dennison, whom Dana thought looked like a younger and even WASPier version of Ivan. Like Tucker Carlson from his bow-tie period. She couldn't imagine he lived anywhere but Greenwich, Connecticut.

And then, just like that, it was over. Dana thought there might be some kind of a receiving line so people could pay their respects to the widow and her sons. But the family made a quick exit, wheeling Blair Dennison out of the church and into a waiting limousine before she could be overwhelmed. Dana understood. Blair couldn't be expected to accept the condolences when it was entirely possible someone in that church was her husband's murderer.

As the rest of the Shopping Channel folks piled back onto the bus for their return trip to Manhattan, Dana lingered in the church, scanning the crowd for the mysterious woman and her daughter. Apparently, they, too, had made a quick exit.

On her way out, Dana stopped at the door, where Ari and his partner stood surveying the crowd. She was dying to ask Ari if he knew the identity of the dark-haired woman, but of course she couldn't. So she simply whispered that she would see him later, and climbed onto the bus.

24

Dana did not want an IKEA couch for her new apartment. She wanted a statement sofa. Something large and comfortable, romantic and pretty, with curved lines and rounded arms. She envisioned it under the living room windows, decorated with beautiful throw pillows.

But since Dana had supplied the deposit for the apartment, Ari wanted to be the one to buy the couch, and insisted on a Saturday morning excursion to the massive retail location in Brooklyn. She knew the place would be big, but she wasn't prepared for the magnitude. This wasn't a furniture store—it was an airplane hangar on steroids, a sprawling waterfront military compound.

Dana was glad she wore comfortable shoes, because even though there was a free shuttle bus from the subway to the store, she logged several miles by the time they reached the sofas, which included a Danish modern couch in beige, a Danish modern couch in olive green, a Danish modern loveseat in black leather and a Danish modern sectional in burlap brown. Since IKEA was actually a Swedish company, she guessed this was considered an international showcase.

"What do you think?" Ari said, as they stood surveying the choices.

"I didn't know there were so many varieties of Danish modern."

"See anything you like?"

"That one's not too bad," she said, pointing to the least Danish modern piece on the floor. It had rounded arms and a skirted bottom, and was upholstered in a mustard color gingham plaid.

Ari cocked his head and she knew what he was thinking—it looked cheap. She couldn't argue the point because it did. She just wasn't sure there were any better alternatives.

"How about that one?" he said, pointing to a flattish couch with a low tufted back and sharp angles. It almost looked like a retro mid-century design, but stopped just short of making the commitment to kitsch. Even the upholstery selected for the display model—a pale grayish aqua—stood timidly to the side, softly suggesting a late fifties look without quite abandoning the Danish modern aesthetic.

She opened her mouth and nothing came out.

"You hate it," he pronounced.

"So very, very much," she said.

He took her hand and they walked around the selections as she said a silent prayer: *Not the one with headrests, not the one with headrests.*

"How about this one?" he asked, stopping at the pleather couch with headrests.

She looked at him, her eyes filled with pain, and he laughed.

"You were busting my chops?" she asked.

He pointed to another couch—a dark gray one she hadn't

noticed. It wasn't beautiful, but it wasn't terrible either. It had a plush cushioned back and narrow, gently sloped arms. The upholstery was a soft imitation velvet.

"I actually like this one," he said, lowering himself into it.

Dana sat next to him and put her head on his shoulder. The piece was downy and enveloping, and her tension didn't exactly dissolve, but she was able to envision the two of them sitting on this couch in their apartment. It was comfortable, at least, and she tried to imagine how it might look with romantic patterned drapes on the windows to compensate for the sofa's bland style. Maybe.

"I can picture this one in the apartment," she said.

He backed up to look at her face. "You're not just saying that?"

She held her thumb and forefinger a quarter inch apart, to indicate that a tiny part of her was indeed "just saying that."

"You want to look at it in another color?" he asked.

She rubbed the upholstery. It was soft and homey, but she was afraid it wouldn't hold up. "That might be a good idea."

She was about to tell him that she was doing her best, really trying to make it work, when a man with white hair and a red tie rounded the corner. From a distance, the resemblance to the dead chairman of the board was strong enough to make her gasp.

"You okay?" Ari asked.

Dana put her hand to her heart and felt it thudding. "I know we're not supposed to talk about the case, but for a second that man looked like Ivan Dennison."

Ari followed her line of vision to study the man, who was now close enough to look almost nothing like Ivan. He was much older, for one thing, and had the kind of skin condition that made his nose large and lumpy.

"Never mind," she said. "It was just a first impression."

But at that moment, a memory came back. It was just a quick flash of something that happened at the party—Ivan, leaning toward her and kissing her on the neck. Had that really happened, or did she imagine it?

Dana couldn't know for sure if it was an actual memory, but it was disturbing enough to make her want to finish this couch business so she could go home and take a hit off a joint.

"Do you want to talk about it?" Ari asked.

Dana shrugged. She *did* want to talk about it. She wanted to tell him what Sherry had said. She wanted to confess that she was terrified she might have lost her temper and shoved Ivan off the roof without even remembering it. She wanted him to take her in his arms and promise that it wasn't her, that he knew exactly who did it and had irrefutable forensic evidence.

"Of course I do," she told him. "But you said the investigation is off-limits."

Ari nodded. "We can talk about anything else."

"Can't you just tell me who's under—"

"I can't." He pulled her toward him and softened his voice. "I'm sorry this is hard for you."

Dana let out a long breath. "It's okay," she said, but what she meant was that it was okay he put so much value on his job. She understood that, and was determined to be a grown-up about it, not a needy child. "I don't ever want you to feel guilty about putting your career first."

"I don't put my career—"

"Let me clarify," she interrupted. "There are *times* when it's first. Times when the job is a priority and times when I'm a priority. I get that."

He kissed the top of her head. "Thank you."

"I'm proud of you." She didn't say it enough, but it was important for him to know. "I'm proud that you're so good at your job."

"Let's hope Covello agrees with that assessment."

Dana moved in closer. She knew the promotion meant a lot to him—not just so that he could afford his share of the rent on their new apartment, but because it meant being recognized. As an actor, Dana could respect that. Nailing a performance felt great. But applause, cheers, appreciation…that was the part that filled you up.

They looked at upholstery swatches, and Dana spiraled into a frenzy of indecision. She really didn't like any of them, but she wanted so badly to give Ari what he wanted.

"You decide," she said, handing him the swatches.

He tossed them down. "Why don't we sleep on it?"

25

The next day, Dana went to her Sunday morning rehearsal eager to dive deep into the scenes. She was discovering layers for her character, and wanted to impress Nathan with the work she had put in. It was important to make him glad he had cast her as Penny Harte.

Today, they were working on the final scene in Act I, where Penny and Curtis—who had been fighting their feelings for one another—have an argument in which their pent-up sexual attraction explodes into a fight. The dialogue was sharp, but it wasn't one of the jokier scenes. Penny was finally off the treadmill, facing her emotions. It was meant to let the audience experience the passionate crescendo between these two, which peaked at the end of the scene, when Penny grabbed Curtis, and kissed him on the mouth just before the stage went black.

Dana and Tyrel were both off book, which allowed them to delve into the characters. Dana identified Penny's rage—she was angry with herself for being so attracted to Curtis, whom she wanted to hate. Tyrel went to a more external place with his character's anger, directing it at Penny. Dana understood his choices, but wasn't sure how it would work in terms of the kiss. She tried her best, but when she moved in for the sexual connection, the moment felt inauthentic as his anger was more off-putting than sizzling.

The actors both sensed a failure in that final moment, and looked to Nathan for input.

He paced for a minute, thinking, then said, "Try the scene again, only let's switch it up. This time, I want Curtis to grab and kiss Penny, instead of the other way around. Let's see if that works better."

He gave them instructions to adjust the blocking so that Dana would be the one exiting at the end of the scene.

"I guess we're done here," she said, in character. She paused, waiting for a reaction from the man she loved, as if deciding whether to stay or go. One tiny moment of softness from Curtis and she would melt into his embrace. But he huffed in anger and folded his arms.

She registered the disappointment, then turned toward the part of the stage where the set would eventually have an exit door, and reached for it. Her back was to Tyrel, so she didn't see him coming, merely felt his hand on her arm as he grabbed it and whirled her around.

It was startling, and Dana went blank in fear as adrenaline rocketed through her. She froze. This didn't feel like love—it felt like an assault. Her reaction was primal. Panicked. Dana's surroundings disappeared and she was nothing but an animal who needed to save herself. Her heart rate pounded in her ears: *run, run, run!* She was about to turn and bolt from the stage when his hands seized her shoulders and his face moved toward her for a kiss. In that moment, she was back on the rooftop. And it wasn't Tyrel grabbing her, nor his character. It was Ivan. Ivan's hand gripping her arm so hard it hurt. Ivan's eyes, dark and menacing. Ivan's face moving toward her. And she did the only thing she could. She protected herself…using more strength than she knew she had.

Her assaulter went toppling backward and landed on his ass.

Reality came crashing back, and Dana gasped, her hand to her mouth.

"I'm sorry!" she cried, realizing she had shoved Tyrel to the floor. "I don't know what came over me." But she did know, and tears spilled down her face.

"What the fuck?" Tyrel asked as he stood, dusting off his pant legs.

"Are you alright?" Nathan asked him.

"I guess," he said, and turned to Dana. "But remind me not to get on your wrong side, honey."

Nathan approached the stage. "Dana, talk to me," he said, concerned.

Her stomach seemed to flip over, and she got that feeling in her jaw that always preceded nausea, as if it wanted to involuntarily unhinge so she could heave the contents of her stomach.

"Can't," she said, and ran to the bathroom, getting there just in time to vomit into the toilet.

When she finished, Dana washed her hands and face, and slurped sink water into her burning throat. Her hands shook, and she stayed in the bathroom as she heard Nathan end the rehearsal and dismiss the cast. A few of them knocked on the bathroom door on their way out, asking if she was okay.

"I'm fine," she kept saying. "I'm fine." But she wasn't.

When she finally emerged, Nathan was the only one left in the theater.

"Do you want to talk about it?" he asked.

She sniffed, wiping her nose. "No."

"You sure?"

"I just…can't."

"Fair enough," he said. "But you need to be perfectly honest with me. Will you be able to play this role?"

She wanted to say, *Yes, of course! You know how important this
is to me. And I would never let anything stand in the way.* But all
she could do was mutter, "I don't know."

Nathan went silent for a few moments as if he expected
her to elaborate, but Dana could barely hold it together. If
she opened herself up to speak, she would collapse into sobs.

"Okay," he finally said. "You take a little time to think about
it. But not too much time. Our next rehearsal is Wednesday,
and I'm going to need an answer by then."

When Dana didn't respond he prodded, "You understand?"

"Yes," she choked out, and then hurried to grab her coat
and purse. All she wanted to do was get out of there. She
needed to be alone and try to understand what had just happened. She didn't even want to get onto the subway, with
those bright lights and all those people. The only thing she
could imagine was hitting the streets to walk and walk and
walk, as if she might find an answer in some loose change on
the sidewalk. But before she could swing open the door to
leave, Nathan stopped her.

"Oh, one more thing," he said. "Before I forget. I asked
around about that dancer. It seems there's a Margaux with an
X who works for a caterer called Garden of Stephen. That's
all I could find out."

It took Dana a minute to absorb the information. But as she
did, she realized it was a perfectly timed gift from the universe. Margaux! She was exactly the person Dana needed to
talk to. The one living, breathing human who might be able
to tell Dana she hadn't killed Ivan Dennison.

26

Dana had just enough presence of mind to call Ari and tell him she had a headache, and would be getting into bed to sleep it off.

"You sound awful," he said, and she could barely hear him as she was trudging uptown against a chill wind.

Dana put her hand over her other ear to block out the noise. "I know," she said. "I think I'm just overtired."

The wind noise was a good excuse to cut the conversation short. So after she assured him that she didn't need anything, and he admitted he had several loads of laundry to catch up on anyway, they agreed to sleep in their separate apartments that night and said goodbye.

At home, Dana stripped out of her clothes and let them fall onto the floor. Then she got into pajamas and a pair of impossibly thick chenille-lined bootie-socks that had been a present from Chelsea. She had called them "reading socks." The idea was that you wore them when you wanted to be alone and comfy, curled up in a chair with a good book. Now, Dana wanted anything that would make her feel protected and safe. But of course, a pair of socks wasn't going to do that.

She poured a glass of cabernet and brought it—along with the whole bottle—into her bedroom. Dana got under the covers and arranged the pillows behind her back, then texted Megan.

Busy?

Her friend responded quickly.

With Jamie. Sup?

Dana stared at her phone, and knew there was just way too much ground to cover in a rushed conversation with a friend who was probably in the middle of something romantic. She took a sip of wine and then typed:

Just chilling. Have fun. TTYL.

She put the phone down on her night table, and seconds later it buzzed with another text.

Just decided we're going to Mexico over Christmas! Me and Jamie.

It was followed by a series of joyful emojis that made Dana want to weep. Instead, she downed the rest of her wine in a long gulp. Then she typed back a smiley face, and told herself they both deserved the respite. Defeated, she threw her phone into a drawer, slammed it shut, and got more stoned and drunk than she had been in a long, long time.

★ ★ ★

The next day, getting out of bed felt like crawling from a coffin. But Dana had to get to work. Thanksgiving was a week or so away, and there were novelty Christmas sweaters to sell, with little sewn-on bells to jingle in delight. Also, she had an early morning appointment with Eleanor Gratz about the Reluven launch. It was all too much.

Dana considered lighting up another joint to face her day. Maybe a toke or two would take the edge off. But then she remembered another piece of important business. She had to track down Margaux and find out exactly what she had seen and heard. And yes, Dana was scared of what she might learn, but a part of her clung to the hope that it was all a big mistake, and that her memory had been false.

So instead of getting high, she took a long, sobering shower, made herself a cup of strong coffee and looked up the phone number for the caterer Nathan had mentioned.

She reached a voice-mail recording. Apparently, the folks at Garden of Stephen were sorry to miss her call, which was important to them. Dana hung up anyway. Her mission was too complicated to leave in a message.

She headed out to work, and kept her sunglasses on when she got to the studio. There were eye drops in her dressing room that would help with the bloodshot remnants of last night's indulgence. In the meantime, she didn't need any questions or gossip. Dana grabbed a cup of coffee from the cafeteria and went straight to her dressing room.

The eye drops did their magic, and Dana sipped her coffee. She was just about to try Garden of Stephen again when Ashlee arrived.

"Y'all okay?" she asked. "You look like you been chewed up and spit out."

So much for the eye drops. "It's about how I feel," Dana said.

"Anything I can do?"

"Just a little moral support. I'm trying to track down the woman bartender from the roof party. Do you remember her?"

"Just that she didn't blink when I asked for an old-fashioned made with Jack Daniel's. What do you need her for?"

"I think she can help fill in some of the gaps in my memory," Dana said. She didn't want to offer too much, but Ashlee was a wily girl and her input could be valuable. "Problem is, I don't even have her last name. I'm going to call the caterer to see if I can wrangle it out of them."

"I've never seen a Yankee wrangle," Ashlee said, "so I'm glad for a front row seat." She lowered herself onto the couch.

"Watch and learn," Dana said. She called the number again and a live person picked up.

"Hi, my name is Penny Harte and I'm from Dance NYC," Dana pronounced, borrowing her Sweat City character's name, but using a voice modeled on a part she had played as a fussy executive. She had the lie already planned out. "I was at a party a few months back—I can't remember whose birthday it was, but one of the bartenders was a lovely dancer named Margaux. Talented girl with an interesting resume, as I recall. I wanted to get in touch with her about an upcoming audition. By any chance, do you have her contact info? I seem to have lost it."

"I'm sorry," said the woman on the phone, "I can't give out that kind of information."

"But you see, we had quite a conversation, and I know she would be eager to hear from me."

"I wish I could help."

"Maybe just a last name? She's probably already in our database."

"Unfortunately, that's not something I can provide. But if you'd like to leave a message, I can try to get it to her."

"I was really hoping to contact her myself," Dana pressed.

"Company policy," the woman said.

Dana sighed. It was no use. She made an excuse to get off the phone and then let out a whine. "I don't know what I'm going to do."

Ashlee looked at her sympathetically. "You think this Margaux knows who the murderer is?"

Dana let out a long breath as she considered how to answer. "No," she finally said. "But she might know who the murderer *isn't*."

Ashlee folded her arms. "Dana," she said pointedly, "are you worried that it might be you?"

Dana stared. She thought she had been so coy.

"You can close your mouth now," Ashlee said. "I'm not as blonde as I look."

"How did you know that's what I thought?"

"It's all over your face, darlin'. You're going to have to call on those acting skills of yours. Also, lay off the weed."

"Noted," Dana said. "But I'm still going to have to track down Margaux."

"Or maybe just have a little faith. There's no way it was you."

"Part of me believes that and part of me..." She searched for the right words.

"Still doubts?" Ashlee offered.

Dana nodded. "If I could just know *for sure*."

"Maybe there's another route to the truth."

"You have some ideas?" Dana asked.

Ashlee leaned forward. "Have you ever considered that Eleanor Gratz may have done it?"

So they were back to Eleanor. Dana wanted to dismiss the idea, because despite what she had learned, her gut instinct was that Eleanor was no murderer. And yet, if she was doubting her own innocence, shouldn't she at least doubt Eleanor's, too?

"Why?" Dana said, folding her arms. "What have you heard?"

"You know Gemma from upstairs?"

Dana could picture her—a dark-haired girl who worked in the bullpen outside Eleanor's office. "The assistant buyer," she said. "From Texas."

"Arkansas," Ashlee corrected, "but yes. That's her. Anyway, she told me Eleanor has been doing some strange things lately."

"Like what?"

"Some meetings she's been sneaking off to without tellin' anyone where she's goin'."

"Is that unusual?"

"According to Gemma, *very*. She's the one responsible for the department's schedule, and Eleanor's appointments are always on it. But since Ivan's murder, she's left the office in the middle of the day three separate times without telling anyone where she was. Gemma thinks it's suspicious, and so do I."

"Maybe she's just busy. I know that Reluven launch is driving her crazy," Dana said.

"But all *those* appointments are on the schedule. These aren't. And Gemma said that whenever Eleanor gets back, she shuts herself in her office and gets right on the phone. But not the office phone—her cell phone."

Dana leaned back to consider the information. It certainly was suspicious.

"You know, I'm meeting with her and the Reluven reps today about the launch. Maybe I can dig a little."

Ashlee clucked. "She's not going to tell you anything."

"No, but I can probe a bit and see how uncomfortable she gets."

"And then what?" Ashlee said.

Dana shrugged. "Margaux is still my best hope. I have to figure out a way to find her."

"We will. But in the meantime, let's figure out what's goin' on with Eleanor. I could follow her the next time she sneaks out. I just have to tell Gemma to give me a heads-up."

Dana had to stifle a laugh. The idea of a six-foot-tall goddess who looked like Charlize Theron on steroids trying to be inconspicuous while tailing someone didn't make a whole lot of sense.

"How about this," Dana suggested. "The next time Eleanor sneaks out for one of her secret excursions, give me a heads-up and *I'll* follow her."

"And here she is!" Eleanor announced to the Reluven reps when Dana showed up at the meeting.

All heads turned toward Dana, and despite herself, she absorbed the warmth of Eleanor's admiration. Because in her entire life, she had never felt even a fraction of that pride from her own parents. She almost wished she could have captured the moment and replayed it for her father. *See?* she would have said to him. *See what the world thinks of me?*

The excitement in the room was electric, and it did wonders for her dark mood. The Reluven people were clearly overjoyed to sell their products through the Shopping Channel. It was a major coup for them. And Eleanor simply beamed. It was a dream come true. She was selling skin care, she was saving the company. And Dana was helping her make it all happen. For the next hour, while the products were discussed in great detail so that Dana would be loaded with info she could use on her show, she was so caught up in the excitement she forgot all about her suspicions. That is, until the meeting ended, and Eleanor said, "Isn't it amazing how everything fell into place!"

"Amazing," Dana repeated, realizing that Eleanor had no idea how much she sounded like someone who had the motivation to send Ivan Dennison off the roof.

27

Two days later, Dana was awoken from a deep sleep by her cell phone. It took her a moment to get her bearings. Was Ari next to her? She glanced over and saw that she was alone in bed. Then she remembered that she had wanted a good night's sleep because it was the day of the Reluven launch, and had told Ari she needed her space. It was just as well, because she was still trying to sort out her memory about Ivan. She could go back and forth on it ten times in a single minute. She did it. She didn't do it. She must have done it. She couldn't have done it.

And poor Ari. He deserved to know the truth. Her secret was putting his career in terrible jeopardy. He was a homicide detective who could well be dating the murderer he sought.

But then, it was all probably a big mistake. A false memory. And if she told him, it would be a nuclear explosion in their relationship. How could she possibly risk that?

At very least, she had made one big decision: she was not going to let her uncertain but traumatic memory get in the way of her Sweat City show. She would play Penny Harte. And she would crush it.

For now, though, Dana just wanted to go back to sleep and forget all about it. But her phone rang again. Who the hell was calling her on the very day she wanted to let herself slumber until the last minute?

When Dana glanced at the caller ID and saw that it was Ashlee, she had a moment of panic. Had she overslept? She glanced at the clock. No, she didn't need to be at the studio for at least another hour.

"Everything okay?" she said.

"Were you sleepin'?" Ashlee asked.

"Trying to."

"Well, you're going to want to get up for this. Eleanor just sneaked out for a secret meeting and I followed her."

"Followed her where?" Dana asked.

"To Central Park. It's like some scene from a movie. She's sittin' on a bench waiting for someone. And it's cold enough to freeze the balls off a pool table."

Dana sat up. "Where in Central Park?"

"You know that arch? Where they shot that film?"

That did little to narrow it down, but as Dana pressed her for more info, she was able to figure out the precise location. It wasn't that far from her new apartment—a fact that gave Dana a tingle. In the near future, some of the most beautiful vistas in the city would be an easy stroll from her front door.

"I think I know exactly where you are," Dana said, as she picked up a pair of jeans from the floor and shimmied into them. "I'll meet you there." She looked under her bed for shoes, and pulled out a pair of ankle boots with a stacked heel. They had seen better days, but they weren't nearly as bad as her combat boots. They would do.

"You sure?" Ashlee asked. "'Cause I can report back."

"I want to see for myself," Dana said.

She got dressed as quickly as she could, dashed out the door, popped into the local bodega for a cup of coffee and hailed a yellow cab. All the while, she was getting texts from Ashlee with updates.

She's looking at her wrist. Think she wears a Fitbit?

Dana typed back:

I think she wears a WATCH.

Ashlee responded with three coffee emojis and three laughing emojis, and Dana caught her drift. She had missed the joke and needed coffee. She took a sip from her steaming cup.

A few minutes later, another text came through.

She's pacing.

And then:

It looks like she's texting someone.

As Dana was getting out of the cab, Ashlee called.

"She's on the move."

"What do you mean?" Dana asked.

"I think they picked another spot to meet. Or maybe she realized she was waitin' in the wrong place, because she looked fit to be tied. Anyway, she's walking now, but not back toward the office."

Shit, Dana thought. This could be trouble.

"What direction is she moving?"

"She's headin' north."

Oh god. Oh god. The cab had let Dana off just north of the arch, which meant she could run smack into Eleanor any minute. And then she'd have some explaining to do. She looked down the path, and thought she saw a figure that looked like Eleanor. Dana needed to make a quick decision. She dashed down a path that headed east. But running while holding a coffee cup and trying to avoid other people in the way wasn't easy. And suddenly, Dana found herself tumbling forward. She tried to wrench her body, and her coffee cup went flying as she windmilled her arms to keep from hitting the ground. At that moment, though, the heel broke off her right boot and her ankle twisted in half. Dana heard an actual crack as a searing pain shot though her leg and sent her tumbling to the ground. Dear god, it hurt.

Fuck, she thought. *Fuck, fuck, fuck,* as she remembered, too late, why she hadn't worn those boots in so long. They needed to be fixed.

"Are you okay?" a jogger asked, running in place as Dana writhed.

Dana could hardly breathe for the agony. "I…need…help."

The man stopped jogging and pulled Dana up by both her arms.

"That…bench," she said, nodding toward it.

"This one's closer," he said, indicating a bench that could be seen from the path heading north.

"Other one," she breathed. "Please."

She leaned on the man as she hopped her way to the bench, each bounce sending an excruciating jolt through her. She thanked him and he went on his way. The pain. Sweet fancy Moses, the pain. It was like an entity. A thing that wanted to kill her. As she tried to breathe into it, a million thoughts rocketed through her mind. But mainly: *How the hell am I going to do my show?*

When she could catch her breath, Dana called Ashlee. "We need to abort the mission," she said, and explained what had happened.

"Should I call an ambulance?" Ashlee asked.

"God no. Just get over here."

They stayed on the phone while Ashlee tried to wend her way to Dana's location. After several minutes it became clear she was walking in the wrong direction, and had to double back. By the time she reached her, almost twenty minutes had passed, and it was getting dangerously close to airtime.

"Oh lord," Ashlee said, when she saw how swollen Dana's ankle was. "You really did a number on yourself."

"I think it was a mistake to take off the boot," Dana said. "I'll never get it back on."

Ashlee scratched her head. "Are you going to call Sherry?"

"Why would I do that?"

"Because she'll need to find a replacement host fast."

Dana was incredulous. There was no way in hell she would miss today's show, no matter how much pain she was in. "Ashlee, I'm going on the air at one o'clock today, come hell or high water."

"Are you sure? I think you need to get that x-rayed."

"I'll go to the hospital after the show. For now, I just have to figure out how the hell I'm going to make it to the studio."

"Aren't you in pain?"

Dana shook her head. "No, this is not pain. This is something much worse. We need a new word for what this is. But I'll take some Advil and I'll manage."

"At very least, you need to wrap that up. I could run to a drugstore and get an Ace bandage."

"We don't have time. Maybe we can wrap my jacket around it."

"No ma'am," Ashlee said. "That is simply not going to

work. But I have an idea." At that, she stood up and took off her faux shearling jacket. Then she reached under her top to pull a strap out over one arm and then the other. At last, she shimmied something beige down below her top and over her hips, and Dana saw what it was—high compression Spanx shapewear. It would make the perfect bandage.

"Genius," Dana said.

"First things first," Ashlee said, and rummaged through her purse. She pulled out a little pill box. "Good thing for you I take this stuff for cramps," she said, and spilled three pills into Dana's palm. She swallowed them dry.

Ashlee folded her Spanx garment and wrapped it tightly around Dana's ankle, slipping the straps under her foot and around to hold it in place. Tears rivered down Dana's face as she endured the agony of the procedure. But by the time it was done, she decided it was better than any drugstore bandage.

"Now let's see if we can get that boot back on."

This, Dana knew, would be the hard part. But she had to do it. Ashlee held the broken ankle boot under Dana's foot and she tried to point her toes into it.

A burn of agony tore through her and she screamed.

"You okay?"

"I just need a minute," Dana said. She was queasy from the pain, and worried she might vomit up the pills she just took. Ashlee looked down at her phone, and Dana knew she was surreptitiously checking the time.

"I know we have to hurry," Dana said. "Just…give me a sec." She closed her eyes and took some cleansing breaths.

"Okay," she announced, when the nausea passed. "I'm ready."

"If I had a bullet," Ashlee said, "I'd let you bite on it."

"If you had a bullet," Dana said, "I'd want you to put me out of my misery."

At last, she held her breath and drove her foot into the boot. It was the worst pain she had ever felt.

"One day," she said, "I'm going to tell some woman about this, and she's going to insist it's not as painful as childbirth. Then I'll have to punch her in the throat."

The two hobbled out of the park together, and saw a man in an expensive overcoat with his hand on the door of a taxi.

"Excuse me, sir!" Ashlee called. "My friend here just had a terrible accident in the park and we need that taxi to get her to the hospital. I know you don't mind. Thank you so much for your kindness!"

Without waiting for a response, she helped Dana into the cab.

"Mount Sinai?" the driver asked, referring to the closest hospital.

"Well, aren't you sweet?" Ashlee said, as she slammed the door shut. "Thank you, but we just changed our minds." She gave him the address of the Shopping Channel, with instructions to get them as close to the entryway as possible.

28

Thirty minutes later, Dana was on set, standing behind a display of Reluven bath sets that were beautifully packaged in shimmery gold baskets threaded with pale silver ribbons. The set was adorned with a brightly decorated Christmas tree, blinking gaily behind her to promote the spirit of holiday giving. The two mature models who had been hired to help demonstrate the products were seated stage right. Dana wore a red cardigan over a cream top, as if dressed for a homey holiday party. She also wore a pair of soft slippers that had been provided by Irini, the wardrobe supervisor, but the viewers wouldn't see them, as the tech director had been told to make sure Dana was only shot from the waist up.

Before the camera blinked on, Dana focused on her breathing. She knew that there was something about being before an audience that could make pain recede. It didn't matter if the people were in the studio in front of her or in homes across the country. An audience sent the pain scurrying. Not that it went away entirely, but it found a different place to reside. A box in which to remain until the lights went down and the performance ended.

And that's the way it was for Dana when the camera went on and she launched into her breathless, exuberant pitch for this brand new life-changing product, offered at such an incredible price. It was the perfect holiday gift. The beautifully packaged luxuriant bath set every woman wanted. Dana talked about the bubble bath (so decadent!), the shower gel (liquid satin!), the scrub (refreshing!), the shampoo bar (perfection!). She practically fainted from joy at the light, delicious scent. She oozed and cooed and was nearly orgiastic in her delight.

Demo the eye serum, Jessalyn whispered through the earpiece. And that's when Dana knew she could be in trouble. Because she had been on the air for over twenty minutes, and had been standing on one foot the entire time. Now she had to walk halfway across the set to reach the first model.

Dana stalled for a few more minutes, extolling the virtues of exfoliating before moisturizing. She went over the prices again, explaining the unprecedented value the Shopping Channel offered on this bath set. She couldn't guarantee this gift basket would ever again be offered at such a low price. By the time she took a breath, it almost seemed as if *not* purchasing this item would be the most foolish extravagance anyone could make.

The demo! Jessalyn whispered again. She sounded frantic, and Dana knew she couldn't delay any longer.

"And I want to talk about the eye serum," Dana said into the camera. "It's not the usual product you find in a bath set, but I am such an incredible fan of this miraculous liquid gold I made a special request to include it. I wanted this opportunity to introduce it to you. And I'm delighted that our beautiful model Vanetta is here so we can see exactly how it works."

That was the cue for the camera to focus on the sixty-eight-year-old model they had brought in for the demo, while Dana hobbled across the set.

Before taking a single stride, Dana looked at the monitor to be sure it showed Vanetta's lovely but lined complexion. She breathed in and sidled a few steps over, holding onto the display table for support. But once she reached the end, the model was still eight feet away. Dana exhaled.

You can do this, she told herself.

And then, she did. She put actual weight on the foot. The pain shot through her like a jagged dart and Dana gave an involuntary yelp. And it wasn't a small yelp, either. It was more like a shriek. Even the models jolted. So much for putting her agony in a box on the shelf.

When the camera was back on her, Dana tried to laugh it off. But there were tears of pain in her eyes. And though she continued with the demo, she sensed a shift in the atmosphere, as if her agony had rearranged the molecules in the air.

People are calling in, Dana! Jessalyn said into her earpiece. Somehow, she managed to sound frantic through a whisper. *They're worried about you. Make up some excuse. Say something. You stepped on a tack or whatever.*

Dana smiled into the camera as she thought about it. What on earth could she say that wouldn't derail the entire launch? She didn't want to take the focus off the products and put it on herself. That wouldn't do at all. In fact, it would be a disaster. She thought about the board of directors and their decision to give the Shopping Channel brand one last shot. If she failed now, that was it. They'd probably follow Ivan's course and make the change to electronics. Half the people here might be out of a job—including her. *Especially* her, because she'd be the one responsible. No, she couldn't let it happen. She wouldn't.

At last, Dana got an idea. She wasn't going to wade into this pool. She was going to swan dive. She wasn't sure it would work, but it was her only option. Standing on the edge of the diving board, Dana took one last breath, and then she launched.

"I have to apologize," she said into the camera, as if speaking to a friend. "I was pretending everything is okay. And that wasn't fair to you." She paused, then spoke directly to the tech director. "Tony, can you pan down and get a close-up of my ankle?" There was a moment of hesitation, and Dana watched the monitor as the camera panned down to her injury. The studio was eerily quiet, as if no one even dared breathe as they waited to see what she was going to do.

Dana lifted her pant leg to expose the terrible swelling, obvious even through the white bandage that had replaced Ashlee's Spanx. Understanding the power of a demo, Dana lifted her other pant leg for comparison. The swollen ankle was at least three times the size. Talk about drama.

"This happened just before I went on the air. The heel broke off my boot—not bought from the Shopping Channel, I'll add—and I twisted my ankle. Now, we have an excellent production staff here, and they could have brought in another host to take my place today. And I'm sure she would have done a *terrific* job telling you about this Reluven bath set." She punched the word *terrific* to show how very much she meant it, and paused for effect before continuing. "But for months, I have been talking to our buyers here about these products. From the moment I opened that scrub for the first time and got a whiff of that exquisite scent, I was hooked."

Dana paused for an extra beat, and the camera panned back up to her face, just as she had hoped. She went on, still addressing her friend at home. "Then I actually tried the products and, well, let me tell you. I knew it would be a game changer. Because I've never fallen more in love with a skin care line. And there was no force on heaven or earth that could keep me from coming on the air today and introducing these products to you. That's how strongly I feel about them." The camera pulled in tighter and Dana gave her dear friend the biggest and most grateful grin, before glancing offstage. "Now, if someone could bring in a chair for me, that would be great. Because I want to get right to the demonstration. It's going to rock your world!"

There. She had not only addressed the elephant in the room, she had tied a ribbon around its trunk. Now she just had to keep going and see if the audience responded to her impassioned confession, believing she would have walked through fire to introduce these products.

Within minutes, Jessalyn was back in her earpiece, saying that sales were going through the roof. *We already exceeded our sales projections for the entire show,* she whispered. Dana kept going, demonstrating the eye serum on both models, marveling as the fine lines faded. In a spirit of sisterly camaraderie, they helped her back to the display table, where the crew had placed a bowl of warm water so Dana could immerse the shampoo bar and show the richness of the lather. She brought her face close to the bowl to inhale the scent. "It's subtle," she gushed, "but so exquisite."

We're now fifty percent over projections! Jessalyn whispered.

Dana demonstrated the exfoliating properties of the scrub. She narrated over a short film that showed the luxuriousness of the bubble bath crystals in action, as a woman in a silk robe filled her tub and delighted in the sensual richness of the experience. She even cooed over the gold-and-silver packaging.

Sherry and Eleanor are in the booth with me now, Jessalyn whispered. *Everyone is freaking out. You've doubled projected sales!*

Dana kept going. She talked about each product included

in the gift basket, and then went back to the beginning and talked about them again. She marveled at the value, explained how much the viewers would pay if they were to buy each product individually. She walked her friend at home through the Easy-Bucks option of spreading the cost into five small payments. Since new viewers were constantly tuning in, she demonstrated the eye serum again and retold the story of her injury.

By the time she signed off, she had sold four times the projected numbers, and she could hear the folks in the control booth whooping. Dana had moved so many units Eleanor had to get on the phone with the supplier to see how fast they could manufacture more inventory to get the Shopping Channel through the rest of the holiday season programming.

Megan and Ari had both shown up on set, concerned about Dana's injury, which they learned about while she was on the air. So as the rest of the staff literally popped champagne, Dana was on her way out the door—one arm around her best friend and the other around her boyfriend—heading to the emergency room.

29

"Broken or sprained?" Ari asked, when the ER doctor returned to the curtained-off area Dana had been delivered to after being x-rayed.

Dana expected him to say *sprained*, as it seemed impossible to break an ankle from something as innocuous as a loose heel. Especially a loose heel she had known about and meant to fix. Besides, Megan had told her a bad sprain could hurt worse than a break, and this hurt like a son of a bitch. Or it had. The Vicodin they gave her took the edge off, and the swelling had gone down. Unfortunately, her mood had only gotten worse, and it was now so frayed she wished she could yank it off and strangle someone with it. Five hours in excruciating pain, she realized, could wear a person down.

"Broken," the doctor announced cheerily, as he slapped the X-ray onto a light box. Dana wanted to hurt him.

As he pointed out the fracture and explained how they would set the bone, Dana's anger morphed into self-pity. Broken? It didn't seem possible. She was twenty-nine years old and had never broken a bone in her life. It seemed so...permanent. Hadn't she heard someplace that once you fracture a bone, it shows up on your X-rays forever?

"You'll be fine," the doctor said when he saw her expression. "We're going to go straight to a hard cast in your case, and you can even choose the color. You like purple?"

She blinked at him. A broken bone wasn't bad enough—he had to treat her like a child?

"Don't you have something with *unicorns*?" she seethed.

"Puppies okay?"

He had meant to make her laugh, but Dana was having none of it. She turned to Ari. "Can you kill him? Pretty please?"

"Calm down, honey," Megan said, "and we'll get you a lollipop."

Dana put her face in her hands. "I hate everyone."

"She's not usually like this," Megan said to the doctor. "I mean, don't get me wrong. She's always a pain in the ass, just not like this."

He gave an understanding nod. "It can be a very painful injury."

Great, she thought. They went from treating her like a child to talking about her like she wasn't there. Dana took a cleansing breath and tried to tell herself things could be worse.

As it turned out, she was right. Because less than a minute later, two unexpected visitors showed up beside the curtain: her father and his wife, Jennifer.

"Knock knock," Jennifer said, to announce their arrival.

"What the hell?" Dana demanded. She felt at once exposed and trapped.

"Don't be mad," Ari said. "I texted your dad while we were in the waiting room."

"Why?" Dana pleaded. "Why would you do such a thing?"

"He's a doctor. And he's your father. I thought he'd want to know."

"Orthopedist?" the ER doctor asked.

While Kenneth introduced himself and explained that he was a neurologist and his wife a cardiologist, Jennifer lifted Dana's wrist and took her pulse.

Dana wanted them gone. She wanted everyone gone. Instead of screaming, she simply said, "Thank you for coming, but I don't need—"

Her father cut her off. "How did this happen?" he asked, an edge of anger working its way into his tone, as if her injury were a personal affront.

"You know me," Dana said. "Climbing that slippery ladder of success."

"Now is not the time for jokes," he said.

"She broke a heel," Megan explained.

Kenneth's brow tightened. "A heel?"

"I was taking a walk with my assistant," Dana said, continuing with the fictional account she had already given to Ari. "The heel snapped off and my ankle twisted."

"You couldn't have been walking at a normal pace," Kenneth said, and Dana realized how annoying it was to have a father with above-average intelligence. Even Ari hadn't asked about that. But then, maybe he just didn't want to interrogate her while she was in pain.

"It's not easy to keep up with Ashlee," Dana said. "Her legs are like a mile long. Did I mention her dad played basketball for the University of Tennessee?"

Dana felt satisfied that she had veered the conversation in another direction, but Kenneth was dogged.

"You have long legs, too," he said.

"Well, she was a few paces ahead. And why are you cross-examining me? I was in so much pain I'm lucky I remember my name."

"You don't need to get snippy," her father said.

Dana exploded. "I have a broken ankle! I went on the air and spoke for four fucking hours in excruciating pain and sold millions of dollars of merchandise and saved my whole damned company. And while everyone else is drinking champagne I'm in the emergency room being told I'll have to clomp around in a cast for god knows how many weeks. So don't tell me not to be snippy!"

Her father shook his head and tsked. "Language, Dana."

But her language was about to get much, much worse, because she suddenly realized how tragic this injury might really be. She stared at the doctor, trying to form the question, but before she could get it out he said, "Why don't we get this bone set so you can get out of here."

Then he slipped away to get the cast technician.

"What's the matter?" Ari asked, when he saw her expression.

Dana looked from her father to Jennifer. "How long does a cast stay on?" she asked, her voice desperate.

"It depends," Jennifer said. "But usually it's three weeks in a hard cast and three weeks in a splint or a boot. But you'll have to ask the doctor because—"

"A splint?" Dana cut in. "That means it's removable, right?"

"Technically, sure. But you're supposed to keep it on unless you're showering. That's the whole idea."

"As long as I know I can take it off," Dana said, realizing she could still pull off the Penny Harte role. It would be by the skin of her teeth, but still.

Megan's eyes went wide. "You're not actually thinking of performing in the Sweat City play with a broken ankle?"

"You heard what she said. I can take the cast *off.*"

"Dana, it's a very physical role. There's a treadmill onstage, for god's sake."

"When is the play?" Jennifer asked.

"Less than four weeks," Megan said.

"It's out of the question," Kenneth said. "You can't rush bone growth."

"Refracturing a broken bone can be very serious," Jennifer said. "Then you're talking about surgery, physical therapy, a long road to recovery."

"I'm so sorry," Megan said.

"I can't do this," Dana said, as if she could unbreak the bone through force of will. "I can't have a broken ankle now!"

"Babe," Ari said, leaning in for a hug. "It'll be okay."

"Maybe Nathan can rewrite the part," Dana said, aware that it was a long shot. "Make it less physical."

Megan put a hand on her shoulder. "You have to be realistic."

"But he wrote it with me in mind. He told me so."

"I know how much this show means to you," Megan said, her voice low and soothing. "But I think you're going to have to let it go. There will be other plays, other performances. You're a talented actor and—"

"Where's my handbag?" Dana said. "I need my phone. I need to call Nathan. He'll figure something out."

Megan handed Dana her purse and they all watched as she fished out her cell phone. She looked up to see them all staring at her. Their eyes were filled with pity, and that filled her with fury.

"Get out!" she cried. "All of you. Get out!"

Later, Ari helped Dana get comfortable in her own bed, a pillow under her cast. "I'm fine," she insisted as he fussed. And she meant it. Because now that the bone was set and the cast in place, she barely felt a thing.

But that didn't mean her mood was any sunnier. Her bedroom, barely big enough for the two of them, now also held Megan, Kenneth and Jennifer, making it claustrophobic. And if that wasn't bad enough, Nathan had just been buzzed in from downstairs, and would arrive any second, bringing good wishes and a bucket of pity. On the phone he had told her he was very, very sorry, but the role could not be rewritten for someone with a broken ankle.

"You guys don't have to stay," Dana said to her father and Jennifer, as Ari and Megan wordlessly scrambled to pick up laundry from the floor and stuff it away.

Jennifer gave her arm a pat. "We want to make sure you're comfortable."

She wasn't, but one glance at her father, stuffed into the corner of the cramped room, made her feel a little better. It was pure schadenfreude, this pleasure at his discomfort. But he damn well deserved it for criticizing her decision to move to a larger apartment. Maybe there was an upside to this.

Minutes later, Nathan came in. His pity took the form of a box of Neuhaus Chocolates, which were Dana's favorites. They couldn't take the place of her role in the show, but they would do for now. He introduced himself to the others, then handed her the box, which she accepted greedily.

"Your cast is blue," he observed, and it took Dana a moment to realize he meant the cast on her leg, not the one he had just left at the theater.

"I wanted it to match my mood. But thank you for the chocolates." She didn't waste any time tearing into the box and popping a truffle into her mouth, and then taking another and another before she even finished swallowing it. When she looked up and realized she had a rapt audience for her self-pitying gluttony, Dana reluctantly passed the box around.

"How do you feel?" Nathan said.

"Do you really need to ask?" she mumbled, pointing to her very full mouth.

"You know, everyone felt terrible when I told them what happened."

Dana took a beat to swallow. "And Carolyn?" she inquired, because Nathan had explained he had no choice but to give her part to the other actor.

"She feels bad, too. I'm sure you know that."

Dana nodded. As much as she wanted to be furious with someone, to rail about the injustice she was suffering, she understood that there was no one to blame. Except maybe herself. She took a tissue from the bedside to surreptitiously dab at her eyes before wiping her chocolatey hands and mouth.

A few minutes later, Ashlee arrived, only Dana couldn't see her face because she was carrying a massive flower arrangement. It looked like the centerpiece from some grand hotel—so large it couldn't have been easy to fit through the door. Dana knew it must have cost a fortune.

"My god!" she said, worried her assistant had spent her whole paycheck on it. "I hope you stole that from a funeral home."

"Even better," Ashlee said proudly. "I got the company to spring for it. Sherry, that little skinflint, wouldn't spend a quarter to see Jesus do a magic trick. But before she could make a stink, Eleanor cut in and said you deserved at least this much. So here we are!"

"Where do you want me to put it?" Megan said.

"Are you really going to feed me a straight line like that?" Dana asked. "With my father in the room?"

Ari took the flowers from Ashlee. "I'll find a place for it," he said, and carried the arrangement into the living room.

"Hey, y'all," Ashlee said to the group, and Dana made the introductions.

Kenneth couldn't even manage a smile. "You're the young lady who was with my daughter when this happened."

It sounded more like an accusation than a question, and Ashlee chirped, "Guilty as charged!"

"Can you explain how she managed to take such a bad fall?" he asked. "I don't understand how this could have happened unless she was running."

Dana shot Ashlee a look.

"Well, I can't rightly say, because I was looking straight ahead when she went down. But isn't it nice that everybody's here visitin'. It sure is cozy."

"It's going to get cozier," Nathan said. "The cast said they'd stop by."

"Maybe we should go," Kenneth whispered to Jennifer.

Dana couldn't blame him. The place was starting to look like the scene from the Marx Brothers movie *A Night at the Opera*, where all the characters are crowded into one stateroom. Normally, Dana would have been happy to see her father go. But she decided this was just too much fun. And she deserved a little entertainment right now.

"Oh, Daddy," she said. "Can't you stay for just a little bit longer?"

"I… I suppose," he said.

A few minutes later the intercom buzzed, and Dana assumed her fellow troupers had arrived. But it was Sherry, Eleanor and Charles Honeycutt. The scent of alcohol followed them into the room, and Dana knew they had spent some solid time celebrating.

After they said their hellos and clucked over Dana's injury, Charles made a little speech about how grateful they were for her performance and quick thinking.

"You went above and beyond," he said. "And exceeded all our expectations."

"Saved our asses," Eleanor added.

Megan elbowed Sherry. "Would this be a good time to re-negotiate her contract?"

"Let's not get carried away," Sherry said. "We had one good day."

"One *very* good day," Megan corrected.

"Even drunk she's hard as a rock," Dana said, shaking her head. Sherry could never lighten up and just go with a joke.

Sherry folded her arms. "I am not drunk."

Dana might have believed it, too, except that her glasses were crooked and she swayed a bit.

"If you ask me," Eleanor said, looking around the cramped room, "she needs a raise. Not that this apartment isn't everything a girl could dream of."

The sarcasm wasn't lost on anyone, except maybe Kenneth. Dana glanced over to study his expression, which gave away nothing.

"I actually just signed a lease on a bigger place," she said. "But my dad thinks this apartment is more than adequate."

"I assume you don't usually have so many guests," he said, and Dana wondered if he had ever, even once in his life, admitted to being wrong.

She turned to Sherry and changed the subject. "I was thinking about how I can manage on the set with my cast. Maybe you could get me a tall stool and I could sit on that behind a display."

Sherry nodded. "It wouldn't be the first time we accommodated a host with a leg injury. But we can talk about it Monday."

"Monday?" Dana said, surprised. "What about tomorrow… and Friday?"

"I already arranged a substitute host for the rest of the

week. I figured we'd see how you feel after that and take it from there."

"But I'm fine," Dana insisted. "I can work tomorrow. Once they got the cast on I—"

"You really should take a little time to rest," Jennifer said.

"But they need me." She turned to the Shopping Channel executives. "Don't you need me?"

"We want you healthy," Charles said.

Ari laid a hand on her shoulder. "I'm sure they can get along without you for a couple of days."

Dana felt a rising panic. Without the distraction of work, she would have nothing to do but dwell in her misery over losing her Sweat City role…and replay her frightening memory about the night of the murder. She might go out of her mind.

"What am I supposed to do with myself?" she asked.

"You're allowed to rest," Megan said.

"But I don't *need* to rest."

Nathan glanced down at his phone. "Uh-oh, the whole gang is coming over. They're on their way." He looked around at the crowded room.

"The Sweat City Company?" Megan asked, incredulous. "Aren't there like eleven of them?"

Worse than that, Dana thought. Her two worlds were about to collide. And yes, she had just been taken out of the show, so technically she was no longer in breach of contract. But if Sherry found out that she had been sneaking out to rehearsals in defiance of her decision, there was no telling what could happen. And sure, maybe none of it mattered anymore, in light of how well the show had gone. But this was Sherry Zidel, who was a bitch even when she was drunk.

Dana gave Megan a pleading look. It took a moment for her friend to register her concern, but in one flash, she got it.

"Hate to be a party pooper," Megan announced, "but I think we need to make room for the second shift."

"We'll leave," Jennifer offered. "These folks just got here."

"That's very kind of you," Charles said.

Dana gave Megan a silent scream for help, and her friend obliged.

"I'm sure Dana would love to visit with you a bit longer," she said to the Shopping Channel executives, "but I think she's getting tired."

"Tired?" Eleanor said, studying Dana's face.

Dana looked at Ari, her eyes pleading for reinforcements, and he understood.

"People," he said, in his authoritative detective voice. "I'm concerned about safety."

"Fire codes," Megan offered.

"Yes, that's right."

At that, her coworkers said goodbye and filed out, followed by her father and Jennifer. Several minutes later, her fellow troupers piled in. Dana knew she should feel grateful for the visit, but her mood went from irritated to morose. Her friends chatted excitedly, trying to cheer her up, but she only got more and more despondent. Losing the role was a terrible blow, and she already felt a hollowness at the thought of all those nights they would be rehearsing without her.

She tried going through the motions and pretending to be cheerful, but she didn't have the energy to perform. At last, they acknowledged that she looked worn out from her long day. Their goodbyes were heartfelt and conciliatory, but after they closed the door behind them, Dana could make out their bright and happy voices in the hallway, and at last, she let herself cry and cry and cry.

30

The cast made it hard to get comfortable, but eventually the long day caught up with her and Dana fell into a deep sleep. The early-morning hours were punctuated by fitful dreams as Ari moved about the apartment getting dressed for work. She stirred as he was leaving, so he bent to kiss her, saying he had an important meeting, but promised to be back soon.

"I'm fine," she said. "Don't worry about me."

"I have a lot of paperwork to catch up on," he said. "Just as easy for me to do it here as in the office."

"Honestly," she insisted, "I don't need to be babied."

Ari ignored her and put the crutches next to her bed. "I made coffee," he said. "And I'll bring back some breakfast."

By the time he returned with food and a large box of files, Dana was awake. She even managed to get as far as the hall-way, determined to practice walking with her crutches so she wouldn't feel like such an invalid. But after one short test drive she stopped. What was the point? She couldn't do her Sweat

City play. She couldn't go to work. She couldn't even try to track down the bartender who might be able to shed light on her memory about Ivan.

"Is there anything I can do to cheer you up?" Ari asked, as they ate breakfast at the small table off the kitchen.

Yes, she thought. *Tell me where you are with the murder investigation. Tell me you know who the killer is, and it's not me.* For a fleeting moment, she even considered revealing her haunting memory to him. She could imagine him saying, *Oh, babe,* and taking her in his arms. *It's not you,* he would whisper. *It's not you.* Or, his face would go stone cold. His winter-blue eyes would ice over. His love would turn to frost.

"Maybe you could give me just a tiny hint on how the investigation is going," she said, trying to look pathetic. Maybe, just this once, he'd give an inch…to appease his poor, suffering girlfriend.

"Babe," he said, his tone measured, careful.

"Please?" she begged. "Just a hint. Do you have a suspect? Someone you're looking at?"

"You know I can't tell you."

Dana sighed and pushed her plate away. "You think it's okay to smoke weed while on Vicodin?"

"Are you serious?" he asked.

"I'm bored."

"If I were you," he said, "I'd spend the day in bed, playing video games and binge-watching whatever I wanted. And I wouldn't feel guilty about it."

"If it's okay with you, I'm just going to sit here and stare into space for a while."

She was laying it on thick, but Ari pretended not to notice. He cleared the dishes and got himself situated on the sofa with his paperwork. It was a challenge, as the massive flower arrangement took over the entire coffee table. He set his heavy file box on the couch next to him, and did the best he could.

Dana was dying to peek over his shoulder, but she knew he wouldn't take kindly to it, so at last she went into the bedroom, where she opened her laptop and searched for something to binge-watch. She settled on a comedy a lot of her friends had been yammering about, but she couldn't get into it.

After a while, she heard Ari on his cell phone, and it was clear he was being summoned to another murder. He appeared at the bedroom door in his coat.

"I have to go out for a while," he said, his face stoic. She could tell he was in murder police mode.

"Someone get killed?"

"A kid."

Dana knew how removed he was when dealing with grisly realities of his job, but it was different when a child got killed.

"Shit," she said.

He nodded. "You need anything before I go?"

"I'll be fine."

Dana got onto her crutches and walked him to the door. When it shut behind him, she turned back toward the living room and saw that he had left his file box behind, but he had put it on the coffee table and placed the massive flower arrangement on top of it. The message was clear: *Do not even think of trying to snoop.*

But how could she *not*? All the answers she needed were inside that box. And even if it didn't lead her to the murderer, at very least she could find out Margaux's last name, and maybe even her contact info.

She knew she shouldn't do it. If Ari found out he would be furious. But he would be gone for hours. If she was careful, he would never know.

No, she told herself. *Do not do it. Go back into the bedroom and find something else to binge on. Maybe rewatch* The West Wing *or something.*

She leaned on her crutches, staring into the living room, and at last decided that what he didn't know wouldn't hurt him. She hobbled over and studied the box as she devised a plan of attack. First, she laid her crutches on the floor. Then, balancing on her left foot, she bent over to see if she could lift the massive arrangement. It was heavy, but she was able to raise it. The problem was carrying it. Dana tried taking a few hops while balancing it, but she teetered. If she tried to move even an inch, either she or the flowers would topple. She set it back down and regrouped. What next?

Dana tried sliding the box to the left while keeping her hand on the flower arrangement to keep it from falling. That might give her just enough room to put the arrangement down next to the box. But the table began to topple from the weight and she didn't have an extra hand or foot to hold it up. So she pushed it back in place and bit her lip, thinking. She considered sliding the centerpiece onto the sofa, but decided it would certainly fall over. *If only I had another set of hands,* she thought.

Then Dana got an idea. Ashlee.

She picked up her cell phone and called her assistant. "What are you up to?" she asked.

"Just shootin' the shit with Felicia and Jo. Not much for me to do here when you're not around. Need anything?"

Dana took a breath. "How fast can you get to my apartment?"

"I can leave this very minute. But I'll need to stop and pick up lunch on the way, if you don't mind."

"As long as you don't bring more flowers," Dana said, "I don't mind at all."

Thirty minutes later, Ashlee arrived carrying a bag from the deli, and the smell of hot pastrami wafted through the apartment. Dana had discovered months ago that the girl couldn't get enough of New York food. *I can't understand why you people don't eat this every day,* she had said, biting into a football-sized sandwich.

"Now, what can I do for you?" Ashlee asked, putting down the deli bag.

"Besides share your sandwich?"

"Oh, darlin'. I wouldn't *think* of sharin'. That's why I bought one for each of us. And also two Diet Cokes."

"I think I love you," Dana said.

Ashlee waved it away. "Why am I here?"

"You see that file box?" Dana said, pointing. "I need to get inside it."

"I'm not sure you'll fit, even skinny as you are."

Dana reacted with a good-natured eyeroll.

"Alright, alright," Ashlee said, as she folded her arms as she assessed the situation. "Why is it under the flowers?"

"Ari did that. He wanted to make sure I wouldn't peek inside."

"Oh, they're Ari's files!" Ashlee exclaimed. "Why didn't you say so." With that, she scooped up the massive flower arrangement and set it on the floor. "You think the identity of the murderer is in here?" she asked, taking the lid off the carton.

"I don't know," Dana said, and walked over on her crutches. She peered into the box, which held a neat array of manila folders labeled with case numbers. They were held in place by a tall pile of slender writing pads filled with Ari's handwriting. These were his notes—the inserts that went into the black leather folio he took to crime scenes.

She picked one up and gave the pages a riffle. Then she took a close look at the top page.

"These are dated," she observed.

"You reckon that'll help?" Ashlee asked.

"If his notes from the night of Ivan's murder are here, they should at least have Margaux's last name."

"Let's find it then," Ashlee said.

The two women sat side by side on the couch, pulling out the pads, and checking the dates. They set them next to the box as they did so.

"We're getting warmer," Dana said, as she found a pad that was dated just days before Ivan's murder.

As she was scanning the notes, Dana heard a key in the door and her heart seemed to stop beating. *What in God's name?* Ari wasn't supposed to be back for hours.

"Shit!" she said, throwing the pad back in the box. "That's him!"

Before she could make another move, the door swung open and Ari's tall form appeared. He surveyed the scene, his eyes going from Dana to Ashlee to the flowers on the floor. Then his gaze lingered on the open box and the pile of his note pads.

"What...the...hell?" He spoke slowly, as if each word needed to contain its own explosion of fury. Dana could feel his white-hot rage from across the room.

"What are you doing here?" she asked.

"I wasn't needed," he said through his teeth. "So I left my colleagues to figure out who would stab a ten-year-old to death, and came back to help my *girlfriend*." He pronounced the last word as if it were in quotes, and the venom in his voice was terrifying.

"Don't be mad!" she said. "Please!"

"Jesus, Dana. Are you kidding me? Are you *fucking* kidding me?"

"Okay, I'm sorry. I should have told you. But I needed to know if—"

"This is beyond anything you could possibly explain."

"I know," she said. "I know. It's unforgivable."

"I think this is my cue to leave," Ashlee said.

"Just one minute," Ari said to her. "I want to understand exactly what happened here." He turned back to Dana. "You saw my files, which you knew were off-limits. And you saw that I had *intentionally* made it impossible for you to get to them. So instead of watching a movie or doing any of a thousand other things, you called your assistant to come and help you get to the information you had no right looking at." He paused. "Do I have that right?"

Dana swallowed against a rock in her throat. "I didn't see anything, Ari," she said. "Really. I was only looking for one thing and—"

"And that's supposed to be a comfort—that you didn't find what you were looking for?"

"It's just that you wouldn't tell me a thing. And I didn't know what else to do."

"There was nothing you needed to do!"

"Yes there was!" she cried.

"What are you talking about?" he demanded. She had never heard him angrier.

Using the couch and the coffee table as leverage, Dana got herself into a standing position and grabbed her crutches. She put her weight on them, and stared at Ari, trying to figure out how to tell him that she might be the one who murdered Ivan.

"That night at the party," she began, but felt the blood drain out of her.

"Yes?"

Dana sat back down on the couch. It was impossible. She couldn't tell Ari she might be the one who murdered Ivan. It would ruin everything between them. As bad as all this was, that would be much, much worse. She could handle his anger, but she couldn't bear the thought of seeing his love evaporate.

"I'm sorry," she whispered. "I'm sorry."

"That's all you have to say?"

He stepped into the room and she looked up at him. "I need to ask you one thing," she said.

"You're hardly in a position to—"

"I know, but this is so important. Because you've told me nothing, and… I just need to know if you've found the killer. Can you tell me that much?"

"For god's sake, Dana."

"Just tell me if you *know*," she said desperately. "That would change everything."

He went silent, and her heart thudded in anticipation. If he knew the killer, then it couldn't be her. He would have left a long time ago.

"Ari?" she pleaded. All she needed was a yes. One simple yes.

"You've already compromised the case," he said, pointing at the file box. "I'm not going to make it worse."

"But—"

"You haven't even told me why you were going through my files! You have no right to demand anything from me."

"I know," she said. "I know."

His voice went cold as the bottom of a quarry. "Is there something you saw at the party that you're not telling me?"

This is it, she told herself. *This is your chance to confess. Tell him what Sherry said to you. Tell him about the memory you had. Tell him you're scared you might have pushed Ivan off the roof. This could all end right now. He might scoop you in his arms and promise it wasn't you.*

But it might go the other way. She looked at him, searching for any softness. But his heart was locked in ice.

"She can't recall anything from the party," Ashlee piped in.

"And how do you know that?" Ari said.

"'Cause we were talkin' about it. And she doesn't remember a thing. This here was all my idea. I came by with lunch and got real curious. I thought maybe we could take a little old peek and see if we could help solve this thing."

Ari shook his head. He wasn't buying it. "Well?" he said to Dana. "Is that your explanation for all this?"

She hesitated. "Yes," she said softly, even though she knew it was an obvious lie.

Ari stood there for a few minutes without saying anything, and Dana could think of nothing to do but avoid his gaze. At last he repacked his box and headed for the door. But before he opened it he reached into his pocket for something and smacked it onto the table. Dana had to lean forward to see what it was. The key to her apartment.

31

"I know this seems like the end of the world," Ashlee said, after Ari left. "But while he was talkin' I got an idea."

"Thanks anyway," Dana said. All she wanted now was to get into bed and shut out the world.

"No, really," Ashlee said. "I know how we can track down that Margaux. Then you'll have your answers. That'll be great, won't it?"

Dana was too bereft to even cry. She couldn't see her way out of the mess she was in. Even if she found out she had nothing to do with Ivan's murder, Ari would never forgive her for this breach of trust. She might as well be arrested for murder.

"I don't see how it matters anymore," she said.

"Of course it matters!"

"He'll never forgive me."

"You don't know that for sure."

"If you don't mind," Dana said. "I'd like to get some rest."

Ashlee protested, but Dana shut her down by hobbling to the coat rack, taking down the white faux shearling jacket and holding it toward her.

"I guess I can take a hint," Ashlee said good-naturedly as she laid the coat over her arm. "But just remember one thing—that boy loves you."

She left, and Dana stood by the door for several minutes trying to decide what to do. But there was nothing. No work. No play. No love. And oh god, the apartment. It would be hers in just a few weeks, and a month after that her current lease would terminate. That meant she had no choice but to move in. Alone. And she would live there. Alone. All that space now seemed like a curse. The embodiment of loneliness.

She knew there were people she could call now. People who loved her. Megan. Her sister. But the thought of listening to them try to cheer her up seemed exhausting. And she was so very tired.

Dana considered the joint in her night table drawer. That was the only friend she needed right now. And maybe a Vicodin. Ari's admonition not to mix it with weed made it even more appealing. Because fuck him. Fuck everything.

She went into her bedroom and opened the pill bottle. There were only five tablets inside—doctors were so cautious about opioids now. *Smart*, Dana thought, as she took one, because it meant she would need to ration these. She took one more, and then lit up a joint.

Dana considered putting on some music, but that would leave her mind free to wander, and she couldn't have that. No, she needed some mindless TV. She put it on and turned up the volume, then clicked through the dial as she smoked her joint. She settled on some show about hoarding. A fat man in a stained T-shirt had made his house into a garbage can. It was shocking. Every surface was under piles of stinking trash with rats and roaches scurrying beneath it. So sad. The man simply couldn't throw anything away. Pizza boxes. Magazines. Rotting food. The idea of parting with a single item seemed to break him. Why couldn't he understand that none of it mattered?

Then the crew arrived at the man's house. An army of people with rubber gloves and surgical masks, ready to dig through the fetid mess and clean everything up. The man's name was Roscoe, but at first Dana thought they said Oscar, like the Grouch who lived in a garbage can. She burrowed deep into thinking about Oscar. He lived the way he wanted. To hell with convention. And to hell with getting along with people. Oscar followed his own path. Fuck, yeah.

Roscoe's army of helpers cleaned out a path by the front door, filling up bags of garbage. He followed after them, and had a meltdown when they tried to throw out an old dishrack. As Dana watched, she wondered why they were so intent on fixing a guy who didn't want to be fixed.

It occurred to Dana that she would normally be on the air at this hour, so she switched over to the Shopping Channel to see who was filling in for her. It was Vanessa Valdes, pulling double duty. Dana listened to her pitch for a gemstone pendant as her eyelids grew heavy and she fell asleep.

She woke up ravenous a few hours later. Dana lit up the joint again and took a few more hits before snuffing it out and trying to get out of bed. Then she remembered about her cast. The crutches seemed impossibly complicated, and so she held on to one surface and then another as she hopped into the living room, trying to remember what she had in her puny refrigerator. When she saw the deli bag on the table, Dana nearly combusted with joy.

Ashlee had left the pastrami sandwiches.

In Dana's current state, this seemed like the one true answer to her existential angst—the pure sensual pleasure contained in this white bag. She sat down and pulled out one of the wrapped packages. The scent of pastrami was like something God had created with one express purpose: to deliver bliss. She opened the paper, grabbed the sandwich with both hands and bit into it. Her mouth filled with textures and flavors so magnificent the entire universe was concentrated into the sensations within it. The ooze of fat. The ting of salt. The punch of pepper. The bouquet of smoke. The zest of mustard. The wet fresh rye bread dissolving on her tongue. Dana was lost in it. She ceased to exist. The universe receded. The physicality of consuming this divine creation was the only thing.

And then. It was over. Dana was back in reality, surprised to discover she had devoured two sandwiches and two cans of soda. She let out a long belch and rested her greasy hand on her distended stomach. Now what?

She turned around to look at her empty apartment, and considered her provisions. Wine. Weed. Vicodin. She had enough to get her through the next few days. And right now, that was all she wanted.

The next morning, Dana woke up to a dry throat, a pounding headache and a buzzing cell phone. *Ari?* For a brief moment a familiar lightness lifted her heart. But no. It was Sherry's direct dial number at the Shopping Channel. She let it go to voice mail. Less than an hour later she called again. And then the calls from Megan began. Dana shut off her phone and got wasted.

Later, when the intercom buzzer sounded, she was listening to music through her headphones at the same time that the TV was blaring. The only reason she even heard the damned thing was because it was so insistent. *Buzz buzz buzz buzz buzz buzz.* Like a goddamned pest.

She picked up one crutch, walked over to the intercom and pressed the Talk button. "New phone. Who dis?" she said.

"Dana, let me up." It was Megan.

"I'm busy."

"I swear to god, if you don't let me up I'm calling the police."

"Just go away."

"I'm serious. Buzz me in. *Now!*"

Her voice was angry enough to break through the haze. "Okay, okay," Dana said. "Don't get so excited." She smashed the button that unlocked the front door to her building. She was still holding it when her doorbell rang.

"Oh my god," Megan said, when Dana opened the door. "What happened?"

"Nothing, nothing, nothing," she said, almost singing the words, because her own voice sounded so strange.

"Talk to me."

"Not that I care, but Ari broke up with me."

Megan embraced her. "Oh, honey."

"Also, I think I might have killed Ivan."

Megan backed up. "I thought we put that to rest."

"Rest?" Dana repeated, trying to understand.

Megan studied Dana's face. "Are you high or drunk?"

It seemed like a trick question. There was Vicodin. There was weed. There was wine. "Very much," she heard herself say.

"When was the last time you showered? Or ate solid food?"

Dana squinted at her. Another trick question. It was like a final exam. "At the same time?"

"Have you even changed your clothes?"

"I can't shower," Dana said, catching up. She pointed at her foot. "Cast."

"Right," Megan said, thinking. "Maybe we can fill up the tub and keep your foot outside."

A bath! It sounded like a magnificent idea. Dana clapped her hands together. "I have Reluven bubble bath crystals!"

"That sounds great, honey."

"Oh, it's better than great. It's *rich* and *luxurious*. And did you know it's one hundred percent natural? Plus, when purchased separately, something something something."

"Okay, Dana. Let's get you soaking. And I'll make some coffee."

A short while later, she was in the tub, surrounded by thick bubbles. Her broken leg dangled over the rim, with the cast wrapped in a plastic garbage bag.

"Can I stay in here forever?" Dana asked. "It's so relaxing."

"If you get any more relaxed you're going to need a defibrillator. Tell me what happened with Ari."

"I did something bad and he caught me."

Her friend hesitated, taking that in. "You cheated on him?" She sounded incredulous.

"I was looking at his files. His…murder notes. You know what I mean?"

Megan considered it. "I guess. I always see him with those little pads."

"Exactly. They were in a box. I wasn't supposed to open it. But I need to know. Because what if it's *me*?"

Megan tsked and shook her head. "Are you still hung up on that thing Sherry said? She's a bitch. She was messing with you."

Dana picked up a handful of bubbles and blew on it. "But I remembered something," she said. Then she immersed her hand into the foamy bathwater and lost her train of thought. The bubbles were so tiny it was easy to see them as a single organism. But no. They were separate entities, struggling against an unfriendly atmosphere that dissolved them as if by magic.

"What did you remember?" Megan prompted.

Dana looked up at her, and it came back. "I think I pushed him. Maybe. I don't know. That's why I need to talk to that bartender. She saw. She was right there."

"And maybe she saw nothing."

"If only I could talk to her."

"Dana," Megan said, "I've known you a long time, and you're not a killer. I promise you."

"But what if I was mad? Or what if I just wanted him off me? Maybe I did it by accident."

"You were drunk and doped. You wouldn't have had the strength."

"Maybe." She wiggled her good toes under the water. "I'm so tired."

Megan helped Dana wash her hair, then she got her into dry clothes, and gave her some toast and coffee. Despite the caffeine, Dana was nodding off at the table. So Megan helped her into bed and let her sleep it off.

It was a blank, dreamless slumber, and when Dana awoke, she saw Megan sitting by her bedside.

"You're still here," she said, feeling groggy but sober.

"Settled in like pneumonia."

Dana was so grateful she wanted to cry. What would she do without Megan? "Thank you," she said. "For everything. You're a good friend."

"I won't argue," Megan said.

"You never told me about this whole Mexico thing. You're going away with Jamie?"

Megan smiled, and Dana wasn't sure she'd ever seen her that happy. "Have you heard of the Riviera Maya, near Cancun? His friend has a resort there, and Jamie got us reservations. And plane tickets. His mother will be staying with her sister, so he's free and clear. We're leaving the day of the Shopping

Channel Christmas party, but we figured we could stop by and go straight from there."

Dana propped herself up on her elbows and listened. But when Megan got to the part about another Shopping Channel party, a thread of anxiety snaked its way back into her consciousness. *No*, she thought. *I can't*. She opened her night table drawer and began rummaging around.

"It's not there," Megan said.

"What?"

"I threw out your weed."

Dana stared at her, stunned. "And the Vicodin?" she asked.

"One flush for the weed, and one for the pills."

"Bitch," Dana said, only half kidding. She was crushed with disappointment. It would be so damned hard to get more weed. Her dealer lived in a second-floor walkup and didn't make deliveries. How would she get through the day? Through the weekend?

Megan stood and approached the bed. "You just said I was a good friend."

"I changed my mind."

"You want something to eat?"

Dana sniffed the air. "Do I smell pizza?"

"I ordered in."

There was pizza. In this very apartment. It seemed too good to be true. Dana realized she'd been so deep in sleep she hadn't even heard the doorbell.

They went into the living room, where they sat on the couch eating pizza. Dana wanted a glass of wine with it, but Megan insisted they drink water.

"I think Sherry was trying to reach me," Dana said.

"I spoke to her," Megan said. "She wanted to know if you were coming to work on Monday."

"What did you say?"

"That you needed a week off."

"What? No! I'm fine. I can go to work on Monday. They need me." She couldn't bear the thought of a whole week off. What would she do with herself?

"Don't sweat it. Next week is Thanksgiving anyway, so you're not even missing that much. They'll manage."

"What am I supposed to do with myself?"

"Chelsea could use some help."

Dana blinked, surprised. "Chelsea?" she echoed. "You spoke to my sister?"

"Apparently her nanny skipped town and she needs you."

"But I'm lame," Dana protested. "What can I even do? It's not like I can chase Wesley around the playground."

"I trust your resourcefulness."

Dana squinted at her. "You think I'm the one who needs a babysitter, don't you?"

"She said she has a spare bedroom on the first floor. It's a win-win. You won't have to worry about cooking and shopping, she gets a hand with Wesley."

"The suburbs," Dana moaned. She had spent the first eighteen years of her life on Long Island, and had vowed she would never move back.

"It's not San Quentin."

"Might as well be."

"You mean because there's no liquor store in walking distance?" Megan asked, though it sounded more like a statement than a question.

"Couldn't I just do community service or something? I don't want to leave Manhattan."

Megan folded her arms. "She said your father and Jennifer have an extra bedroom. I'm sure they would be happy to—"

"I almost forgot how lovely Long Island is this time of year."

32

The days went by in a lazy, languid blur, like she was a Thorazined zombie in some nineteen-fifties sanitarium. Only Dana wasn't drugged. Or lobotomized. Yet her senses were dulled, her emotions existing at the bottom of some milky pool. She knew they were there, but had no desire to dive through the lacteous bog to find them. No thank you. Better to stay right here on the surface, reading stories to a four-year-old in between setting the dinner table and watching reruns of *Say Yes to the Dress*.

Ari hadn't called or texted. Not once. But even that didn't send her into an emotional tailspin, because as long as she was living this limbo life, it didn't count. There were times she considered reaching out, but she didn't want to risk the anxiety of waiting for a response, or the heartache of dead silence. And so she coasted.

Dana understood, now, why they used to send people away for a "rest." When you plucked someone from their life and delivered them to a place with no responsibilities or worries, their spirit could simply float untethered.

"Oh for god's sake," Chelsea had said one night as they sat in front of the TV watching a bride try on an outrageous ball gown. "Those feathers! She looks like an exploded chicken."

"I guess," Dana said.

"And she wants to wear it with high-tops!"

"That sounds comfortable," Dana said.

"Seriously? High-tops? With a wedding gown?"

Dana shrugged, and Chelsea's brow creased. During the commercial, she muted the volume and studied her sister. "Are you still planning to go back to work next week?"

"I don't know."

"You think you need more time off?"

Dana exhaled, already exhausted by the conversation. "Can we talk about it later?"

On Thanksgiving morning, Chelsea asked Dana if she could keep Wesley busy while she and the housekeeper got dinner together.

"Don't you need me in the kitchen?" Dana said. "I can sit at the table and slice or dice or mix or whatever."

"You'll be more useful with Wesley," Chelsea said. "Brandon is at a friend's helping to set up a new big-screen TV—god forbid he should have to watch football on a regular television—and Wesley needs some attention."

That's how Dana found herself on the bed in the guest room, her sweet-smelling nephew tucked under her arm as she read from *Charlotte's Web* by E.B. White. Dana was certain she had read it as a child, but didn't remember much beyond something about a spider who could spell and a little pig named Wilbur. So when she began, and the beautiful sentences washed over her like a cleansing tide, something stirred.

"What's the matter, Aunt Dana?" Wesley asked.

Dana touched her cheek and realized it was wet. This wasn't good. She didn't want to feel anything. "Sometimes grown-ups cry when they like something a lot," she explained. Or when they've been suppressing emotions so much that a few tender words break their heart. She grabbed a tissue and blew her nose.

"Like at weddings?" he asked.

"Yeah, like at weddings."

"I cry when I get hurt," he said. "Or when I'm really, really mad." He wrinkled his brow, and Dana could tell he was picking at a memory.

"What gets you really, really mad?" She brushed some hair from his soft, pale forehead.

"Do you know Jonah?"

She shook her head. "Is he your friend? Like Harper?"

"He lives next door to Harper. His mom lets him eat Hershey's Kisses after lunch. Just two." He held up his fingers to illustrate. "That's the rule."

"Good rule," she observed.

"I went there after soccer, and his mom gave two to Jonah and two to me. Guess what he *did*."

"He took one of your Kisses?"

"How did you know?"

She sighed, thinking about her history with men before Ari. "I dated Jonah in another life."

He ignored her and continued. "I took the silver off, and before I could eat it he just put it right in his mouth! Can you believe it?" His expression was so earnest, so incredulous, it broke her heart. He couldn't fathom the betrayal.

"Unfortunately, yes," she said, then asked if they were still friends.

He looked surprised by the question. "We always make up, Aunt Dana."

She went back to reading and soon the lessons about death began, as Wilbur learned that his new friend, Charlotte the spider, lived by killing flies and drinking their blood. And the reader learned that Wilbur was scheduled for slaughter. Dana glanced at Wesley to see how he was receiving this news. He was rapt but unfazed. She continued reading, and toward the end, as Charlotte the spider was dying, Wilbur asked why she had done so much for him when he had done nothing for her. Her reply was simple. He had been her friend.

At that, a wave of sorrow crashed and broke. Dana had not been a good friend to Ari. She had betrayed his trust. She was more like Jonah than Wilbur, only what she had done was unforgivable. She deserved all this misery.

Dana took a steadying breath, and relied on her acting skill to keep her voice even as she finished reading the book, barely listening to the words she spoke. If the agony showed in her face, Wesley was too engrossed in the story to notice.

"Can you read it again tomorrow?" he asked when she was finished.

"I don't know," she said. "If I'm not too tired." She told him to go see if his mom needed any help. Then Dana burrowed under the covers and fell asleep.

She was awoken a few hours later, aware that the house was buzzing with guests. Chelsea appeared at the open doorway of the room and Dana bolted up, alarmed. She had been dreaming about Ari, and her semiconscious mind leapt to an illogical thought. Had Ari come? Was it possible? Had he decided to surprise her and show up, full of forgiveness and Thanksgiving?

"You okay?" Chelsea said.

Dana's heart raced. "I… I was in a deep sleep."

"Dad and Jennifer are here," Chelsea announced.

"Is that it?"

"My in-laws, my friends from Atlanta, the Wassermans with their little girl. We're still waiting for Bill and Jan."

Of course, Dana thought. *Of course Ari isn't here.* It had been a dream. She let her head fall back on the pillow. "I think I'm just going to sleep through Thanksgiving," she said.

"Like hell you are."

"It's too much for me, Chelse."

"Then go through the motions. Play the part of someone who gives a shit."

"You're mad," Dana observed.

"My patience is wearing thin."

Of course it is, Dana thought. All week, her big sister had been placating her. Still, everything was so overwhelming. And Dana didn't feel like facing anyone, especially her father.

"No one will miss me," she said.

"Of course they'll miss you. It's Thanksgiving. Now get up and brush your hair. Put on that purple sweater dress that looks so good on you."

Dana sighed. She knew there was no use fighting it, so she did as her sister asked.

When she emerged from the guest bedroom on her crutches, Dana was bombarded with attention. Chelsea's father-in-law—an affable man with a pleasant smile, a bald head and a teal sweater he had probably received as a gift sometime in the 1990s—leapt from the easy chair and insisted she sit down. Someone put a plate of hors d'oeuvres in her lap. And then the questions started. How did she feel? When would the cast come off? What was it like working at the Shopping Channel? Did she ever get recognized on the street? Was Vanessa Valdes as nice in person as she seemed on TV?

Brandon's tiny nonagenarian grandmother—who somehow

seemed even smaller than last year, as if aging were an act of disappearing—pulled on Chelsea's sleeve.

"Who is that pretty girl? Is she an actress or something?" The old bird wore a vintage Chanel jacket that threatened to swallow her whole.

"That's my sister, Dana," Chelsea said loudly, over-enunciating each syllable. "You remember her, don't you?"

"She's the one who always went around with such terrible men."

"I'm done with all that, Mrs. Schiff," Dana said.

"Men like that only want one thing," said the old woman, wagging a finger. "You know what that is?"

"I have a pretty good idea," Dana said.

"In my day we called it hoochie-coochie. Now they say pussy."

"Pussy?" Wesley asked.

He was sitting on the floor with a six-year-old girl in patterned leggings. She looked up from her coloring book. "I think they're talking about vaginas."

The girl's mother jumped in to change the subject. "Didn't I read the Shopping Channel might switch from fashion to electronics?"

"Looks like we dodged that bullet," Dana said.

"And all because of my little sister," Chelsea said, coming up behind her. She put her hands on Dana's shoulders. "She got the idea to sell a skin care line, and then went on the air with a broken ankle and saved the day."

"Don't give me too much credit," Dana said. "I wasn't the first one with the skin care idea."

"I saw you that day!" Chelsea's friend gushed. "I couldn't believe you powered through that injury. You must have been in agony."

"It was pretty bad," Dana admitted.

"Damned foolish," said her father, who sat nearby with Jennifer. "She could have done permanent damage."

Dana gritted her teeth, and Chelsea gave her tensed shoulders a squeeze.

"We're all so proud of you, sis," she said.

"*All* might be a bit of a reach," Dana corrected, nodding toward their father. "But I appreciate your support."

"I'm sure your father is proud of you," said Chelsea's father-in-law. "Aren't you, Ken?"

"She's come a long way," he conceded.

"That's about as much as I'll ever get from my dad," Dana said.

"It's a compliment," Kenneth insisted. "Everyone wants to improve. Am I right?"

He said it as if he expected everyone in the room to rally round, but his comment was met with uncomfortable silence. It was almost as if they preferred talking about pussies.

"Why don't we move to the table?" Chelsea said. "I'm sure everyone is hungry."

Dana got up on her crutches and moved with the crowd to the dining room. Normally, she would have been among Chelsea's worker bees, getting the table set and ready. But today, that was impossible, and so the impact of the room took her by surprise. The soft amber lighting was perfect, and the table was beautifully set with rustic colors and a centerpiece of fire lilies, sunflowers, peach roses and other autumn-colored blooms in a pumpkin planter. Flickering candles of assorted heights completed the look. Dana had to hand it to her sister—she had an impeccable eye. Even the hand-lettered place cards, decorated with colorful turkeys stamped from Wesley's thumbprints, were charming. Dana wondered if there was one with Ari's name on it in the bottom of the trash bin.

As the dishes were passed around and everyone filled their

plates, Dana retreated into herself. It was easy, as conversations buzzed around the table and attention scattered. For the past several days, she had managed to keep her mind off Ari, and to forget her memory about the night of the murder. But now, both her crushing sadness and her crippling anxiety bubbled up from the muck of sublimation, threatening to pull her under.

Dana pushed food around her plate as she wondered how she would get through this meal. Or worse, the days that followed.

Almost reading her mind, Brandon's father elbowed her and asked, "Are you still seeing that police detective?"

"She's seeing a police detective?" asked old Mrs. Schiff. "Good for her."

"Actually, we broke up recently." The words sent ripples of goose bumps down her body. It was the first time she had said it out loud.

Her father put down his knife. "What?" he said. "How come I didn't know about this?"

"Didn't you wonder why he wasn't here?" Dana asked.

"Your sister told me he was working."

Chelsea gave a sheepish shrug. "He *might* be working."

"What happened?" Kenneth demanded.

"That's none of your business, Dad."

"I thought you two were moving in together. Now what are you going to do?"

"You just heard Chelsea say I saved the company. You really think I can't make a living and pay my own rent without a man?"

"Don't twist my words," he said. "Manhattan is expensive. I'm sure that lease you signed is unaffordable."

"It's not unaffordable. I told you that."

"But you still didn't tell me what happened with Ari."

"I screwed up, okay? Is that what you want to hear? I'm a

complete fuckup. Every time something good happens in my life I sabotage it. So I betrayed Ari's trust and he got pissed off and he walked out, and I spent the next forty-eight hours stoned and drunk, until Megan picked me up and shipped me off to my sister's house so I could have a perfectly classic nervous breakdown. But the icing on the cake? That's you. Judging me. As always." Dana stopped, aware that the room had gone quiet, and everyone was looking at her.

"That's because you never learn," her father said.

"You know what? You're right. I don't. Because no matter what you do, I keep thinking that one day…" Dana paused to swallow against a gourd-sized lump in her throat. "One day, you'll stop thinking of me as a loser, and maybe, just maybe, offer me a crumb of support. A grain of pride. I can never seem to learn that one simple lesson. But guess what, Dad? I'm done. I no longer give a shit what you think of me."

With that, Dana hobbled back to the guest room, packed her bags, called an Uber and left.

33

"It is so great to see you back!" Ashlee said, when Dana showed up for work on Monday.

She held open the dressing room door and Dana—by now an expert on crutches—maneuvered her way to the couch and sat. She was glad to be back, too, determined to steer this ship. She wasn't the loser her father thought she was. Sure, she had made mistakes, but it wasn't too late to set her course. She could sell her heart out and make sure the Shopping Channel never again teetered on the brink. Dana knew she was damned good at it, and no one could take that from her.

Also, she could find Margaux the bartender and prove to herself, once and for all, that she didn't murder Ivan.

Then, she could fix things with Ari. For now, of course, she had to keep her distance to protect his career. Finding the bartender was her first step. Once Dana knew she was innocent, she could go back to Ari and apologize, beg his forgiveness for her betrayal. That was the only part where her confidence got shaky. She couldn't even manage any creative visualization. Because no matter how many times Dana tried to play it out in her mind, she couldn't get to the point where he accepted her apology and they fell into each other's arms. The scene didn't work, because deep down she knew she didn't deserve his forgiveness. But she would try. And if she failed, at least she would make peace with her mistake. Learn from it and move on. Dana wanted to become the kind of person who wouldn't betray the trust of someone who loved her.

Of course, it could all turn out the other way. Margaux might say that yes, she had heard Dana fighting with Ivan by the roof's ledge—and that it was just before the lights went out. If that was the case, well. She couldn't think about it. She needed to focus on the positive.

And also, she needed to come to grips with the reality that she would be moving very soon. Dana had arranged for a one-month overlap with her current apartment and her new one. That meant she would officially take possession of the new place on December 1, and would need to move out of her old one by January 1. It still didn't seem real to her. But cognitive dissonance or not, she would need to spend the next few weeks staring at paint chips and choosing furniture.

Ashlee sat across from her and they swapped stories about their Thanksgivings. Dana kept hers brief. Ashlee had gone home to Tennessee, and went into colorful detail about her big, noisy, loving family.

"Sounds like you grew up in a Norman Rockwell painting," Dana said.

"The supersized version. With beer and wrestlin'."

Dana nodded. It was time to broach the subject she had been thinking about. "That day in my apartment," she began. "You said you had an idea for tracking down Margaux."

"I sure do," Ashlee said, digging her cell phone from her pocket. "You still have the phone number for that caterer?"

That was the idea? Calling the caterer again? Dana sighed, deflated. "What makes you think you'll be any more successful than I was?"

Ashlee clucked. "Bless your heart," she said, "but I been thinkin' on it, and decided you went about that all wrong."

"Trust me," Dana said, "they're not going to give out her last name."

"I didn't say they would."

"So what are you suggesting?" Dana asked.

"I suggest you let a Southern girl pour on a little charm."

Dana shook her head. Clearly, Ashlee had something up her sleeve. But Dana wasn't sure it was right to let the girl get more involved in her mess. She had already asked so much of her.

"I don't know, Ashlee," she said.

"Why not?"

"I just don't think it's fair to put you in this position."

"Fair?" Ashlee put a hand to her heart, offended. "No ma'am—you don't decide what's fair for me. This is something I want to do."

She was so imperious Dana could only smile. "You sure you want to get involved in this?"

"I enjoy using what the good lord gave me. Now let's get on with it."

And so they did. Dana read off the number for Garden of Stephen, and Ashlee punched it into her phone. She put the call on speaker.

"Hey!" she said in her cheeriest pageant voice when the receptionist answered. Dana had never imagined anyone could pack so much Tennessee into a single syllable, but this girl had managed it. "My name's Ashlee St. Pierre and I got your number as one of the best caterers in New York City. Is that true?"

The woman laughed. Clearly, she was charmed. "We like to think so."

"Great!" Ashlee chirped. "I am in New York for one little old week before I go on home, but I'm coming back next year to get married. My mother-in-law-to-be wants to use her own caterer and I don't trust that woman's judgment. She squeezes a quarter so tight the eagle screams, and I think she's bargain hunting for *my* wedding. Can you imagine such a thing?"

"I guess not," the woman said.

"So I was wonderin' if there was any chance I could sample your food and services before I leave town."

Dana held her breath. She was in awe. Ashlee poured it on thicker than she could have imagined. Dana wished she had recorded this—it would come in handy if she ever needed to study a Tennessee accent for a part.

"Just hang on one second and let me see if we can accommodate you," the woman said.

Ashlee flashed her proudest smile at Dana.

"You're amazing," Dana said in a whisper, even though the hold music was playing.

The woman got back on the phone. "Any chance you're free tonight? We're catering an art gallery event downtown and I can put your name on the list."

"Well, aren't you the sweetest thing!" Ashlee cooed. "Can I assume that event is fully staffed? I'd also love to see what kind of service y'all provide."

The woman assured her it was, and Ashlee asked her to hold on. She took the phone off speaker and whispered to Dana, "How well do you get around on those things?" She nodded toward the crutches.

"Pretty well now."

Ashlee nodded and put the phone back on speaker.

"Okay if I bring my future sister-in-law along? She's *so* sophisticated. Knows the subways like a worm knows dirt. I don't know what I'd do in this big city without her."

"Yes, of course," the woman said, and provided all the relevant information for the event. Ashlee thanked her, said goodbye and ended the call.

Dana looked at her impressive new assistant and found herself choked with gratitude. "Ashlee, I—"

"Oh, hush," the girl interrupted. "Never you mind. Let's just get you ready for your show."

"But I have something to say."

Ashlee put her hands on her hips. "Alright, then. Out with it."

The crutches made her unsteady, but Dana moved in for an awkward, one-armed hug. "Bless your heart," she said.

Using a tall stool during her show was easier than Dana thought it would be, especially since there were no models on the set, and she could stay in one place. Today's show featured microfiber tops and elastic waist skirts. It was strategic post-Thanksgiving positioning, as people struggled with extra pounds and welcomed the flowing skirts with forgiving waistbands. The trick was to try to get viewers to buy mix-and-match separates for themselves and as holiday gifts. Fortunately, the challenge was mitigated by the sale prices.

Plus, since it was Dana's first day back on the air, Jessalyn made the decision to open the phone lines, letting viewers pour out their affection and concern for the injured host. It was an effective strategy, as it made the show especially warm. Viewers were receptive to Dana and by extension, her pitch.

She finished on a high, and went back to her dressing room, where she took a call from Megan. Her friend was flattering and solicitous, as if dealing with a fragile ego. Dana couldn't blame her. She'd been such a wreck the last time they had seen one another.

"You sure you're okay?" Megan asked.

"Nothing a little cocaine won't cure."

Her friend went silent as if she wasn't sure it was a joke.

"I'm kidding," Dana piped in.

Megan exhaled. She didn't seem convinced Dana had recovered. "What are you doing tonight?" she asked, trying to make it sound casual. But Dana understood Megan was keeping tabs on her to be sure she wasn't going home to get stoned and drunk.

"Actually, I'm going to an art gallery with Ashlee," she said, leaving out the reason for the excursion. She didn't want Megan to worry that she was still obsessing on her vague memory about the night of Ivan's murder.

"Oh!" Megan said, sounding surprised, and possibly a little hurt that she wasn't invited. "That's great. Enjoy!"

Dana exhaled, suppressing a twinge of guilt. She would find a way to make it up to her friend.

Subways were still too difficult to navigate with a broken ankle, so Dana and Ashlee got into a cab and headed downtown. Dana was excited, but tried to temper her expectations; there was no guarantee Margaux would be working at the gallery's party that night, even if it *was* fully staffed.

The driver let them out at the curb, several yards from the entrance. Dana was doing pretty well on her crutches, but not well enough for the impatient couple walking behind them.

"Excuse me," the man said brusquely as the couple darted around them and pressed through the glass doors of the Warren Erstein Art Gallery. He gave the door a mock-polite push behind him, as if Dana could catch it before it shut. As if she wasn't already using both hands to hold on to her crutches.

"Hey thanks!" she called sarcastically, as she stuck out her crutch, missing the door. "I've always wondered what a random act of kindness felt like."

"Well, this should be fun," Ashlee said.

The interior of the gallery was packed like a subway car at rush hour. The patrons were mostly well-dressed, and more interested in one another than the paintings, all of which seemed to be highly stylized portraits in vivid colors.

"How on god's green earth are we supposed to make our way through this crowd?" Ashlee asked.

It did indeed look like it would take a grenade to break through the mob, but Dana was determined. "Don't worry," she said. "I'm going to get through to Margaux no matter what it takes."

There was a table by the door, staffed by a young woman checking people in. She had the translucent skin of someone who lived underground, offset by bottle-black hair, black clothes, purple lipstick and a tattoo climbing up her neck.

They approached the young woman, who checked them off a list and handed them preprinted adhesive name tags.

"Y'all know where the bar is at?" Ashlee asked.

Dana wondered what this urban creature, who had probably never been south of Canal Street, made of Ashlee's accent. But she seemed unfazed. "If you can push through the crowd, you'll see it." Then she looked at Dana's crutches and shrugged, as if to say, *Hey, sucks to be you.*

"I can handle it," Dana said, as if the girl had expressed concern, and set off.

But when she approached the thick crowd, her confidence faltered. Dana wasn't usually overwhelmed by packed rooms. After all, she'd had plenty of experience squeezing through crowded bars, doing the sideways shuffle as she moved aggressively toward the bathroom or the exit doors or a friend in the back. But never on crutches.

"Let me give this a try," Ashlee said, and then called, "Excuse me, ladies and gents. Would y'all mind if my friend and I got through? We are having a vodka emergency and need to get to that bar in the very back of the room. Thank you *so* much!"

It was hard to disarm jaded New Yorkers, but a few appreciative titters spread through the crowd. Still, there was no parting of the Red Sea—merely an opening just wide enough for Dana to wedge her shoulder into.

"Excuse me," she announced loudly, and no one moved. She tapped a woman on the shoulder and said it again.

"Sorry," the woman said, and moved aside about six inches.

Dana couldn't help noticing that everyone was avoiding her eye, pretending they didn't see the woman with a broken leg. They had all claimed their precious little piece of art gallery real estate, and weren't willing to budge.

"I'm going to need just a little bit of cooperation here," Dana called out, and nothing happened. This was one stubborn crowd. In fact, a guy in a blazer used his elbow as a weapon to keep her from passing, and a skinny woman in a vintage dress shot her vicious looks. It was as if they thought she brought the crutches as a prop to help her displace them.

She tried again. "Broken ankle, coming through!" she called.

It made only a small difference, but Dana could feel an atmospheric shift. She had scared them. They thought a mental patient had infiltrated their cultured ranks.

She said it again, louder this time, as if she were on the brink of psychosis. Again, the crowd shifted. She had to repeat it three more times, but at last she and Ashlee managed to jostle their way to the clearing at the back.

Dana glanced around, and could make out what looked like a bar at the rear, but the line around it was too thick for Dana to see if Margaux was working.

"Come on," Ashlee said. "We got this."

They stood at the back of the line at the bar, and Dana thought she saw the top of a blond head. So not Margaux. But there seemed to be two bartenders, so maybe.

In another minute, Dana got a better look at the blonde bartender. She was dressed just as Margaux was at the last event, in a white shirt and black vest, with a yellow bow tie and matching hair ribbon.

And then, at last, Dana stood face-to-face with her. She wore a name tag that said *Isabel*, and her partner was crouched down, retrieving something under the bar.

"What can I get for you?" asked Isabel.

Dana hesitated, trying to see over the bar. She pointed and said, "Uh…who is that?"

"Excuse me?"

At that, the other bartender stood. She was a striking Latina woman who looked a lot like Salma Hayek, and nothing like Margaux.

Dana exhaled, crushed. "Margaux isn't working tonight?" she said.

"You know Margaux?" Isabel asked.

"Sort of," Dana said. "I needed to ask her something."

"She's away—taking an extended Thanksgiving vacation."

"Y'all know when she'll be back?" Ashlee asked.

"First week in December, I think." She looked at the other bartender for confirmation.

"Yeah, she'll be back by the third. Can I get you ladies a drink?"

Dana hesitated, but only for a moment. "Hell yes," she said.

34

With no other avenues to Margaux available, Dana had no choice but to wait it out until the bartender was back from vacation. And so she distracted herself by making plans for her new apartment, and spent the next few weeks getting price quotes from painters and choosing colors. She had the keys now, and went over several times to examine the paint chips in the light and imagine how everything would look. It still felt like she was playing make-believe, pretending this place would soon be hers.

And while the apartment felt like a fantasy, the job felt more grounded than ever. Dana poured everything into it, and was delighted she had the chance to go back on the air with Reluven merchandise several more times. The viewers always responded enthusiastically. They loved the products, and Dana was on her way to becoming a Shopping Channel legend.

She and Ashlee had circled a date on the calendar—a Monday in early December. They knew Margaux would be back by then, and hoped she would be working as many bartending gigs as she could.

By the time that day arrived, Dana's leg was in a splint instead of a hard cast. She rested it on the coffee table as Ashlee called back the Garden of Stephen. Using her bride-to-be persona, Ashlee explained to the receptionist that she had absolutely loved the catered food and just needed to convince her fiancé. Since she was back in New York for the holidays, she wondered if it would be possible to let her betrothed sample the food service.

Once again, the receptionist was accommodating. "Are you going to be in town on Thursday?" she asked.

"As a matter of fact I am."

The woman went on to say that a fancy new hair salon was opening on the East Side with a catered party to mark the event. Since it was open to the public, Ashlee was free to attend with any guests she wished.

"Well, ain't that just perfect!" Ashlee cooed.

On Thursday, Ashlee and Dana took a crosstown bus and braced themselves against the icy December air as they walked toward the salon. The sidewalk was jammed with shoppers and workers, hurrying and scurrying. New Yorkers always had someplace to be, but there was an extra rush when it got this cold. Still, Dana thought the holiday season took a little edge off the impatience.

There were Christmas decorations everywhere, but it was easy to spot the new salon, as it was the only place that had white-and-silver Grand Opening flags flapping in the chill wind. Ashlee held the door for Dana, who was greeted by a burst of warm, humid air and a server holding a tray of champagne flutes. Dana was about to wave her off when she stopped cold, staring straight into the symmetrical face of a dancer with a pronounced widow's peak.

"Margaux!" she blurted.

The young woman blinked at her, taken back. She looked just as she did the night of the Shopping Channel party, in a white shirt and black vest, only now she was accessorized with a silver bow tie and hair ribbon to match the salon's colors.

"Do I know you?" Margaux asked. Her posture was alert and defensive.

Dana tried to smile nonthreateningly. But it was hard to mitigate a stalker vibe when you were, in fact, stalking someone.

"I'm Dana Barry?" she said, lilting it like a question, hoping her name rang a bell. "And this is Ashlee St. Pierre."

"Okay," Margaux said, her face tight and wary.

Dana was using only one crutch now, and leaned on it, hoping to look pathetic and harmless. "From the Shopping Channel," she said. "You were the bartender at our party the night that—"

"Oh god—the rooftop party," Margaux said, her eyes widening in recognition. Her voice was big and throaty. There had been so much noise that night Dana hadn't really heard it. "Yes, I'm sorry. I should have remembered you."

"It's okay," Dana said. "I was hoping to talk to you about what happened."

"Me?"

"I think you might have seen something that would help me."

"I doubt that," Margaux said. "I told the police—the lights went out and I couldn't see a thing. I was in the middle of pouring a drink and spilled it all over the bar. Dewar's, I think. Under normal circumstances, my boss would have been furious."

Dana nodded. "I understand, but do you have a minute to talk in private? There's something else you might have witnessed that would help me."

Margaux looked confused and hesitant. Dana couldn't blame her—it was an odd request.

"Please," Dana added. "It'll only take a minute."

Margaux shrugged. "I go on break in half an hour, but I really doubt I can—"

"That's great," Dana said. "Thank you. I'll wait."

With that, she and Ashlee accepted champagne flutes and went to the back of the room, where they nibbled hors d'oeuvres and pretended to admire all the carefully lit posters of models with interesting haircuts. A couple of stylists stopped to talk to them about their hair, and they listened, accepting business cards as if they were truly interested in makeovers.

When Margaux finally approached, Ashlee excused herself so Dana could have a one-on-one conversation with her. This was a tactical move they had discussed earlier, deciding it would be best if the woman didn't feel ambushed.

"So how did you track me down?" Margaux asked.

"I'm an actor," Dana said. "We travel in overlapping circles. It wasn't that hard." She didn't want to go into details about her stalkerish behavior, and hoped that would put it to rest.

"How did that happen?" Margaux asked, pointing at Dana's ankle.

She explained a bit about the accident, and how she had to power through for the show. That seemed to impress the dancer, who knew a thing or two about injuries.

"You know, I'm sorry you went to so much trouble when I don't have much to offer. I have no idea who pushed that guy. I would have told the police if I did."

"I figured that," Dana said. "But I have gaps in my memory from that night and I thought you could help."

Margaux nodded. "Vodka martinis, right?" She looked proud of herself for remembering.

"It wasn't just that," Dana explained. "Someone slipped me a roofie."

Before Margaux could react, a stylist approached and said he'd love to talk to them about their hair.

"Do you mind?" Margaux said. "We're having a conversation."

"Touchy, touchy," he said, backing away.

"Asshole," she muttered, before looking back at Dana. "I'm sorry. I'm just… I had no idea. Are you sure…about the roofie?"

"I went for a drug test that night."

"Jesus," Margaux said, shaking her head. "Are you okay?"

"Fine," Dana assured her. "Nothing happened. But that's really all I can remember from that night."

"Does that mean you don't know who spiked your drink?"

"The police are trying to figure that out."

"I didn't see it happen," Margaux said. "I swear. If I had, I would have—"

"I know, I know," Dana said. "That's not even why I'm here."

"Then, what?"

"Someone told me I had words with Ivan Dennison at some point."

"That's the guy who died?"

Dana nodded and Margaux squinted, thinking. "Yeah, you did. You guys were pretty close to the bar at one point. Now I remember. You were enraged."

"What else do you recall?"

"I think you told him to take his hands off you. You sounded really drunk so I wasn't sure what was going on."

"And then what happened? Did you see somebody pull me away?"

Say yes, Dana prayed. *Please.*

Margaux's eyes seemed to light up in memory. "Oh yeah! That's right. Some guy."

Dana's could barely contain herself. This was exactly what she wanted to hear. It wasn't proof, of course, but it was damned close.

"What guy? What did he look like?"

"White, I think. Not sure I remember. There were a lot of people at that party."

"Think," Dana said. "Please. Was he old? Young? Short? Tall?"

Margaux sighed. "I'm sorry. It's not coming back to me."

"And this all happened right before the lights went out?"

Margaux stared into the distance, as if searching for the memories. "Probably."

"Margaux," Dana said, "do you think it's possible that whoever pulled me away was the person who pushed Ivan off the roof?"

Margaux shook her head, but said, "I don't know. I'm sorry. I wish I could be more helpful."

"You've been *very* helpful, actually," Dana said. "Thank you." She took out her business card and wrote her cell phone number on the back. She pressed it into Margaux's hand. "Will you call me if you can remember anything about the guy who pulled me away?"

"Of course," Margaux said. "But you know, I'll see you tomorrow."

Dana stared, confused. "Tomorrow?"

"Yeah, I'm booked for your company's holiday party."

"Oh!" Dana said, nearly laughing in surprise. She knew, of course, that the party was tomorrow—the Shopping Channel held their celebration early in the month because so many people took the holiday off. But it hadn't occurred to her that Margaux would be there. She smiled at the irony. She had worked so hard to track this woman down, and if she had waited just one more day, she would have run into her. "I had no idea. But that's good. Maybe you'll see someone there who jogs your memory."

"Maybe," she echoed, but added a doubtful shrug.

They said goodbye, but before Dana could leave, Margaux stopped her. "Will you do me a big favor?" she asked.

"Of course," Dana said. "What is it?"

"Never again let a drink out of your sight." The dancer raised a graceful finger and wagged it at her. "*Never.* You understand?"

"Trust me, I learned my lesson."

Dana hobbled off to rejoin Ashlee and told her how well the conversation had gone. As they headed toward the exit, Dana quietly debriefed her on the details. They were at the door when Margaux came dashing toward them, sliding gracefully through the crowd.

"Dana!" she called. "Wait a second."

"What is it?"

"The guy that pulled you away—I just remembered. He had tattoos."

35

Lorenzo DeSantis. It made so much sense. If anybody at the party was watching out for her, it would have been him. He was street-smart and wary—just the person who would have been alert to a problem. And they had a history that dated back to her early days at the Shopping Channel. In fact, it started even before she was officially employed. Lorenzo had given her a tour of the place, taking her up to the roof. Dana had been attracted to his earnest intensity, and initiated a kiss. Of course, it didn't hurt that she was, at that moment, ebullient with hope. And also a little stoned.

He came with a ton of baggage, and the relationship was probably doomed from the start. He was a single dad, who happened to be on parole at the time, and so he had other things on his mind. And anyway, Dana was distracted by the too-tall homicide detective nosing his way around the company, with particular attention to the one ex-con in the building.

Dana and Lorenzo had parted amicably. In fact, he was all set to move to another state when the Shopping Channel made him an offer that was hard to refuse. And so he and his precious daughter, Sophie, were still living uptown, in Washington Heights.

"What are you doing?" Ashlee asked, when Dana took out her cell phone. They had stopped to grab some dinner and were in a restaurant near the salon.

"Texting Lorenzo to see if he's free," she said. They had already agreed that he had to be the man Margaux saw.

"Now?" Ashlee said, checking the time. "He's going to think it's a booty call."

"So?" Dana wasn't necessarily looking for someone to distract her from Ari, but now that she thought about it, why not? Maybe it was just what she needed to help her accept that it was over.

Her phone pinged with a response from Lorenzo. He said he wasn't doing anything, and she could come by if she wanted. She signaled the waiter for the check.

Dana had become so adept at ambulating with the splint that she didn't think twice about getting onto the subway to head uptown. She arrived at the private entrance to Lorenzo's semi-subterranean apartment and paused before pressing the buzzer, realizing Sophie, his five-year-old, might be asleep. Dana sent a text to let him know she was there, and a second later he opened the door.

Lorenzo was lean and ropey, with black hair and large dark eyes so earnest she trusted him from the moment they first met. Today, he greeted her in a worn gray T-shirt that looked like it had been through several hundred laundry cycles. His lived-in Levis sat low on his hips and his feet were bare. There was a beer bottle slung between his knuckles.

"Come in," he said.

She followed him inside and glanced around the familiar living room. It looked mostly the same, with a collection of antique radios high on a bookcase, and Sophie's toys arranged below it. She noticed he had bought himself a new TV, and wondered if this indulgence was a celebration of the significant raise the Shopping Channel had given him. Next to it, there was a stack of video games, and it was hard to tell if they were father's or daughter's. The glass ashtray still rested on the windowsill, which meant he hadn't quit smoking. She took a whiff, and caught the scent of Febreze coming off the furniture.

Lorenzo offered her a beer, which she accepted as she lowered herself onto the couch. Seeing him at the studio every day, it had been easy to forget how sexy he was. But here, relaxed in his apartment, he exuded an undeniable radiation. She remembered how much she liked being close to his heat.

"How's Sophie?" she asked, keeping the conversation innocent. She still wasn't sure if it was smart to get involved with him again. Maybe it was better to stick to the business at hand and get out.

He sat next to her. "Great," he said. "She's with her mother tonight."

"Oh?" Dana said, surprised. When she and Lorenzo dated, Sophie's mother was in prison. She had no idea the woman had been released. "When did she get out?"

"About two months ago. So far she's sober, living with her mom in the Bronx, trying to get her shit together."

Dana looked down, contemplating a twinge of guilt. She knew none of this. At work, she'd had hundreds of opportunities to ask him about his life, and refrained, as if even a simple kindness might rekindle something. In retrospect, it seemed absurd. Why had she been so distant? But she knew the answer. Ari. He had a jealous streak, especially where Lorenzo was concerned. That's why she kept things so cool. But Lorenzo didn't seem to mind. Or at very least, he understood.

She recalled, now, what he had told her about his ex, Evy. She was batshit crazy. Jealous. Volatile. Drug-addicted.

"You trust her with Sophie?" she asked.

"I do now," he said, looking thoughtful. "At first I supervised the visits, and when I saw she was okay, I backed off. She's still fucked up in other ways, of course, but I think she'll be alright. Got a crappy job at a restaurant that should keep her out of trouble. Tell me what's going on with you."

Dana shifted, trying to get comfortable. He seemed to think it had to do with her ankle, and moved a stool for her to rest her leg on. In truth, she was readjusting to the idea that Sophie wasn't in the next room. It changed the dynamic. Not that the girl's presence would have necessarily kept them apart. In fact, they'd often made quiet love out here in the living room during the dark late hours of the night while she slept. But in Dana's mind, the idea of his daughter being there kept this visit innocent. Now, she was alone in an apartment with a single man…a single man she'd had a sizzling sexual relationship with.

Dana took a swig of her beer, and launched into her story, starting from the beginning, as she hadn't said much in her text.

"That night of the party," she began. "I know I seemed pretty wasted."

"Out of control," he agreed.

She exhaled. "It's worse than you think. Someone slipped something into my drink."

"Really?" He looked shocked. "Why didn't you tell me?"

Dana sighed. She didn't want him to take the omission personally. "I haven't told anyone at work," she said. "It's part of the police investigation so I thought it was best to keep it quiet."

"Did you get a drug test?"

She nodded. "Positive for Rohypnol."

He grunted, disgusted, and rubbed his arm against a chill. "Who did that to you?"

"Probably Ivan, but I can't be sure."

"I wouldn't put it past that piece of shit."

"Here's the thing," Dana said. "I remember almost nothing from that night. But Sherry told me I had some huge fight with him. I thought and thought about it, trying to find a piece of it in my memory. And then I had this vague idea that...that maybe it was me—maybe I was the one who pushed him off the roof. It nearly drove me crazy."

"Dana," he said gently, "your mind was playing tricks on you."

She nodded. "I had these two competing memories. One was that I pushed him, the other was that someone came to my rescue and pulled me away. But now I think the second one is correct. And I believe that someone was you." She looked at him, waiting for confirmation.

He gave a small nod and put his beer down on the table. "It *was* me. It was a bad scene, and you were so messed up."

Dana could barely breathe. "Just to be clear," she said, "you pulled me far enough away to keep my hands off him?"

"I promise," he said. "I brought you over to the bar so I could get you a Coke. I thought it might sober you up."

"Thank you," she whispered, and wanted to cry with joy. This was the final piece. The one thing she needed to know to assure herself she didn't kill Ivan. Until that moment, Dana hadn't even realized how tense she had been. But now, her muscles relaxed as if going from a frigid downhill slope to a warm fireside. Still, a question plagued her. If she didn't kill Ivan, who did?

"Do you remember anything else?" she asked. "I mean, what happened next?"

He rubbed his stubble, thinking. "We were standing by the bar and that nerdy dude came over—his son."

"Jamie," she prompted.

"Yeah, Jamie. He wanted to know what happened and I told him. Man, he was *pissed*."

I'll bet, she thought. "What did he do?" she asked.

"He went charging over to Ivan. If it was anyone else, I would have suspected him of killing the guy. But it was his *son*. That would be fucking *cold*."

She nodded, agreeing. It would be monstrous, and that wasn't Jamie. He was a normal guy. Nerdy and gentle. Only psychopaths killed their own fathers. Not mild-mannered reporters for the *Daily Beast*. And besides, Jamie was too protective of his mother to put her in the position of losing her husband. Dana simply had to believe he was innocent, especially since Megan was getting deeper and deeper into the relationship.

But what if he wasn't?

"So you really don't think he could have killed Ivan?" Dana asked.

"I doubt it."

Dana was relieved. She trusted Lorenzo's ability to size up someone's character. He'd seen the worst of human behavior, and didn't easily let people off the hook.

"Where was Megan?" she asked.

"I don't know," he said. "I didn't see her at that point, though those two had been pretty thick most of the night. Maybe she was in the bathroom or something."

Dana closed her eyes to concentrate, trying to picture the scene. "What was the timing? I mean, you saw Jamie charging over to his father in a fury. How long after that did the generator die?" She looked at him now, and his brow was tight in concentration.

"I don't know. To be honest, I was a little buzzed myself so it's hard to piece together every detail."

"But do you think it could have happened right after that?" Dana asked, hoping for just a scintilla of proof that Jamie was innocent.

He shrugged, as if he just couldn't summon the information. "Maybe someone else remembers."

"Who might have seen?" she asked.

"A lot of people. We were right by the bar so it was a crowded spot. Maybe you can ask Ari. I'm sure he has detailed notes."

She let that sit for a minute as she took a sip of her beer. "*Very* detailed."

"What's his take on the whole thing?"

Dana shook her head, shifted again. "I don't know. He was under strict orders not to discuss the case with me. His lieutenant was adamant about that."

"So you didn't even tell him what you told me?"

"None of it."

Lorenzo looked surprised. "That's got to put a strain on a relationship."

She gave a bitter laugh. "So strained it snapped in half."

He backed up to get a better look at her face. "You broke up?"

She hadn't meant to tell him, but it felt good to let it out. "Just before Thanksgiving."

He picked up his beer again and took a long pull. Dana could feel the oxygen in the room shift. Until this moment, he was sitting on the couch next to his ex-girlfriend. The one seeing a jealous cop. And now, everything was different. She could sense him recalibrating the evening, from the text she had sent to this very moment. He was weighing his options. His concentration was palpable.

"Sounds rough," he said.

"Hasn't been easy," she admitted.

"I'm sorry, Dana. Guys can be such pricks—even the good ones."

She considered that, and realized he had leapt to the conclusion that Ari cheated on her. "It wasn't his fault. It wasn't anyone's fault. Well, maybe my fault. I wasn't a very good girlfriend."

He raised an eyebrow.

"Nothing like that," she said. "I didn't cheat on him. I was more of a generic asshole, and he couldn't take it anymore."

"I'm sure you didn't do anything that bad," he said.

"You have too much faith in me."

He stood. "Can I get you another beer?"

She looked at him then, and understood that it was the moment of decision. He wasn't just offering another beer. He was asking if she was going to stick around for a while. And if she was, well, they'd probably wind up in bed.

She picked up her bottle to look at it. Still half full. "I'm good for now," she said, which was a noncommittal answer. But she knew she would have to decide soon.

Lorenzo got himself another beer from the fridge and came back to the couch. He sat down close to her, and she could feel the heat of his thigh mingling with the heat of hers, and the urgency sent a desperate pulse to a spot between her legs. She wanted him. She wanted his kiss, his hands. She wanted enough passion to forget about all the pain of her loss. She put her fingers on his thigh. It was her yes to the question he was thinking.

Lorenzo leaned over and kissed her on the mouth. He was still holding his beer, so it wasn't an embrace, just the tenderness of his lips. They came apart, and he looked at her. When she didn't back away, his put down his beer and pulled her toward him, burying his face in her neck.

Her body responded with a shudder. She wanted this. Needed it. He put his mouth on hers for a long, deep kiss, and she needed to be naked with him. To feel her skin against his. Then he touched her hair. It was so delicate, like a feather, and the intimacy of it reminded her of Ari. A breath caught in her throat. It was such an intense déjà vu that she almost expected to pull back and see Ari's face.

"Oh god," she said.

"What's the matter?"

Dana put her hands on his chest and gently pressed him away. "I can't do this," she said.

Lorenzo waited a long beat before reacting. Then he scooted away from her on the couch. "You're sure?" he asked.

"I'm sorry."

"You're not over him," he said.

"No, I'm not," she agreed, but realized it was so much more than that. She wasn't done with Ari. And she didn't think he was done with her, either. She would win him back. She had to.

36

The next morning, before she got dressed to leave for work, Dana called Megan to fill her in on everything that had happened. There was so much to unpack.

"I tracked down Margaux yesterday," she began.

"The bartender?" Megan asked. "How did you manage that?"

"Long story, but if you want a coupon for ten percent off a very expensive haircut, let me know. Point is, you were right. I didn't push Ivan off the roof."

"Of course you didn't!"

Dana was standing in her tiny kitchen, where she had just poured hot water into her coffee press. She drummed the countertop, waiting impatiently for it to finish steeping. "I needed to hear it, needed to be sure."

"You can't let Sherry get inside your head. That bitch will mess you up."

"She wasn't lying, though. That's the thing. I *did* get into a screaming fight with Ivan. Margaux confirmed that some guy pulled me away."

"What guy?" Megan asked.

"At first she couldn't remember. But then one small detail came to her: the guy had ink."

"Tattoos?" Megan said, and Dana could almost hear her mentally walking the halls of the Shopping Channel. "Lorenzo?"

"Check," Dana said.

"You talked to him?"

Dana paused, unsure how her friend would react to the next part. She exhaled. "I went up to see him. In his apartment."

"Now this is getting interesting!" Megan said, a smile in her voice.

The kitchen timer dinged. Dana pushed the plunger and poured coffee into her favorite red ceramic mug. She tipped in a splash of milk and had a sip as she considered how to veer the conversation in the right direction. It would need to be delicately played, because she had to stop short of accusing Jamie of murder. It was just too outlandish. And deep down, she really didn't believe the guy could have killed his father. But there was that tiny pinhole of doubt, and she wanted to test the waters with her friend to see if there was even a hint of suspicion leaking through.

"We talked for a while," Dana said. "He remembered pulling me off Ivan, bringing me back to the bar to get me a Coke."

"And you don't recall any of this?"

"Not a thing."

Megan paused, as if she was probing her own memory about the event. "I wonder if I was on the dance floor at that point."

"I think you were in the ladies' room, because Jamie came over and he was alone."

"The ladies' room!" her friend said with a laugh. "I remember that, because things were heating up with Jamie, and while I was in the bathroom I checked my purse to see if I had a condom. Just in case."

"And did you?"

"Always prepared."

Dana walked carefully over to the table, putting weight on her splinted foot so she wouldn't spill her coffee. She sat. "Apparently, Jamie witnessed what happened between his father and me. At least part of it."

There was a pause before Megan quietly said, "I know."

"What?" Dana said. "You knew?"

"Jamie doesn't keep secrets from me."

"But why didn't you tell me?"

"Because you were already wigging out. I was afraid you'd go to a dark place. And anyway, I didn't know the particulars. Jamie just told me he saw you having an argument with his dad."

"And did he tell you how angry he was?"

"Of course he was angry!" She sounded defensive now. "He put the pieces together. He knew Ivan had come on to you and you had to fight him off. It's not easy having a father who's such a pig."

"So what did he say to his dad?"

It was Dana's loaded question. Her version of *How often did you beat your wife, Mr. Smith?* Because Dana had no proof Jamie actually confronted his father at that point.

"I don't think he had a chance," Megan said. "The generator blew and he came to look for me."

A chill rippled over Dana's flesh. She put down her cup too hard and a bit of coffee splashed out. The timing, she thought, as she grabbed a napkin and dabbed at the spill. This meant Jamie went to confront his father just before the lights went out, and that's when Ivan was pushed off the roof. For several moments, she wasn't able to speak.

"You still there?" Megan asked.

"Yeah, sorry. I just spilled my coffee." Dana kept her voice even, but inside she was roiling. Because now it looked like there was a good chance Jamie had done it. She wasn't going to say anything to Megan until she was sure, but it had to be soon. Because that night, her friend was jetting off to Mexico with a man who might well be a murderer. They'd be making just a brief appearance at the Shopping Channel's annual holiday party before heading to the airport. Dana had to uncover the truth before that happened.

She changed the subject. "Are you packed yet?"

"Almost done," Megan said. "In fact, I should probably go. We have tickets to Radio City this afternoon and I need to finish up before I leave."

For as long as Dana knew her, Megan had never missed a chance to see the Radio City Christmas Spectacular, Rockettes and all. She always said it wouldn't be Christmas without it. Usually, she insisted on dragging Dana along, past the iconic orange neon sign, through the historic lobby and into the celebrated auditorium. It was fun the first time, tolerable the second time, and then it was all Dana could do to make it through without wishing one of the Rockettes would fall and knock down the whole line like dominoes.

"You got tickets?" Dana said.

"Are you kidding? When Jamie asked me to go to Mexico with him, I wouldn't say yes until I was sure we could see the show before we left. He's such a peach he ran out and got us tickets."

"That's the best news I've heard in a long time," Dana said, trying to keep the conversation light.

"You're just happy you're off the hook," Megan said.

Dana took a sip of her coffee. "It's a Christmas miracle."

There was a lot to think about. Dana turned her cell phone over and over again as she tried to figure it out. She needed more information about Jamie, and she needed it now. She was so lost in thought that by the time she remembered to pick up her coffee again, it was cold.

There was one person who would have answers—Ari. But he was off-limits. Or was he? Now that she knew she had nothing to do with Ivan's murder, she could reach out to him without jeopardizing his career or the case. Of course, he wouldn't want to talk to her, but this was too important to let their fight interfere. And so, after nearly chewing her lip in half, Dana tapped out a text to him:

Something important has come up and I need to talk to you. Please call asap.

She read it back to herself three times and decided he would almost definitely call her back. Even if he was furious, he was responsible. She took a breath and hit Send. Then she got dressed and headed off to work.

But even as she reached the studio and checked in at the security desk, Ari still hadn't responded. She got into the elevator and looked at her cell phone again, as if she could will a text to appear. The doors were about to shut when a voice called out, "Unless you're an ax murderer, hold that elevator." It was Eleanor.

At that, Dana realized she'd been overlooking an obvious source of information. Why hadn't she thought of it before? If she wasn't going to talk to Ari, Eleanor Gratz was the next best thing, because she still had some terrible secrets that Dana was sure related to the murder. She had already connected some of the dots. Eleanor had gone to the Dennisons' house to threaten Ivan. She was going to expose his affairs to his wife if he didn't cease and desist with his plans to gut the Shopping Channel's branding in favor of computers and robots and whatever other high-tech gadgets would supposedly sell like digital hotcakes. But Ivan counter-threatened, using the paper trail of a decades-old kickback. Still, there was one other piece that didn't make sense. Eleanor had been sneaking off to meet someone. She had a rendezvous that day in the park. And if Dana hadn't broken her ankle, she might have had the answers by now.

Dana held open the elevator door. "The only place I kill is on the air," she said.

"Ah, my favorite assassin," Eleanor replied.

Dana decided not to follow up with another murder joke. "Mind if I tag along with you up to your office?" she asked. "I wanted to talk to you about something."

"Dana Barry gets whatever she wants, sweetheart."

They exited the elevator together on the executive floor and walked toward Eleanor's office. Her assistant, Gemma, held out a steaming mug of coffee and Eleanor took it without breaking stride.

"Can you get a cup for Dana, please?" she said.

Dana waved it off. "I'm fine."

They settled themselves into Eleanor's office and the busy buyer shuffled through papers on her desk. "So what can I do for you?" she asked, distracted.

Dana didn't see any reason to ease into the conversation. There was just too much at stake. "I know we spoke about that day you visited the Dennisons' house," she said. "But I have some questions."

That got Eleanor's attention. Her posture went rigid. "I told you everything," she said quickly.

"Not quite everything," Dana insisted.

"You're wasting your time." Eleanor folded her arms. "This is nonsense."

"Then help me out here. Because I still don't understand

why you decided not to go through with your plan to tell Ivan's wife about his infidelities."

"That's what you're so worried about?" Eleanor said, as if it were the most ridiculous question imaginable. "I didn't tell her because I knew it wouldn't make any difference, so why torture the poor woman. He was going through with his plan no matter what."

"I think there's more to it," Dana said.

"And why would you think that?"

Dana reached down to scratch an itchy spot inside her splint. When she looked up, Eleanor's face was pale. The woman knew something was coming. Dana saw no reason to drag it out. "Eleanor," she said pointedly, "I know about the kickback."

"What?"

"Don't worry, I didn't tell anyone."

Eleanor stood. "What are you accusing me of?"

"Hartsdale Marketing—a shell company set up by your husband. You funneled fifteen thousand dollars into it from the Shopping Channel."

Eleanor's eyes went dark. "Are you blackmailing me?"

"No! For god's sake. I don't give a damn about a stupid kickback from 1999. It was so long ago."

"How did you find out?"

"Does it matter?"

Eleanor's jaw went tight as she considered her next move, and Dana knew she was trying to figure out if there was still a way to deny it. But of course it was too late. She collapsed back in her chair. "One goddamned time. We were so desperate, so deep in the hole. And the company was flush. Phil was gambling, that stupid shit. We nearly lost our home."

Dana paused to take it in. She'd walked the edge of financial collapse, and understood the terror. But she had never considered stealing to save her own ass. Okay, maybe once. But she didn't go through with it.

"And it never happened again?" she asked.

Eleanor shook her head. "I sent Phil to Gamblers Anon. I told him that next time I would throw him out." She took a long pause and stared hard at Dana. "If you don't give a damn about the kickback, then why are you bringing it up?"

"Because I think there's another piece you're not telling me, and it might have to do with Ivan's murder."

Eleanor folded her arms. "If there was another piece— and I'm not saying there is—it has nothing to do with Ivan's murder."

"How do you know for sure?"

"Just leave it alone, Dana."

The two women stared at one another, and Dana knew she had to put her whole messy, outrageous hand on the table. And she did it with one word.

"Jamie," she pronounced.

Eleanor blanched. "What about him?"

"I have reason to believe he might have killed his father."

"No!" Eleanor's hand went to her chest, as if she needed to protect her heart. "That's not possible."

"What aren't you telling me!" Dana demanded.

"You go first. Why do you think it was him?"

"Because he knew his father came on to me at the party, and knew I literally had to fight him off. And then, right before the lights went out, Jamie was seen charging over to him in a rage. And you know what happened next. Ivan was pushed off the roof."

Eleanor went still for a long time. "Are you sure of this?"

"I'm sure the events happened in exactly that order with that exact timing. So now I need to know if there's anything you're not telling me."

A faraway look crossed over Eleanor's face. "I didn't think he was capable of that."

"Neither did I."

Eleanor rested her head on her hand and closed her eyes.

"What is it?" Dana pressed. She could sense that Eleanor was on the brink of opening up.

There was a long pause as the executive wrestled with whatever was on her mind. At last she said, "He knew about the daughter."

"What?" Dana said. "What are you talking about?"

"Jamie. He knew about Ivan's illegitimate daughter."

"There's a daughter?"

"He was trying to keep it from his mother. He was so furious when she showed up at the memorial service."

Dana remembered. The girl in the peacoat who came in late with her mother. Jamie and his brother had stared at them before Brock charged over.

"How did you find out about it?" Dana asked.

Eleanor sighed. "I know a lot of people, a lot of suppliers. Ivan had a terrible reputation in the electronics industry, despite his success. He took a lot more kickbacks than I did, though I could never prove it. But I found out about the daughter. The mother worked for Ivan. Karen Clifford—she was his marketing director. Everyone at the company seemed to know the kid was his, but it was all whispers. People knew about Blair's condition and felt sorry for her, so they kept it on the down low. Personally, I don't believe she's as fragile as everyone thinks she is."

"And this is what you tried to blackmail Ivan with?"

"I told him I thought she deserved to know. I still believe that. The guy had a kid, for god's sake."

"So you went to his house and threatened to—"

"I was trying to save the company! I knew we couldn't make

it with electronics. And I think Ivan knew it, too. That's the irony. I took a kickback twenty years ago. He'd been taking kickbacks his entire career. And I bet that if we did some digging, we'd find out that he stood to make millions while wringing the Shopping Channel dry." She shook her head. "I was trying to be a hero, Dana. And I really thought I could do it."

"How did he even find out about your ancient breach?"

"He dug and dug and dug. People like that always know where the bodies are buried. Or they have people who do. And apparently I had tipped my hand before I showed up at his doorstep. Ivan got wind that I had been nosing around him, so he hired a forensic accountant to dig up dirt on me. By the time I visited his house, he already had a paper trail. There was nothing I could do."

"And you think Jamie knows about the daughter?" Dana asked, though she was pretty sure his expression at the church said it all.

"I know he does."

Dana thought about the anger Jamie harbored. He knew his father was a cheater. Knew he had a hidden daughter. Knew he continued to screw around, hurting Blair again and again and again. And then, when he witnessed it firsthand at the party, his rage got the better of him. Years of pent-up anger exploded in one terrible moment. He might have been in the middle of an argument with Ivan when the lights went out. And then, with his fury at a fever pitch, he put his hands in the middle of his father's chest and sent him over the railing to his death.

It all made so much sense. But there was still one thing Dana didn't know.

"That day in the park," she said to Eleanor. "Were you meeting with Jamie? Was he paying you off not to tell his mother?"

"He tried to. We had already met several times by then, and I told him he could keep his damned money. Then he found the proof about my kickback."

Dana felt sick. She was the one who had helped him with that.

"So what was the park rendezvous about?"

"I don't know. He said he needed to talk to me. But he never showed up."

"Did you tell the police any of this?"

Eleanor shook her head. "I couldn't. It would have led them straight to my kickback."

"That was twenty years ago. Isn't there a statute of limitations for these things?"

"Don't you understand? If that got out, I'd lose my job in a microsecond."

"I'm so sorry, Eleanor," Dana said, and she was. Because she was going to tell the police, and then everyone would know.

In her dressing room, Dana checked her cell phone again. There was still no message from Ari, and she wondered if he was busy or ignoring her. But it didn't really matter—not right now. Because there was something more pressing Dana needed to do. She needed to reach out to Megan and warn her to get as far away from Jamie as possible. And no matter what, she couldn't get on that plane to Mexico with him.

But Megan didn't answer her call. Dana checked the time and understood. Her friend was already snug in her seat at Radio City Music Hall with her phone turned off. By the time she got the message, Dana would be on the air and unable to talk to her.

She was trying to decide what to do next when Ashlee came in.

"Gracious!" she said when she saw Dana's face. "What's

wrong? You look like something just snatched a knot in your tail."

Dana opened her mouth to respond, but the truth she just discovered overwhelmed her, and she fought a surge of nausea, unable to speak.

"You need a glass of water or something?" Ashlee asked.

Dana waved away the offer.

"What is it?" Ashlee said. "Tell me."

Dana took a long, ragged breath to center herself. "I know who murdered Ivan," she finally said.

Ashlee's eyes went wide. "Who is it?"

"It's his son," Dana said, swallowing hard. "It's Jamie."

Her words hung in the air for several moments before Ashlee reacted with a gasp. "Jiminy Christmas," she whispered, "are you sure?"

Dana told her the whole story, starting with the conversation with Lorenzo, and finishing with the information she just got from Eleanor.

"Did you tell Megan?" Ashlee asked.

"I tried. She and Jamie are at a matinee and her phone's off."

Ashlee paced, her hand over her mouth as she thought. "Ari," she said. "You have to call Ari."

"I tried texting him," Dana said. "But he's not getting back to me."

"Well, you just pick up that phone and *call* him. This is no time for pride."

Dana nodded. She knew Ashlee was right, and so she dialed Ari's number. She wasn't surprised when it went straight to voice mail. Keeping her tone even, she left an emphatic message. "Ari, I need to talk to you right away," she said. "It's about the murder. Please, this is urgent. Call me as soon as you can."

She hung up and looked at Ashlee. "You think he'll call me back?"

"I know he will."

Dana went over to the counter and poured herself some water. She chugged down half of it in one long, desperate pull.

"What am I going to do now?" she asked Ashlee.

"Now, you are going to get ready for your show. You have some merchandise to sell."

Dana was grateful that she had an easy program planned that day. One of the Shopping Channel's favorite designers, Bastina, would be live on the air with her, selling a line of knit loungewear. Viewers loved the affectionate relationship between them, and the minute the red light blinked on, Dana played it up, projecting her fondness for Megan onto the older woman. Dana modeled and swirled and cooed, while she and Bastina chatted like besties about what made the garments unique. The design. The craftsmanship. The comfort. The fit. The value. They moved from one style to the next, and Dana kept interjecting with appreciation for the designer's talents. And then, just like that, the four hours were over, and Dana held still while Lorenzo came on set to unclip her mike.

"Everything okay?" he asked.

"We'll talk later," she whispered. Then she gave Bastina a quick hug and hurried to her dressing room to check her phone for messages. But the only one who had called her was Chelsea.

"I don't understand," she said to Ashlee, while staring down at her phone. "Why hasn't Megan called me back? Why hasn't Ari?"

"Maybe they knew not to bother trying since you were on the air," Ashlee suggested.

Yes, Dana thought. That made sense. They were probably just stalling until they knew she was ready.

But Dana wasn't going to wait to hear from them. She ignored the message from her sister and called Megan. But once again, it went straight to voice mail. Dana could only assume her friend forgot to turn her phone back on after the show. She left a frantic message to call her back as soon as possible.

She tried Ari next, and almost threw her phone in frustration when he didn't pick up. What the hell!

"Why can't I reach anyone?" she cried.

"Sometimes people don't get messages," Ashlee said. "You know that. Batteries die, phones fall into toilets. But you'll hear from them. I promise."

Dana tried to comfort herself with the knowledge that, no matter what, she would see Megan in person in just a couple of hours. Because even if her phone was turned off, she'd be coming to the company's holiday party. She'd have Jamie with her, of course, but that didn't matter. Dana was going to tell her the truth, and make sure she didn't get on that plane.

She was in the middle of changing out of the Bastina loungewear and into her streetwear when her phone rang. She dashed for it, but it was neither Megan nor Ari. It was Chelsea.

"Oh, I'm sorry," Dana said. "I was just going to call you back."

"Thank god," Chelsea said, when she heard Dana's voice. "Thank god you're there."

"What's wrong?"

"I've been trying to reach you…or Dad…or Jennifer…no one was picking up."

Join the club, Dana thought, but kept it to herself. Chelsea was too distraught to hear about Dana's problems. "What's the matter?" she asked.

"I don't know. I have a fever. I thought it was nothing, but my OB wants me to go the hospital for something called a nonstress test."

"I don't understand," Dana said.

"It's this thing where they monitor the fetal heartbeat. My doctor is worried because I have a hundred-and-one fever but no other symptoms and she thinks it might be an infection. I said it's probably just something I caught from Wesley, who just got over a stomach bug. But she's worried. I mean, she tried to sound calm but she wouldn't be sending me to the hospital if she wasn't concerned."

"Oh, honey, I'm so sorry. I'm sure you'll be fine."

"Can you come out here and babysit?"

"Me?"

"I know it's a pain in the ass, but I don't know what else to do. Brandon is coming with me to the hospital and I have no one to stay with Wesley."

"But I'm so far away," Dana said. "Wouldn't it be better if you asked one of your neighbors?"

"They all have kids, Dana. And this thing Wesley had is like the plague. No one wants to go near him. I tried Dad and Jennifer first, because I know how busy you are. But I couldn't reach them."

Dana was about to put up an argument. To explain about the holiday party and the murder and Megan's plans. But her sister started crying, and it suddenly seemed like none of it mattered.

"I'm scared," Chelsea said through her tears. "I'm scared I'm going to lose this baby."

"I'll take a car service," Dana said. "I'll be there as fast as I can." And then Dana's stomach dropped like a rock. Because somehow, some way, she would have to make it back to the city to keep Megan from getting on that plane.

37

Now Dana had two more people she desperately needed to reach: her father and Jennifer. Where the hell was everyone? It was as if the universe was conspiring to keep her on edge. There was nothing she could do but leave a message and explain the situation, pleading with them to come and relieve her so she could head back to Manhattan.

When she reached her sister's house, Chelsea and Brandon were already standing by the front door in their coats. Dana leaned her crutch against the wall.

"Thank you for doing this," Chelsea said, as she wrapped her arms around Dana. "I'm afraid I don't know how long this is going to take."

"It's okay," Dana said. "Where's Wesley?"

"The den. I put him in front of a cartoon to distract him. There's macaroni and cheese in a pot on the stove. I tried to get him to eat but—"

"Macaroni and cheese? I thought he had a stomach bug."

"It passed, and the doctor said to give him his favorite food. He said whatever he would eat was okay." She shrugged apologetically. "So I asked what he wanted and—"

"It's alright," Dana said, understanding that her sister's maternal guilt never got put on hold. Not even when she was on her way to the hospital. "I'll work it out."

Brandon gave Dana a hug. "We appreciate this," he said.

Dana looked into her sister's worried face, and laid a hand on her cheek. "Let me know what happens."

Chelsea nodded. "See if you can get him to eat," she said, nodding toward the den. "He needs something in his stomach."

"I promise."

After they left, Dana stood by the door for a moment, absorbing her sister's pain. Chelsea was so worried about losing this baby. It was almost like she was already in mourning. Dana closed her eyes and tried to send her sister strength. *And please*, she added. *Please. Let the baby be okay.*

Dana walked into the den, forgoing the crutch and putting careful weight on her foot. Wesley sat cross-legged on the floor, a bag of gummy worms in his lap as he stared up at the television screen. Dana was pretty sure that wasn't on the menu.

He barely glanced her way. "Hi, Aunt Dana," he said, as if it there was nothing unusual about her presence in his home on a Friday evening while his parents were rushing out to the hospital.

"What do you have there?" she asked, pointing at the gummy worms, though she knew perfectly well what they were.

"Mom said I could."

She laughed, because it was such an obvious lie. Chelsea might have been a little lax on the nutritional content of dinner, but she wasn't going to let him fill up on sugar. "Let's each take one and then put it away, okay?"

That seemed like a pretty good deal to Wesley, and Dana congratulated herself on her negotiating skills. Who said this parenting stuff was hard?

After taking the bag of gummies away, she sat on the floor next to him and watched the brightly colored cartoon, featuring adorable dogs with expressive, oversized eyes. Wesley was in a trance, his milky skin bluish in the glow of the TV, his eyes wide and gleaming.

When it was over, she clicked off the television and struggled into a standing position. "Time for supper."

"I'm not hungry."

"Well, I am," she said, figuring he might eat if she put a plate of food in front of him.

He shrugged. "So?"

"Come keep me company. I'll be lonely in the kitchen all by myself."

"I want to watch more *Paw Patrol*," he whined.

"We can watch it after dinner."

"Please?" His eyes filled with the pain of longing. He was pouring it on, but that didn't mean he wouldn't burst into bona fide tears if she misstepped. She sensed he was on the brink.

Dana knew Chelsea wouldn't have given in, but she figured if her negotiation tactic had worked once, it could work again, and so she agreed to one more cartoon before dinner.

As they watched, she held tight to her cell phone, certain she would hear something soon. But the later it got, the edgier she became. What if she never heard back from Megan? What if she didn't hear from her father and she was stuck here until it was too late?

Then she had an idea. Jennifer was a working cardiologist. Maybe she had an emergency service that had a way to reach her? But no. The service would just call her cell, which Dana had already tried. If it was turned off, it meant someone else was on call.

There was nothing to do but wait. As the cartoon wound down, her heart began to sink. Maybe the best she could hope for was to ask Ashlee to waylay Megan, and tell her she had to call before she left for Mexico. But there was no guarantee Megan would follow through. Maybe she'd be in such a hurry she'd head for the airport with the intention of texting after she landed. And then what? And what would happen if Jamie was in Mexico when he discovered that Dana knew the truth…and that he'd be arrested if he returned home?

Dana took a deep breath and tried to tell herself it was all going to be okay, and that she was just letting her anxiety spiral out of control. Then her phone rang at last. It was her father.

"Dad!" she cried, as she walked into the kitchen so she could explain the situation out of Wesley's earshot. It was the first time they spoke since the fight at Thanksgiving, but of course that meant little. They never worked through their differences. They just ignored them. Dana launched into an explanation of what was going on, but before she could get too much out, her father cut her off.

"I know," he said. "I got Chelsea's message. Jennifer was giving a talk at a symposium and we had our phones off. But we're on our way there."

"Oh, thank god. I have to get back into the city." She knew how selfish that sounded and added, "It's kind of an emergency. Do you know what time you'll get here?"

"Friday night traffic," he said. "We're doing the best we can."

She made him promise to text her when he was getting close, and got off the phone. By the time she went back into the den, the cartoon episode had ended and another one began.

"Okay, let's put this on hold," she said, shutting off the television. Dana wanted to have Wesley fed and in his pajamas by the time her father and Jennifer arrived. If not, she knew exactly how she would look to her father—like the self-absorbed, irresponsible, useless daughter who couldn't even manage to take care of her nephew before rushing back into her own life.

"Hey!" Wesley protested. "I was watching that."

"Guess what?" she said. "Grandpa and Jennifer are coming over!"

"I don't care!"

She put out her hand. "Can you show me how the stove works?"

"I'm four-and-a-half. I don't know how the stove works."

"Maybe we can figure it out together."

He hesitated.

"Come on," she said. "Let's get this over with so we can come back and watch more of this Poor Control."

"*Paw Patrol*," he corrected, and then went with her into the kitchen.

The macaroni and cheese was congealed in the pot. After letting Wesley point out where the knobs were, she turned on the heat, but worried it would just turn too dry and sticky. She considered adding a little milk, but decided the microwave might be a better option. So she shoveled some into a bowl and nuked it for a few seconds. She put it in front of Wesley with a spoon.

"Can you tell me if this is okay?" she said.

Wesley ignored the food and rested his face on his hand, looking so sad it broke her heart. She understood, then, that his behavior was simply his way of coping with a bad situation. She knew Chelsea and Brandon hadn't told him what was really happening, but clearly he sensed something was wrong. She brushed his hair from his forehead.

"Your mom and dad will be home soon," she said.

He picked up a spoonful of food and flung it across the kitchen. It narrowly missed her, hitting the cabinet behind her head. A clump of the orangey goo stuck to the cherry-wood in gravity-defying tenacity.

"Wesley! That wasn't very nice!"

He began to cry. "I want my mommy."

The blob of food plopped to the floor as if in sympathy.

Dana approached her nephew. "I know, sweetie. I know," she said, hugging him. "I promise she's going to be home soon and everything will be fine."

She let him cry and rubbed his small, warm back. When his sobs subsided into hiccups, she asked, "Is there something else you want for dinner?"

He took a jerking breath. "I guess I'll have macaroni and cheese."

As he ate, Dana cleaned up the mess. And when he was done, he seemed like an entirely different child.

"Pajamas?" she asked.

He agreed, and they went upstairs, where she ran him a bath. She rolled up her sleeves and washed his hair, letting him splash her a bit. He got into his pajamas and she rubbed a towel over his hair before brushing it in place. Then she helped him with the toothpaste and watched as he carefully brushed his teeth.

"Do you want me to read you a book?" she asked.

"Can I watch one more *Paw Patrol*?"

"Sure," she said. He'd been so good she wanted to reward him.

By the time her father and Jennifer arrived, everything was perfect. Wesley was calm and happy. He was fed, bathed and in his pajamas, the fresh smell of shampoo rising off of him. The kitchen was clean.

"I gave him dinner," Dana said, as she led Jennifer and her father into the den. "And a bath. He's ready for bed."

She surveyed the scene through their eyes. A beautiful little boy, all scrubbed and safe and well-cared-for. Dana beamed. She had done it. Even her father looked impressed.

Her Uber was waiting outside, so Dana kissed them goodbye. As she was heading toward the door she heard Kenneth say to Jennifer, "She let him watch this garbage?"

38

Oh, the traffic! Dana wanted to kick herself for taking an Uber instead of the Long Island Railroad, but it was too late now. They were approaching the Midtown Tunnel into Manhattan when she got a text from Ashlee.

Megan arrived 10 mins ago. Made her promise to wait for you.

Dana wrote back:

TY. On my way!

A few minutes later her phone pinged again. Dana looked down expecting another text from Ashlee, but it was from her brother-in-law, Brandon, whom she had messaged earlier to let him know all was well at home and that Dad and Jennifer were with Wesley.

Baby seems okay. Chelsea on IV antibiotics. Will be in touch later.

Dana reread it several times. It sounded like good news. She texted back: Give her a kiss for me, and returned to fretting about the traffic.

The car continued crawling forward into the brightly lit tunnel, and they were stuck behind a driver with Connecticut plates who left far too much space between his car and the one in front of him. It was maddening. Did he think a plane was going to need a place to land, right here in the Midtown Tunnel? Dana wished her driver would at least honk.

When they finally emerged from the fluorescence of the underground tube into the darkness of the New York night, they were behind the same slow driver as they tried to inch their way toward the West Side. She texted Ashlee.

Almost there! Make sure she doesn't leave.

"Please hurry!" she said to the driver.

At last they arrived. Dana pulled her single crutch out of the car after her, but didn't bother using it. She carried it horizontally as she hurried across the lobby of the Shopping Channel to Studio E, a cavernous, unused space the staff nicknamed the planetarium, as the massive, high-ceilinged room was normally pitch dark. Today, the tinkling of a piano playing "Carol of the Bells" poured from the maw, the pace becoming more frenetic as Dana approached. When she reached the open doors, she saw that the expansive interior had been transformed. The room was softly lit, with Christmas decorations along the walls, and pots of poinsettias adorning the red-draped tables. A grand piano had been brought in, which Dana imagined took quite a bit of planning and effort. The pianist was elegantly dressed in tails and a white tie.

People were lined up with plates at the long buffet set up on the left side of the room. Directly to her right, by the door, there was a bar that looked almost exactly like the one from the rooftop party. Margaux was there, next to the same male bartender, wearing the same coordinated uniforms, complete with yellow bow ties.

Dana did a quick scan of the room and her eyes registered all the colors. She saw Charles Honeycutt and his wife, Victoria, and noticed that his red pocket square coordinated with her gown. Felicia and Jo stood by the bar. They were both in black cocktail dresses, but Jo's had hot pink tulle netting peeking out from the hem. Sherry Zidel sat at a table next to her partner, Anna, sipping a brown cocktail. At the gold-draped buffet tables, dozens of people were lined up for food, including Eleanor and her husband, Phil, as well as Vanessa, Gemma, Lorenzo, Brenda, Jessalyn and Robért. Dana's eyes continued down the line until she spotted Ashlee, waving furiously at her. And then she saw them—Megan and Jamie—standing in front of her assistant.

Dana put her crutch back under her arm and crossed the room to them.

"I've been trying to reach you all day," Dana said to Megan.

"I'm so sorry!" her friend said. "I forgot to turn my phone back on. What's going on with your sister? Is she okay?"

Dana glanced at Ashlee and understood. Her assistant had told Megan that Dana had to rush out to Long Island for Chelsea, and Megan just assumed that's what Dana had been calling her about.

"I don't know yet," Dana said. "I think so. She's still at the hospital."

Megan reached over for a hug. "I'm so sorry I wasn't there for you."

"I need to talk to you," Dana said into her ear. "It's important."

"Can we get a quick bite first?" Megan asked. "I'm starving."

Normally, Megan would have picked up on Dana's despair,

but she was clearly giddy with excitement over her impending trip, and all hyped up on Christmas.

Dana shook her head. "This is urgent."

Megan studied her for a moment and then looked at Jamie. "It's okay," he said. "I'll fill up a plate for you."

"I want those little meatballs," she said, making a circle with her thumb and forefinger.

He crossed his heart in solemn oath, and Megan set off with Dana, heading toward the exit. They were almost at the center of the room when Dana stopped short. There, standing in the doorway, was Ari. He came! She wanted to cry with joy.

She realized he hadn't seen her yet, and she watched as he stood there, scanning the room. Then his eyes found her, and he froze. She couldn't read his expression from that distance, but she sensed the stirring in his heart. And she knew what it meant. She knew it as well as she knew how to find her own feet in the dark. It lifted her with hope.

Then, the spell was broken. He seemed to collect himself and strode across the room.

"I was in court today," he explained, and she understood. It was why he hadn't called. As a homicide detective, it wasn't unusual for him to take the witness stand in a case. And she knew he wasn't allowed to keep his phone on during a trial.

Dana nodded. "I should have figured."

"What's going on?" There was no warmth in his tone, and she understood. It could be a long road back for the two of them. But they would find a way. They had to.

"Let's talk outside," she said, and started to move Ari and Megan toward the door. Her heart thudded in anticipation of what she was about to tell them. It was a terrible thing. A man had murdered his own father. He would be arrested, his life ruined. His mother would probably never recover. And Megan. Poor Megan. She had fallen so hard for this guy.

But what choice did Dana have? She had to tell the truth.

As they neared the bar, Dana saw Margaux in profile, and something seemed off. It took her a second to realize what it was—the hair ribbon. At the rooftop party, she had worn a yellow one to match her yellow bow tie. At the salon party, she had worn a silver ribbon to match her silver bow tie. But today, she was in a yellow bow tie but wore a black hair ribbon.

At first, Dana was ready to dismiss it as one of those ridiculous details she couldn't help noticing. And besides, didn't people lose hair ribbons all the time?

Still, she couldn't ignore the feeling deep in her gut that this was significant. And sure—maybe it was wishful thinking, a way to avoid breaking the terrible truth that would destroy so many lives. But something pushed at the back of her memory. The lost yellow ribbon. She had seen it somewhere…hadn't she?

"You okay?" Ari asked.

"I just need a minute," she said, and continued thinking as the pianist transitioned into "Have Yourself A Merry Little Christmas," and began to sing. It helped get her brain to shift gears and a memory came into focus. The photo in Jo's cell phone. Was that it? Was that where she had seen the ribbon? There had been something in Ivan's hand that looked like an off-white strand of fabric. But maybe it wasn't off-white. Maybe it was yellow.

She could barely breathe now, and hoped her suspicion was right. Because she didn't want to think it was Jamie. She had never wanted to believe it was Jamie. She took out her phone and scrolled to the photo Jo had forwarded to her. The strip of fabric in Ivan's hand did indeed look like a hair ribbon, but the picture was too blurry to know for sure. If only the image were crisper. She bit her lip, considering her next move.

"What's the matter?" Megan asked.

"Hold on," Dana said. And then she called out to the people nearby, "Excuse me. Did anyone take a picture of...of the body? Of Ivan?"

Her question created such a strange hush that the piano player stopped. The whole room went silent, as everyone looked at her. Dana took a deep breath. She had to test this new theory, no matter how strange it seemed.

"The night of the rooftop party," she called out, addressing the whole room now. "Did anyone happen to take a picture of the body with their cell phone?"

Her question hung in the silent air for several long moments. And then, there was a burst of activity and suddenly dozens of hands reached toward her, each holding a cell phone showing a photograph of Ivan's dead body. Of course. Nearly everyone had taken a picture.

"What's going on?" Megan asked.

Dana ignored the question, and took a loop around the room, examining the images. Most were taken from the rooftop, and the pictures were indistinct. But then, she found a photo that had clearly been taken by someone on the ground next to the body. It was sharply focused, and the scene was well lit from the overhead streetlight. Dana took the phone and zoomed in on Ivan's hand. And there it was. As clear as could be. She held it toward Ari.

"See that?" she said. "In Ivan's hand? It's a hair ribbon. A *yellow* hair ribbon."

Ari studied the photo. "I remember that. We sent it to the lab, along with other pieces of evidence. We're still waiting for the results."

It was like they were onstage now, with a riveted audience. Every face in the room was turned toward them, listening. Dana called upon her acting skills to take a mental test drive of her theory. If a character had a dark enough history—complete with a past that included a violent assault—it might be enough to push her over the edge. That was why Margaux had originally struck her as so paranoid—a feeling reinforced yesterday in the salon. Dana understood. Margaux didn't just see herself as a bartender, but as a protector of women. She had a mission. And if she had witnessed Ivan trying to assault Dana, it might have been enough to trigger violence. Someone like that wouldn't see it as a crime. She would see it as justice.

It might be mental illness, Dana thought, but her sympathy only went so far. The woman was a murderer and needed to be held accountable.

"You don't need to wait," Dana said to Ari. "The hair ribbon is hers." She pivoted and pointed to Margaux. "She was wearing it the night of the murder."

"No!" Margaux cried. "That's not mine!"

"I'm sorry," Dana said. "But when they get the results, it's going to have your DNA all over it."

"Is that what you wanted to tell me?" Megan asked her.

Dana shook her head. "Until one minute ago, I thought it was Jamie."

"Jamie?" Megan looked shocked.

Dana shrugged apologetically. "There was so much damning evidence. He saw me fight with his father. It sent him into a fury."

"I can vouch for that," Lorenzo called out.

"But I never even got to him," Jamie insisted. "The generator died and the lights went out. I was worried about Megan and went to look for her. I told the police all of this."

"How could you think he was a killer?" Megan asked.

"I didn't at first. But then I found out Ivan had a bigger secret than we realized. A secret that added a much deeper layer to Jamie's resentment. And he was set on making sure no one found out."

"You mean his affairs?" Megan asked.

"I mean his daughter."

Ari put a hand on Dana's shoulder. She nearly melted into him, but she knew she needed to stay focused.

"What are you saying?" he asked.

"Do you remember the dark-haired mother and daughter who came in late to the memorial service? Jamie's brother, Brock, rushed over to have words with them."

"I was told they were estranged family," Ari said, frowning. He hated when people lied. And hated even more when he didn't see through it.

Dana shook her head. "They were Ivan's big secret. That girl is his daughter."

Megan turned to Jamie. "Is this true?"

His head was down, and when he lifted it, his face was drained of color. "We wanted to protect my mom," Jamie said. "I was afraid this would kill her."

"She's stronger than you think," Megan said, and then turned to Dana. "You thought he would kill his own father because of this?"

"I thought it explained the reason for all his anger," Dana said. "When I added that to what I already knew—that Jamie was seen rushing toward his father just before the lights went out—all the pieces seemed to fit. He hated his father for what he'd done, and when he saw him assaulting me, well, that was the last straw. At least, that's the way it looked."

Megan's eyes looked pained. "I can't believe you would have such a low opinion of him."

Since so much was out, Dana couldn't stop now. She had to tell her friend everything she knew about Jamie. "There's something else," Dana explained. "Jamie was threatening someone—someone at the Shopping Channel who knew about the daughter."

"I wasn't going to hurt her," Jamie said. "In fact, I tried to keep her quiet with money. When she said no to that, I found something on her that—"

"And you used me to get it," Dana said. "You used Megan, too."

"Who are we talking about?" Ari asked.

Dana looked at Jamie, expecting him to tell everyone it was Eleanor, and that he had found out she had taken a kickback many years ago. But he just shook his head and said, "It doesn't matter."

Dana looked at him. Now that everything was out, he could have pointed a finger at Eleanor and destroyed her career. But he hadn't. And in Dana's mind, that said something about his character.

"Of course it matters," Ari said.

"Can we just let it go?" Jamie asked. "I don't want to get her in trouble."

At that, a voice from the back of the hall called out, "It was me. I was the one who knew about the daughter." Eleanor walked to the center the room and told everyone present about the terrible thing she had done twenty years ago. She explained the circumstances, but took responsibility.

When she finished, there was a hush in the room. And Dana knew it was over for Eleanor. She might be admired for coming clean, but there was no way the board of directors would let her stay, even if Charles Honeycutt forgave her.

"I still don't understand how this leads back to the bartender," Megan said. "Why would she have killed Ivan?"

"Because she saw him trying to assault me, and that brought something up for her. Some trauma from her past that haunts her, shapes the way she looks at the world." Dana turned to Margaux. "Isn't that right? It's why you were so concerned from the beginning. You warned Megan and me about sleazy guys, like it was your mission, like part of your job was to make sure women were safe from predators."

Margaux folded her arms. "They're out there," she seethed, "just waiting to pounce."

"You killed my father!" Jamie said. "You killed him!" Dana had never heard him use that tone of voice. It was as if the reality was just now breaking through.

Margaux turned to him, her eyes blazing. "I saw him! I saw him slip something into her drink. And the next thing I knew he was trying to force himself on her."

"But you didn't need to—"

"I was protecting her!" Margaux cried.

And that was it. The confession. Ari produced a pair of handcuffs from somewhere in his jacket. When Margaux saw them, she tried to dash for the door. But even her dancer's quick-footedness was no match for Ari's long stride and even longer reach. He managed to put her in handcuffs before she even knew what was happening.

And then, Jamie did something Dana didn't expect. He put his face in his hands, and wept.

39

"If one more person tells me they like my couch, I'm going to take a knife and rip it open," Dana said to Megan.

It was New Year's Eve. Dana had moved in only four days earlier, and this was her housewarming party. It just happened to fall on December 31, so she bought champagne and silly hats.

Dana had fallen in love with a massive $9,000 sofa that was on clearance sale for $3,900. It was like something out of a dream, in a pale silvery gray, with a round tufted back and elegantly curved armrests, inlaid with carved wood painted to match the upholstery. Formal but romantic, it would look exquisite beneath the living room's large windows. She imagined them draped with heavy curtains and tiebacks, making the couch take center stage.

And it wasn't only beautiful, but symbolic. The end to all her years of financial struggle. The realization that yes, she was successful. And stable. It wasn't all going to disappear in a puff of smoke.

And okay, that didn't mean she was suddenly going to become the kind of person who didn't look at price tags. The bargain hunter trait was ingrained far too deeply. But an extravagance and a sale all at once? Now that was intoxicating.

And then, of course, there was Ari. The decision to purchase this sofa was a way to convince her heart what her head already knew—he wasn't coming back.

But when it came time to pull out her credit card, Dana froze, her heart and head locked in battle. They were not going to make this easy.

"Miss? Your credit card?" the salesman had repeated.

Dana didn't answer. She was replaying what had happened since the Shopping Channel's holiday party. Ari had agreed to meet her for coffee so they could talk things over. But no matter how many times she apologized, he couldn't move forward. The trust, he said, had been broken. It shattered her heart in a million pieces, because she knew he loved her. He was just too hurt to let her back into his life.

I take responsibility, she had said. *It's my fault. I messed up. It'll never happen again.*

But Ari was immovable. She had hurt him for the last time. It was over.

So yes, purchasing this beautiful sofa was the right decision on every level. And the perfect symbol for moving on. And yet. Dana couldn't pull the trigger. At that moment, she understood that she wasn't done trying, and the couch could be her last chance. A signal to Ari that she could make whatever sacrifices were needed. For him.

So she told the salesman she changed her mind. Then she went to IKEA and bought the not-too-ugly couch he had favored. It made her a little queasy, this compromise, but love, she reasoned, was worth a little nausea.

"Will you come to my housewarming?" she had asked Ari on the phone. "It would mean so much to me. And there's something I want you to see."

"You really think that's wise?" he'd responded.

"Please, Ari," she'd said. "Even if it's just for a few minutes."

He said he would think about it, but his tone of voice suggested he was just trying to get off the phone. So here she was, with a house full of people, a couch she didn't really like, and no Ari.

She tried to console herself with the knowledge that she now lived in a dream apartment…an apartment that could handle such a large crowd without feeling like the subway at rush hour. She had invited friends and family, including her entire theater group, several coworkers from the Shopping Channel and a few others she was close to.

Chelsea and Brandon hadn't been able to make it, because she was now on bedrest. The unidentified infection that caused the fever had put her into preterm labor. It stopped when they started the antibiotics and got the fever down, but her cervix had already started the process of dilating for birth. So Chelsea was ordered to stay in bed for the rest of the pregnancy. Fortunately, their babysitter had come back, and so she had someone to care for Wesley while Brandon was at work. Now that Dana had her splint off, she planned to go out there on weekends to help out whenever possible.

Dana glanced around at her guests. Nathan, her Sweat City director, was there with his wife, Lisa. There had been whispers among the cast that they had split up for a time, but were back together now. Dana wondered if the separation accounted for the weird vibe she got off him that day. Ultimately, it didn't matter. She never had any intention of hooking up with him.

Lorenzo, of course, was another story. She had told him he could bring a plus-one. It would, she reasoned, keep her from being tempted to do anything impulsive. But he came alone, and she couldn't help noticing how often he glanced her way.

Megan held up a glass of champagne. She and Jamie had just returned from Mexico, looking tanned, happy and relaxed.

"To your new place," she said, offering a toast.

Jamie raised his glass. "In the words of Oscar Wilde, take everything in moderation...including moderation."

Kenneth and Jennifer were standing nearby, so Megan called them over. "What do you think of the apartment?" she asked. "Isn't it great?"

The last part, Dana knew, was an attempt to lead the witness.

"It's lovely," Jennifer said, and turned to Dana. "I'm so delighted for you."

"It's a hell of a neighborhood," Megan went on, trying to prompt a positive reaction from Dana's father. "Safe...beautiful... and there's a Trader Joe's just a few blocks up."

Dana wanted to tell her to save her breath. Kenneth Barry would never approve.

"I'm jealous," Jamie said. "It's like a rare gem."

"How about you, Dr. Barry?" Megan pressed. "Can you believe the steal she got on this place?"

"It's a big improvement from her old apartment," he conceded, and raised his glass to Dana. "To many healthy and productive years here."

Dana gave Megan a look to let her know her father's reaction was just enough. Not a rave, but about as positive as she could hope for.

"Thanks, Dad," Dana said, tipping her glass toward his.

"And I like the sofa," he added.

Megan patted Dana's arm. "We're going to keep you away from sharp objects tonight," she whispered.

Dana made the rounds, chatting with her guests, accepting their toasts and congratulations. She no longer wore a splint, so it was a relief to have freedom of movement. She had invited Eleanor and her husband, Phil, who seemed to be enjoying themselves, despite the turn their lives had taken. After the holiday party, Eleanor had offered her resignation before the board could fire her, so she was officially unemployed. Dana felt terrible about it. Eleanor loved the Shopping Channel. It was everything to her. And sure, she had committed a pretty serious crime. But that was twenty years ago. Water that had long since passed under the bridge and evaporated.

Dana was glad to see that tonight Eleanor looked cheerful and relaxed, in a flowing black dress with ivory piping, a patterned silk scarf and an arm full of bracelets. Her husband, in a wool sweater, button-down shirt and broad smile, looked like someone who had just won *Jeopardy*—a little dorky and decidedly happy. Dana wondered if exposing their dark secret had a freeing effect on the couple.

They thanked her for inviting them and complimented the apartment, but Dana glossed over the small talk and asked them how they were coping with everything.

"Not too bad," Eleanor said. "I got a call from my friends at Reluven this week. They offered me a position as marketing VP."

Now that was a welcome surprise. Dana smiled. She knew that Eleanor wasn't ready to retire, and they had spoken about how hard it could be for a woman her age to get a new job, especially after a scandal.

"Are you going to take it?" Dana asked.

"I'm seriously considering it."

Dana continued chatting with her guests. Everyone wanted

to toast her, and all those sips of champagne eventually sneaked up on her. Dana found herself getting a little woozy, so she went into the kitchen for a glass of water, and had to remind herself that she had a new, full-size refrigerator with a water dispenser. In her old place, the fridge had been a tiny relic of another era, when appliances were built ruggedly enough to roll into war.

Dana pressed a glass into the dispenser and watched it fill like she was a time-traveling anthropologist paying her first visit to twenty-first-century America.

"How are you doing?" said a male voice, and Dana looked up to see Lorenzo.

"A little too much to drink," she said.

"You're overflowing."

She squinted at him, confused.

"Your glass," he said, pointing.

Dana turned and saw that she was spilling water all over the floor. "Shit," she said, pulling out the glass. She glanced around, not sure where she had put the paper towels. Lorenzo found them and stooped to clean up the mess.

"You don't have to do that," she said.

"It's okay." He looked around for a place to deposit the wet paper towels and she showed him where the trash can was hidden. He stuffed it in the garbage and washed his hands.

"Thank you," she said, and fought a wave of melancholy at the ordinary domesticity of the scene. It should have been Ari standing in the kitchen with her.

"You look a little sad," he said.

Dana didn't want to get into it. "It's the champagne," she said. "And New Year's Eve. I seem to be on the brink of maudlin."

"Brink of maudlin," he repeated, "could have been the name of a grunge band."

"I think I had their first album."

He smiled. "Feeling better?"

Dana shrugged.

"Are you expecting Ari?" he asked.

She shook her head. "I invited him. A last-ditch effort."

"I'm sorry," he said.

Dana studied him. Lorenzo wasn't exactly handsome, with his crooked nose and narrow face, but he was virile and sexy. More important, he was fundamentally decent. And sure, he carried a boatload of baggage—a criminal record, drugs, a history with batshit crazy women that colored his view of the world. And that was just the stuff she knew about. But if she was going to move on from Ari, maybe he was the one. She could see in his face that he still liked her. And lusted for her. His eyes lingered on her throat and her body responded to his desire. This night, she thought, could be a new start.

Standing inches apart from her now in this space, he had to sense that something was stirring. But he was too respectful to make a move. And that was even hotter than his longing. Dana decided she would kiss him at midnight. Only it wouldn't be like that day in his apartment, where she changed her mind. Because if Ari didn't arrive by midnight, it meant that things were over.

So yes, she would press her body against his and let herself melt into him. The thought of it made the heat rise up in her neck. She might even ask him to stay overnight. When they were dating, that wasn't possible. But now that Sophie's mom was back in the picture, everything would be different. Dana thought of that big bed she had slept in alone last night. It would be so comforting to share it.

She knew, of course, there was a risk she'd feel heartbroken in the morning that the man next to her wasn't Ari. But maybe this was exactly what she needed to convince herself the final note had been played.

They moved into the living room, with Dana clutching a glass of water.

By eleven thirty, a few more people had arrived. Her theater friend, Tyrel, had taken over door duty, so Dana only became aware of new guests when she saw them floating around. She realized it was too late to expect Ari. He wasn't going to show up just before midnight like in some rom-com. Unless, of course, he wanted to make a dramatic entrance. *Don't get your hopes up*, she told herself. Yet she kept glancing at the door.

And then, Lorenzo was at her side again. So be it, she thought. At midnight, they would kiss.

"Dana," he said, "I'd like you to meet Rafaella."

She turned to look, and there, at his side, was a petite woman with shiny black hair and a silver nose ring. She was young. Pretty. He put his arm around her. Lorenzo had invited a plus-one, after all.

"Thank you so much for having me," Rafaella said, shaking Dana's hand.

Dana braved the introduction with a polite smile, and then grabbed a glass of champagne and downed it like a shot. She burped into her hand and grabbed another.

At midnight, the group counted down and cheered. Couples kissed, friends hugged. Dana was surrounded with well wishes by dozens of people who loved her, and never felt lonelier.

40

When her buzzer rang the next morning, Dana was in such a dead sleep she had no idea where she was. She opened her eyes, expecting to see her familiar cramped bedroom, and it took her a minute to remember. She was in a large bright room that didn't yet have window coverings. Her throat burned, her sinuses pounded, and she realized it was New Year's Day. She had finished the night by polishing off what was left in several open bottles of champagne, and had fallen asleep on top of the quilted white bedspread on her king-size mattress. She let out a breath and glanced down. She had gotten a lipstick smear on her brand new bedding. Damn.

The buzzer rang again. Dana wondered who would be visiting at this hour of the morning and glanced at the time. It was almost noon.

She padded over to the intercom and pressed the button. "Who is it?" she asked, trying to blink herself into full consciousness.

She didn't hear anything so she pressed the Talk button again. "Who the hell is it?"

When she heard nothing, Dana realized this new intercom actually had a volume knob, and it was dialed all the way down. She turned it up.

"Sorry," she said. "Can you repeat?"

"It's Ari, Dana."

Ari?

Dana was stunned, but there was no time to process it. She dashed into the bathroom to brush her teeth and wipe the mascara smears from under her eyes. The buzzer rang again, and she realized she hadn't let him in. She ran back to the intercom and pressed the button to unlock the building's front door. She hurried to her bedroom to change into a fresh shirt, and run her fingers through her hair.

"Hello," she said, when she opened the door. She had no idea what to expect, and studied his face. Her head was still pounding, making it hard to concentrate.

"I bought you a housewarming gift," he said, holding up a white paper bag.

"Thank you." She took it from him. It was warm and smelled of bagels. An odd gift. If he had brought flowers, she would have melted into his arms. But this? It seemed more about moving on than forgiveness. Dana was determined to be stoic, but her eyes burned from the effort.

He stood rigidly in the doorway, as if he needed an invitation to cross the threshold. So she swallowed against a knot and asked, "Will you come in?"

He nodded, and she led him into the living room. "I didn't think you were going to come," she said.

He exhaled. "I didn't think so either. But…I changed my mind."

"Why didn't you come last night, then?" Dana asked, realizing this could have played out very differently. If Lorenzo hadn't invited a girl to the party, he'd probably be in her bed right now.

"I considered it," he said. "But to be honest, I thought it might be awkward to show up at the party—making small talk with everyone. I figured it was probably better to see you alone."

"How did you know I'd be alone?" she said.

Ari's eyes turned serious. "Are you?" he asked, glancing from corner to corner.

"Would you care if I wasn't?"

It was an earnest question, and it seemed to rattle him. Dana saw him go deep into himself to find the answer. "Of course I'd care," he finally said, and his eyes roamed the room again, as if scanning for a clue to another man's presence. The place was still a mess from the party, and she knew he was in detective mode, analyzing the scene.

"I'm alone," she finally said. It was meant to appease him, but the words felt thick with meaning, and Dana's throat tightened. She had to turn away from him. She wasn't going to break down in tears now. She wasn't.

"So what do you think of the apartment?" she said, changing the subject. With a sweep of her arm, she indicated the entirety of the living room. There were no shades here yet, either, and the space was flooded with morning light. She knew that despite the mess, it was impressive.

"Wow," he remarked. "Windows."

"And walls," she replied. "Floors and ceilings, too." Dana was trying to keep things light so she wouldn't cry. This might be the last time they would be alone together. Once he walked out the door, it was really and truly over.

Ari's eyes landed on the sofa. He looked at her and back at the couch. "The one from IKEA?" He seemed confused.

She shrugged.

"I thought you didn't like it that much," he said.

"I don't."

"So why did you…" He trailed off and looked at her.

Dana said nothing, and the silence throbbed in her temples as she considered shrugging it off. After all, the truth would do nothing to change the situation, and might just leave her more vulnerable. But when she looked up and met his gaze, something shifted. This was Ari, and she still wanted him. So it was worth telling him the truth, even if it meant another rejection, more stress on a wound that wouldn't heal.

"I needed to do *something*," she said. "I didn't feel like we were over and I thought you might take it as some kind of symbol of what I was willing to do for you. For *us*."

The atmosphere went thick as her words hung between them, and she knew what his silence meant. He was looking for a way to let her down kindly.

Ari did a loop around the room, inspecting it like a real estate agent. Or like a cop. But Dana sensed he was just buying time, trying to find the right words.

"You don't have to say anything," she told him.

"But I want to," he said, inspecting an empty champagne bottle as if there might be answers inside. He put it down and turned to her, straightening his posture. He was backlit from the window, making it hard to see his face, so she walked toward him and stood by his side.

"Okay," she said, looking into his eyes. "I'm ready." Dana took a steadying breath. If he was going to give a speech—one last lecture on her unforgivable behavior—she would take it head-on, no matter how painful. And then she would let him go.

"Remember that day you told me how brave I was?" he said. "It was right after that kid pulled a gun."

"I remember," she said. It was at the beginning of their relationship, and it had terrified her, thinking of how close he had come to getting shot.

"I don't think I'm nearly as brave as you," he said. "If they gave awards for emotional courage, you'd take all the prizes. Me? I'm just a coward."

"No," she protested, but he held up his hand to stop her.

"It's true. I mean, you hurt me—you know that. I responded by shutting it down. I didn't want to revisit it, didn't want to risk feeling like that again. But you were hurt, too. I walked out, and you were heartbroken. I know that. But you didn't give up. You faced it again and again, Dana."

"Because I still love you."

"And I still love you," he said. "That's not news to you. You know it. You've always known it. The difference is that you've been braver about all this than I have."

Dana picked up a used cocktail napkin and wiped her face, then blew her nose. "So where does that leave us?"

"When you called to invite me to your housewarming, I was nearly knocked out. I thought for sure I'd hurt you so much you couldn't possibly try again. But there you were, like a soldier who charges into a hail of bullets."

"Reckless?" she asked.

"Maybe a little," he said. "But mostly determined. And fearless. It inspired me. I thought, *God, this woman. I must be crazy. She's so strong. And she loves me so much. How can I walk away from that?*"

Dana knew her eyes were wet, but she didn't care anymore. She looked straight at him. "So it wasn't the couch?"

He looked at the sofa and back at her. "Are you having buyer's remorse?"

"I'm not sure."

"Look at it this way," he said. "If we get a dog, you're not going to care if he gets hair all over it."

We. It was all she needed to hear. "If we get a dog," she said, "he can slobber on that thing and bury his kibbles in the cushions."

He took a long moment to respond. "Are you hungry?" he asked. "Because I am."

"Was it the slobber and the kibbles?"

Ari laughed. "In a way," he said. And she knew what he meant. He'd said *we*. And she'd responded without hesitating.

So they pulled stools up to the bistro table she had brought from her old apartment. Her new kitchen table and chairs hadn't yet been delivered, so it would have to do.

It felt a little disappointing, having this auspicious meal at her rickety old table. It was, after all, their first meal of the New Year, and they were having it together. She wondered if there was something she could do to make it more special. Because they had sat at this very table dozens of times eating bagels.

"Should I heat them up?" she asked.

Ari touched the bag, testing the temperature. "Not necessary."

She reached out to see for herself, and realized he was right. The warmth was still there. And when she thought about it, that was all she really wanted.

EPILOGUE

They named him Ham. The rescue dog was a two-year-old black lab mix with a white stripe on his head and a worldview that love was all. It was clear Ham believed he could get anyone to love him, if they would just stop long enough to be sniffed. His tail was in constant motion, thwacking back and forth in joy. Nothing thrilled him more than his long walks on the Upper West Side, because every stranger was just a friend he hadn't met. A new opportunity for love.

Ari had moved in with Dana shortly after New Year's Day, and his promotion came through a few months later. That was when they started visiting shelters.

On a Saturday afternoon in April, as the three of them walked back from the West Seventy-Second Street Dog Run, Dana got a call. It was her brother-in-law, Brandon. Chelsea had gone into labor—three weeks early.

"Nothing to worry about," Brandon assured her.

Dana wanted to go to the hospital immediately, but Brandon asked her to stay put.

So they kept their plans for that evening—dinner with Megan and Jamie at a neighborhood Italian restaurant. Dana was distracted, checking her cell phone every five minutes. She was excited, but also nervous. It had been a difficult pregnancy, and it was hard to be entirely confident.

By the time they went to bed that night, the baby still hadn't arrived. Dana texted Brandon to say they could call her even if it was the middle of the night.

And it was. Dana's cell phone rang at 2:48 a.m.

"I'm holding her in my arms right now," Chelsea whispered. "She's perfect."

"What's her name?"

"Beatrice Jade Schiff. Six pounds, fifteen ounces."

"I love her already."

Dana and Ari arrived at the hospital the next day bearing gifts—clothes for the baby, a toy for Wesley and flowers for Chelsea.

"Nothing for me?" Brandon joked.

"You got everything, man," Ari said.

Brandon's eyes went wet. "I do," he said, looking down at the small bundle in his arms.

Dana peered over his shoulder at the baby's peaceful face. "Can I hold her?"

"Wash your hands," Chelsea said, pointing to a stainless steel sink in the corner of the room.

Dana had already washed her hands *and* used the sanitizer pump on the wall outside the room, but she wasn't going to argue. She scrubbed in like a surgeon and sat in the orange vinyl chair next to Chelsea's bed. Brandon lowered the burrito-wrapped infant into her arms.

The newborn's smell took her by surprise. It was so intoxicating she leaned in for more, taking a long sniff off the baby's head. She didn't normally think of heat itself as having a scent, but that's what the infant smelled like. It was so profoundly familiar that Dana could only assume the recognition was built deep into her DNA.

"Bea," she cooed, staring into the little face. She studied the baby's nose, so tiny it was hard to understand how she could possibly breathe. "Will you open your eyes for your aunt Dana?" she asked, touching the newborn's smooth cheek.

The baby's head turned toward her breast, her little bow lips opening, and Dana was awed. This tiny perfect creature was born less than twenty-four hours ago, yet knew how to turn toward nourishment.

"Did you see that?" she said to the group.

"That's the rooting reflex, Aunt Dana," Wesley explained.

Dana turned to Brandon and Chelsea, surprised. "Have you enrolled him in medical school or something?"

"What do you mean?" Wesley asked.

She looked into the sweet face of this child whose whole life had just shifted. "I mean that you're going to be a terrific big brother," she said. "With lots to teach your sister."

Soon, it became clear the baby was hungry, and Dana transferred her to Chelsea's arms. As she was happily suckling, Kenneth and Jennifer arrived. Dana knew that her mom was on her way from Florida, and things could get awkward fast. Rhonda Barry Spector never enjoyed being in her ex-husband's presence. And since it would be her first time meeting Jennifer, it would be even more uncomfortable. But for now, the atmosphere was joyous.

A few months later, Dana was in her dressing room when Megan came by with some news. A producer was creating a new panel talk show, like *The View*, but more geared toward culture and entertainment than current events. It would be taped in New York.

"He wants to talk to you," Megan said.

"Me?"

"They're looking for people to put on the panel, and they've had their eye on you."

Dana lit up. She didn't even know if she was interested, but the very idea of being courted like this made her light-headed. "Tell me more," she said.

Megan went on to explain what she knew about the format, and how Dana would fit in. She said that the timing could be perfect, because it was in the early planning stages and might not get off the ground until Dana's Shopping Channel contract was up.

"And even if it happens faster," she said, "they might be willing to buy out your contract. I'm telling you, Dana—they really like you!"

"I'm reeling," she said. "I never expected this. I mean—"

"Before you get ahead of yourself," Megan interrupted, "there's one thing you should know. The contract will be even more airtight than the one you have now. Acting would be off the table."

"No acting?" Dana said, already trying to imagine how she would be able to sneak off to Sweat City once her face was that famous.

"It's a serious commitment," Megan explained.

Dana felt short of breath. "I'm going to have to think about this."

That night, she did her thinking out loud as she and Ari walked uptown, with Ham straining at the leash to greet every animal and human they passed. She started by relaying everything Megan had said. Ari leaned his head toward her, listening. She gesticulated madly as she went on and on about the opportunity, insisting it would be fun and exciting, a great path forward. Before she got to the part about a contract that would lock her out of acting opportunities, Ari gave a little tug at Ham's leash and stopped. There was concern on his face.

"What is it?" she asked.

"Babe, if this is what you want to do, I'm behind you, but…" He looked down the block, as if the words he wanted were somewhere west of Manhattan, perhaps floating over the Hudson River.

"But what?" she pressed.

He let out a breath. "It sounds like you're trying to talk yourself into it."

Dana checked an impulse to be defensive and insist that she might never get an opportunity like this again. "I am," she admitted.

"So what's the downside?"

She sighed. "It would mean giving up my acting career. At least for now."

"Is that really what you want to do?"

Of course not, she thought. But how could she say no to the money, the fame, the excitement, the lifestyle? She realized, then, that somewhere deep inside she had already imagined the high of telling her father and getting his full approval at last.

And that, she knew, was not the reason to give up her dreams.

You're an actor, she told herself. *An actor*. The Shopping Channel gig was meant as a stop on that journey, not a whole new trip.

Dana took the leash from Ari, and Ham gave a little skip, anticipating some new excitement, even though he had no idea where they would end up.

She knew just how he felt.

★ ★ ★ ★ ★

ACKNOWLEDGMENTS

Like many novelists, I have to rely on the kindness of strangers willing to get on the phone and answer my oddball questions. In researching this book, I was fortunate enough to connect with Newark homicide detective Jerry Simons—a real-life Ari Marks—who gently and generously filled in the large gaps in my understanding of murder investigations. Jerry was thoughtful, patient and insightful. I later found out how sick he was at the time of our chats, and sadly, Jerry died shortly thereafter. I hope his family knows how very grateful I am for his input. This book would not have been possible without his help. May his memory be a blessing.

I was also lucky enough to connect with other professionals who were able to round out my limited knowledge of law and order, including Mike Espinoza and Anitra Wheeler.

My good fortune also extends to the incredible team at MIRA. My brilliant editor, Kathy Sagan, offered the guidance I needed to usher Dana through her adventures. Thanks, too, to Nicole Brebner, Margaret Marbury, Rachel Bressler, Samantha McVeigh,

Ashley MacDonald, Natasha Shaikh, Lucille Miranda and the rest of the gang.

Much love and thanks to my talented writer friends and beta readers for their support and input, which was more important than ever during the trying times of Covid quarantine. Saralee Rosenberg, Susan Henderson, Alix Strauss, Myfanwy Collins and Susan DiPlacido mean the world to me and then some. And a big thanks to the writer friends who never stop inspiring me, including Robin Slick, Amy Ferris, Debbi Honorof, Carol Hoenig, Peggy Zieran, Jordan Rosenfeld, Lydia Fazio Theys, Debbie Markowitz, Mary Ellen Walsh, Dina Santorelli, Greg Correll, David Toussaint, Debbie Ann Ice, Melanie Benjamin, Elinor Lipman, Susan Isaacs, Tami Hoag, Hank Phillippi Ryan, Jonathan Vatner, Candace Bushnell and Caroline Leavitt.

To my dear friends Wendy Baila DeAngelis and Stephen DeAngelis, and their daughter Alexandra, thank you for the daily love and guidance!

To the hosts, staff and management at HSN, QVC and other real-life shopping channels, my humblest thanks for the inspiration and apologies for the creative license I took with your business models. I hope you can accept this fictional world as homage to the work you do so very well.

Love and gratitude to my agent, Annelise Robey. I couldn't have done it without you. I'm also grateful to the whole team at the Jane Rotrosen Agency, including Andrea Cirillo. I'm so lucky to have you.

As always, thanks to my kids—Max, Ethan and Rook—for keeping me laughing and living in this actual century. And most of all, thanks to Mike, for everything.